the RETURN of
KID COOPER

the RETURN *of* KID COOPER

A NOVEL

Brad Smith

Arcade Publishing · New York

Arcade Publishing books may be purchased in bulk at special discounts for sales promotion, corporate gifts, fund-raising, or educational purposes. Special editions can also be created to specifications. For details, contact the Special Sales Department, Arcade Publishing, 307 West 36th Street, 11th Floor, New York, NY 10018 or arcade@skyhorsepublishing.com.

Arcade Publishing® is a registered trademark of Skyhorse Publishing, Inc.®, a Delaware corporation.

Visit our website at www.arcadepub.com.

10 9 8 7 6 5 4 3 2 1

Library of Congress Cataloging-in-Publication Data is available on file.

Cover design by Erin Seaward-Hyatt
Cover photo by Randy Nyhof

Print ISBN: 978-1-62872-871-2
Ebook ISBN: 978-1-62872-872-9

Printed in the United States of America

One

A RECENT ISSUE OF THE *Police Gazette* had been circulating through the prison population for some time and on the Wednesday after the hostage incident, the magazine landed in Nate Cooper's hands. He took it back to his cell after a breakfast of mealy porridge and lukewarm coffee and lay down on his bunk to read. The front cover featured a photograph of the colored prizefighter Jack Johnson standing in a ring somewhere, the boxer stripped to the waist, his right fist cocked and ready and his left hand open and extended as if in defiant warning to anyone who dared come close. The palm was as big as a saddlebag. Inside the magazine was a story about Johnson, who was about to meet the former champion Jim Jeffries for the heavyweight title.

As Nate read, Bo came out from a narrow crack in the wall and approached the cot noiselessly across the stone floor. He jumped up onto the wool blanket and then scrambled onto Nate's pant leg, stopping just below the knee, where he sat on his haunches, whiskers twitching. Nate had pilfered a stale crust of bread from the breakfast table and now he produced it from his shirt pocket and offered a pinch to the mouse, which took it in its front paws and began to nibble away. Just as Nate was about to deliver a second helping he heard footsteps approaching along the corridor and then the key as it hit the lock in the door. Bo, his breakfast thus interrupted, was off the bed in a flash, his tail disappearing into the wall as the hinges creaked open.

The guard entered and walked to the center of the small cell, looking around suspiciously before turning to regard Nate, his legs spread and his thumbs hooked in his belt. He indicated the top bunk.

"Where's Bilanski?" he demanded.

"Working the laundry," Nate replied, continuing to read.

The guard's eyes fell on the periodical. "That black bastard's gonna get his yellow ass whupped by Jeffries," he said.

Nate glanced up at the comment but had no inclination to argue with the man. He preferred to avoid imbeciles, whether they happened to be inmates or guards. He went back to the magazine.

"Warden wants to see you," the guard said.

The announcement was so unexpected that it naturally got Nate's attention. He almost asked the guard for the reason behind it but then checked himself. In all likelihood the man wouldn't know the answer and anyway Nate would find out for himself soon enough.

Warden Conley sat behind his desk, two-finger typing on a Remington machine, when Nate arrived on the heels of the guard, who interrupted his continued disparagement of the fighter Johnson to announce their arrival. Conley dismissed the man with a nod of the head before waving Nate into the office.

Nate took a couple of steps before stopping, glancing briefly toward the warden before giving the room the once over, his eyes shifting from the vaulted windows on the west wall to the high bookshelves opposite. Watching, it occurred to Conley that the prisoner had never been in the room before. Nate had removed his cloth cap and was holding it carelessly in his left hand. His hair was brown, with considerable gray in it, and he wore a mustache, also going to gray, that drooped past the corners of his mouth. His eyes were blue and sharp, taking in the room and its contents but also showing a glimmer of a question, the question being—*why am I here?*

Conley indicated a chair across from him. "Have a seat, Nate."

Nate walked across the room to the chair, pulled it back a few inches and sat. Conley noticed that the man, in spite of his many years at Deer Lodge, had never developed the prisoner's shuffle, that peculiar gait of men who had spent time in leg irons. And Conley knew that Cooper had worn the irons in his day. Still, he retained the bowlegged, rambling step of a cowpoke, like the throwbacks Conley often saw on Main Street on a Saturday; ranchers in town for supplies, or cowhands blowing off their wages. He saw them less and less though, he realized. Their numbers were dwindling.

"I always wanted to ask you a thing, Nate," Conley said to begin. "With regards to your vegetable garden behind the stables—where did you get your green thumb? Were you always good at cultivating or did you turn your hand to it here?"

"I never grew nothing bigger than a bunion before I come here," Nate said. "I was a cowboy and a cowboy ain't much for digging in the dirt. Most won't stoop to it. I demeaned myself here only in an effort to stave off boredom. Might have saved my sanity. If it has been saved, that is."

"You have a talent for it nonetheless," Conley said. "Wherever it came from."

Nate shrugged. "My ma always had a sizable vegetable garden. Nine kids, it was required."

"Where was this?"

Nate took a moment, watching warily across the broad desk. Apparently he'd been summoned to the warden's office, for the first time ever, to discuss the growing of greens. "Missouri, two days out of St. Louis."

"Have you ever grown trees?"

"No, sir," Nate said. "I have not. But I spent a good portion of my youth cutting them down, at my father's bidding. Heavy forest in that part of Missouri, and my father was a dirt farmer. Trees were in the way."

"That's a story very familiar to me," Conley said. "My lumberjack days were along the Chesapeake Bay. In the years before I was born, my grandfather outwitted the local Indians for a section of virgin hardwood forest. Grandpa wasn't much for physical labor and so the tree clearing was left to my father and me. Looking back, I'm not so sure the Indians weren't the ones doing the outwitting. They got the gold coin and without ever wielding an axe."

Nate nodded, thinking of something to add to the conversation. "It wasn't the cutting so much as the stumps that got to a man."

"You're preaching to the choir," Conley said. He got to his feet and walked to the window, where he looked down at his spindly oak saplings. "But now I find myself trying to grow them here. With very limited success."

"I've seen those trees of yours," Nate said. "I wouldn't call that any kind of success."

Looking yet at his project, Conley didn't smile. "You would be right. Watching you grow those tomatoes and pumpkins and corn over the years, I was hoping you might have some insight in growing eastern oak, something with a taproot. Or maybe a hard maple. I miss the syrup on those Sunday mornings when I can persuade the wife to cook up some flannel cakes."

Nate looked evenly at the warden's back. Waiting. Wondering if this little visit had any purpose, other than that of idle talk about trees and pumpkins and flannel cakes.

Now Conley turned. "Under different circumstances, perhaps you and I might tackle the problem together. But I'm getting discouraged to the point of surrender. And you won't be around anyway."

"How's that?"

Conley sat down and opened a desk drawer. He drew out a manila envelope and carefully extracted a document from within.

He held it in his hands for a moment, as if admiring it, not reading it. He placed it on the desk, halfway between himself and Nate.

"I appreciate your help last week," he said. "With the Indian boy."

Nate shrugged. "I was helping him, if anybody. Hostage or no hostage, we both know what was gonna happen, if he'd of walked out that door."

"Yeah, we do," Conley said. "Nevertheless, this institution is not immune to the concept of gratitude."

"I once heard that the quality of mercy is not strained." Nate took a moment to search his memory. "I believe it was that old forger Baldwin said it, while speculating on them he'd swindled."

"That's from Shakespeare."

"I never said that Baldwin come up with it first."

Conley smiled and, with the flat of his hand, slid the document across to Nate. "We're releasing you, Nate. As of tomorrow morning."

Nate, his eyes on the sheet of yellow paper, said nothing for several moments. He hadn't been expecting a conversation about the cultivation of root vegetables or maple trees, and he sure as hell hadn't been expecting this. He gathered himself.

"Releasing me?" he said. "Hell, I just got here."

"You've been here twenty-eight years," Conley said.

Nate looked past the warden, to the high windows, where the morning sun was just now showing on the snowy slopes of Mount Powell.

"I know that, Warden. I know how long I been here."

The suit was of some brown worsted material, a step or two up from burlap. The jacket fit fair to middling, but the pants were short in the legs and pinched in the crotch area. The clothes came in a cardboard box, dropped off in his cell the night before. Also in the box were two pairs of shorts, two pairs of wool socks, and a boiled linen shirt. There was another box as well, and inside was a straw boater. The shoes they gave him were shiny patent leather. They had thin laces and were cut low on the sides, barely covering the feet.

Nate was wearing the new clothes, save the boater which he held in his hand, the next morning, as the warden escorted him to the front gate. It was a gray day, and cool for May, the north wind whipping through the stone walls of the prison. The warden extended his hand and Nate tucked the package containing his extra socks and underwear under his left arm before taking it.

"You have any notion where you're going?" Conley asked.

"None."

Conley pointed vaguely toward the center of Deer Lodge. "There's a boardinghouse with a passable reputation on Buckle Street, just off Main. Colored woman named McKee runs it. You might give that a try until you get your bearings. I trust you got your money from administration?"

"Yes, sir," Nate said. "One hundred and sixty-three dollars and fourteen cents. Should last me the rest of my life, so long as I don't live any more than a month or two."

"You should find work easy enough," Conley said. "You're good with horses and growing things. You have more common sense than most men I walk out these gates."

Nate was doubtful about the last statement but held his opinion.

"You intend to stay out of trouble, I assume?" Conley added.

"Staying out of trouble has always been my intention, Warden. I expect that's true of most everybody. Don't always work out that way. But yes, I would say that I should be able to manage it. I hold no ill feelings toward any man."

"Good." Conley hesitated. "You're going to find it's a different world out there than the one you knew. Telephones and electric lights. Automobiles are here and here to stay, I suspect. Might take some getting used to."

"It's a better world, is it?" Nate asked.

"I'll let you make up your own mind about that," Conley said. "But it's a better world than the one you just left."

Nate nodded, then held up the boater. "I only got one question. What am I supposed to do with this?"

"That's a hat," Conley said. "You wear it on your head."

Nate handed it to the warden. "Not my head. If a cowpuncher in my day showed up wearing a thing like that, we'd of trussed him up like a Christmas turkey and tossed him in the Republican River. I wish you luck with your tap roots, warden. I'll be seeing you. Or rather, I hope not to, if you understand my drift. No intention to offend."

"No offense taken. Good luck to you."

Conley watched as Nate Cooper walked through the gates and headed into the town of Deer Lodge. And he kept watching, thinking the old cowboy might turn for a last look at the place. He never did.

Wilson's Haberdashery & Quality Men's Wear was on Main Street, kitty-corner from the New Baltimore Hotel. Established in 1897 by Rufus Wilson, freshly arrived from Nashville, the store sold custom-made suits, work clothes, beaver hats, shoes and boots, belts and suspenders, and everything else a man might want or need by way of apparel.

When Nate walked through the front door, Rufus himself was behind the counter, a stubby fellow of fifty-six years, with a balding pate and skin as pink as a new born piglet. Looking up from the ledger in front of him, he removed his wire spectacles and his eyes went knowingly over Nate's rough serge suit.

"Good day, sir," he said. "Something I can help you with?"

Nate nodded in the direction of a display of headwear along the wall. "I'll be needing a hat. And a pair of good boots, if you got them."

"We have shoes and work boots and western boots," Rufus told him. "Fresh out of the institution, are you?"

"I'm fresh out of prison, if that's what you're driving at," Nate said. "How'd you know that?"

"Your suit," Rufus said. "I supply the prison with clothes for the inmates. Those being released, that is."

"You made this suit?" Nate asked. "I suspect it was a gunny sack in a previous life."

"I don't make those," Rufus said. "They come in from California. The prison is not willing to pay much. I do make custom suits, if you're in the market."

"This one will do for now," Nate said. "If I don't bleed to death, getting cut from one of those bristles. You the man behind these shoes, too?"

"Well, yes. Is there a problem?"

"Not if you got a pair of good Frye boots you can sell me."

Fifteen minutes later, Nate walked out onto Main Street, twenty-eight dollars poorer, wearing a dun-colored Stetson on his head and brand new Frye boots on his feet, high in the heel and rounded in the toe, in the cowpuncher fashion. The boots were tight across the top of the foot, but Nate would rather have boots that would conform to his feet than a too-big pair that would never be anything but that. The hat had a wide brim and tall crown. It would require some creasing before it would show any personality, but Nate could accommodate that too. He had attempted to barter with Rufus Wilson, hoping to get something in trade for the new prison shoes, which had been worn a total of maybe an hour. Rufus wasn't budging, although he did offer to take them off Nate's hands for nothing.

"And you'll sell them back to the prison," Nate said. "You're like a story I once heard about Davy Crockett. Seems that old Davy traded a coon pelt for a jug of moonshine in a tavern. Every time the owner would put the pelt behind the bar, Davy would steal it back and trade it for another jug."

"I don't get the comparison," Rufus said.

"You might, if you was Davy Crockett," Nate said. He gave the shoes to a man sitting on a bench in the town square. The man was mainly toothless, wearing a moth-eaten wool coat. His own shoes were past worn out.

Nate found the boardinghouse Conley had mentioned. The owner was a large woman, three hundred pounds or more, and she said her name was Thelma McKee. The room she showed Nate was on the third floor, small and clean, with a single bed, a tall dresser and slat back chair. The rate was three dollars a night or seventeen for the week. Nate paid her for a week and left the package he'd been carrying on the dresser. Then he returned to Main Street, for another look at the world he was now a part of, whether he felt that way or not.

Walking into town earlier, he'd been passed in the street by a couple automobiles. Of course, Nate knew of them, from periodicals he'd read inside the prison. What the magazines never fully conveyed was how noisy the machines were, or the odor they emitted—a nasty noxious smell Nate had never before experienced. They constantly belched and farted and backfired, causing enough racket to frighten the horses and mules, which on the main street of Deer Lodge outnumbered the motorcars by ten to one.

Nate stopped at the town square, where he sat on a wrought iron bench and watched the traffic for a while—pedestrians on the move, men on horseback, mules pulling wagons, more of the rattling motorcars. The square was in the center of the town's business district. The sidewalks were of concrete and occupied by men and women, hurrying to and fro, on errands or business. The women were mainly dressed alike and seemed to favor high felt hats with feathers in the bands. Nobody paid much attention to Nate but then why would they have reason to?

There was a diner called Dimaggio's directly across from the square and as he watched, a man in a white apron came out and erected a placard on the sidewalk out front. The sign read:

TODAY'S SPECIAL—CHICKEN & DUMPLINGS 45 CENTS

Nate looked at the sky. It was an overcast day, the sun just a smudge behind the clouds, but he figured it to be nearly noon. He made his way across the street, stopping to allow a rig to pass by, the buggy occupied by a young red-haired girl and her swain. The boy held the reins carelessly in his right hand while twirling a long cheroot in his left. His eyes flicked over Nate without seeing him. As they passed, the girl laughed at something the boy said, her giggle high pitched and exaggerated.

Inside the diner Nate was the first customer of the day. He took a table by the front window and waited for the man in the apron to approach. When he did, he gave Nate's suit the same look as had the haberdasher earlier.

"The special then?" he asked, his voice flat.

"Does this place offer beefsteak?" Nate asked.

"It does."

"That's what it will be then," Nate said. "With potatoes and fresh bread and any kind of vegetable you might have to offer."

"That will run you a buck," the man said. "The chicken is the special and it's only forty-five cents."

"Except I'm not in the mood for chicken," Nate told him. "I've spent many years eating charred gristle disguised as steak. If you claim to have the genuine article back there, then bring it on out. And I would prefer it on the bloody side, if it's not too much to ask."

The meal arrived as ordered. Nate ate slowly, savoring each bite. He drank two cups of coffee and had a slab of apple pie for dessert. By the time he paid his bill, the diner was filling up, merchants and businessmen coming in for lunch. The chicken was doing big business.

His belly fuller than it had been in memory, Nate set out on foot for the train station on the north edge of town. It was the same building where he had stepped down from the passenger car, manacles on his wrists, nearly thirty years earlier. It had been kept in good repair in that time, the walls painted a blood red, the roof newly cedar shingled. Inside the depot, Nate asked about a train running south to Opportunity and the station agent, who was playing checkers with a man dressed in greasy blue coveralls, handed him a schedule before returning to his game without a word.

Walking back into town, Nate stopped at a dry goods store to buy a watch; having a train schedule was of no use if he didn't know the time of day. He chose a Walther pocket watch for a dollar. After setting it by a clock on the wall, he noticed a display of pistols in a glass case by the cash register. Nate looked them over before indicating a Smith & Wesson that had obviously been used hard. The price tag said twelve dollars.

"I'd like a look at that revolver."

The merchant was a bean pole of a man with a shock of jet black hair, parted in the middle and plastered down with grease of some sort. "That .38 needs repair," he said. "The pawl is worn, and it don't always advance."

"Does it fire?"

"It does, but the pawl is worn and don't always advance."

Nate took the revolver from the man and looked at the bore, then half-cocked the hammer and turned the cylinder with the ball of his thumb. "I'll give you eight dollars if you throw in a half dozen shells," he said.

The skinny man considered it briefly and then nodded. "On the understanding that the revolver needs repair."

Nate paid the man and tucked the revolver into his waistband inside his coat.

Across from the dry goods store was the Great Western Hotel, a rundown two-story affair that Nate remembered from the early days. He went inside and bought a beer at the bar, then sat down at a table by the dirty front window to read the schedule. The place was nearly empty. Aside from the saloonkeeper, there were two men drinking at the scarred bar, both dressed in overalls and work boots. They had soot-lined faces and appeared to be miners. Another man, dressed in a gray suit and wearing bushy side whiskers, was drinking hard liquor at a table in the corner, a half full bottle in front of him. He stared openly at Nate until Nate returned the favor and he looked away.

Nate folded the schedule and put it in his pocket, then leaned back to enjoy his beer. He wondered if the Great Western Hotel had any sporting ladies in the rooms upstairs. There had been several the last time Nate was there. He'd gotten to know one quite well, a red-haired woman named Hannah. She was a natural redhead, maybe ten years older than Nate, and a good deal of fun to be with, both in and out of bed. She and Nate had once gone on a picnic together, taking a buggy into the foothills. He wondered what had become of her. She could be dead and if she wasn't, she'd be an old woman. But, sitting there with his beer, Nate couldn't help but miss the younger version of her. He'd been half in love with her, in spite of her profession. That part hadn't bothered him in the least; in his opinion a whore was honest in ways that most people were not.

He drank two more five cent beers before leaving and as he walked back toward the town center he could feel the effects of the alcohol. He passed the remainder of the afternoon wandering around the town, covering all the streets eventually, looking at the fancy new houses on the west side, and the shanties out along the tracks to the east. There was a baseball field on the east bank of the river, where several youths were playing scrub. Nate watched for a bit. He drew looks, in his prison suit and new hat. For supper, he had another beer and two pickled eggs at a small hotel not far from the prison. The bartender was a man named Doge, who had served time with Nate before being released ten years ago. A decade gone and he hadn't made it any further than a few hundred yards from the prison gates. They visited for a time but there wasn't enough in common between the two of them to sustain much conversation.

It was dark when Nate arrived back at the rooming house. Inside the front door to the left was the parlor, where a man in a checkered suit sat, playing solitaire on a drop leaf table. The man greeted Nate heartily, as if to invite his company, but Nate just nodded and climbed the two flights of steps to his room.

He lit the lamp on the night stand. Sitting on the bed, he pulled the stiff boots off with considerable effort and then took the revolver from his waistband and put it beneath the pillow. He sat on the bed for a time, looking at the wall. There was a painting there, or at least a print of a painting, of a locomotive out on the prairie. An assortment of men, eastern dandies, was hanging out the windows of the passenger cars, shooting down a herd of buffalo in the distance. The men wore expressions of rapture on their faces.

Nate stood up and undressed. Turning off the electric light, he got into bed and lay there, looking at the ceiling. There was a rustling in the wall behind the baseboard and it made him think of Bo. He'd had a notion to sneak the mouse out of the prison with him, tucked in the coat pocket of his new suit. In the end he had decided against it. Out here in the real world, the mouse would probably get eaten by a cat or squashed beneath the wheels of a motorcar. Nate couldn't help but feel that his own future was equally uncertain. He was a long while going to sleep.

Two

AFTER LUNCH ROSE PUT ON A pair of Harry's old pants, and a blue chambray work shirt. Both were too large but she cinched the pants with a cowhide belt that was, like the trousers, too small for him anymore, and rolled the sleeves of the shirt up past her elbows. Downstairs, she laced up her boots, tied her dark hair back behind her neck, and went out to plant her garden.

She had cultivated the ground the day before, enlisting young Donnelly's help, starting with the mule-drawn tiller and finishing up with rakes and shovels. She had made note of—and ignored— the fact that the youngster was somewhat mortified and downright embarrassed to be doing such work. He'd hired on the previous fall as a hand, and Rose was quite certain that he considered scratching around in the soil to be beneath his station as a cowboy. Of course, the boy was too polite and well-mannered to make mention of this directly to the boss's wife. Rose didn't know much about his background; he'd come from the Milk River country and arrived already somewhat accomplished with regards to riding and roping and cutting. She was sure he hadn't had a nickel in his pocket the day he signed on. But he was willing and responsible; Rose suspected he'd been raised dirt poor but right. That didn't change the fact that he had been none too happy about playing farmer for a day. The country was changing, and not always in a good way, but one truth remained—a cowboy didn't want to do anything he couldn't do from the back of a horse.

She raked the tilled soil again and then, using a roll of twine and some wooden stakes, she laid the garden out. The plot was along the south wall of the main barn, on an elevated piece of ground she covered with rotted manure every fall. She put in the tomato plants first, seedlings she had started weeks ago in the kitchen, planting them hard against the barn wall so the vines could be tied there when they grew heavy. The rest of the vegetables—corn, beans, peppers, squash—she sowed in rows running at right angles to the wall. She stayed at it steadily for a couple of hours, carrying buckets of water from the horse trough at the base of the windmill in the corral, and was soon sweating in the May sun.

Mid-afternoon young Donnelly came riding up to the remuda where they grazed on the slope a hundred yards or so from where Rose was working. He slid down from the tired gelding he was aboard, pulled saddle and bridle from the animal and deftly roped a tall bay mare. Saddling the horse, he took extra care not to glance in Rose's direction. She waited until he was back in the saddle, and thinking he was in the clear, before calling him over. He came at a reluctant trot, wiping his sweat-stained face vigorously with his bandana as he approached, apparently concerned about his appearance.

"Just changing my mount," he said, hoping to discourage any notions Rose might have of enlisting his help again. "Heading back out."

"I see that," she said. "Garden's coming right along."

"Yes, ma'am." The mare, not ridden of late, was somewhat rank and Donnelly was required to keep a tight rein or she would have trampled the just-planted ground. "Well, I best be getting back."

"You did a good job here yesterday," Rose said. "I was telling Mildred Parsons about it, and she inquired whether you'd be interested in helping her with her own vegetable patch. She puts in a sizable crop every year. Does a lot of preserving. Of course, she would pay you. I was thinking you could work for her on the weekend, if you were interested."

It was quite evident young Donnelly would rather hunt grizzly bear with a buggy whip than help Mildred Parsons with her vegetable patch. Rose looked steadily at the young cowboy.

"Well, ma'am," Donnelly said, and then stopped to formulate his argument. "Well, ma'am, the thing is, we got the gather right now, and I feel I should devote all my energy to that." He paused, his mind racing. "It's my opinion that this will be our best gather ever, but it's going to take considerable effort and it would not be right for me to divide my—"

"But this will be your first gather," Rose reminded him.

"That's true, ma'am. That is true." Donnelly glanced longingly toward the foothills. "It's just—it's just that I feel obligated to concentrate on my ranch work."

"Well then, I guess I'll have to send Mildred your regrets." Rose watched the relief wash across the young cowboy's face.

"I best be getting back, ma'am."

"Now if you change your mind—" Rose began, but Donnelly had already kicked the mare into a lope. He rode off without hearing her, or at the very least he rode off pretending not to hear her.

When he was out of sight she walked to the house for a drink of water, that in the horse trough being suitable for livestock only. Harry had installed indoor plumbing in the ranch house three years earlier, drawing the water from a spring-filled cistern. Rose ran the tap until the water was cool and poured a glass full. Standing looking out the kitchen window to the road in front of the ranch, she arched her back where her muscles had stiffened while working the garden. Another harbinger of her years, along with some gray in her hair, problems with her teeth (having had two pulled in the past eighteen months), and a growing impatience with stupid or unreasonable people, although some would argue that Rose had always suffered from that particular ailment. Those concerns aside, she was fortunate that she didn't feel any older. She still weighed the same, more or less, as she had in her twenties. And, aside from the diminishing of certain desires, she felt the same as well. She would turn fifty-three in a month.

Moving away from the window, she noticed the copy of the *Helena Statesman* on the table. Harry must have brought it home with him the night before. Rose flipped it open to find a picture of her brother inside the front page, standing in an office somewhere with Governor Toole and a couple of other state senators, all looking mighty pleased with themselves about something, the details of which could be found, no doubt, in the accompanying story if a person was inclined to read it. Rose was not.

When she walked back outside, intending to carry more water to the garden, she heard the motorcar before she saw it, the loud cacophony of bleating and barking, as if a mutant strain of sheep had invaded the range. She stood watching the road where it crested to the north and after a half minute the machine came into view, shiny black, with brass adornments, meandering its way back and forth through the ruts of the rough dirt road.

Harry was behind the wheel of the thing, wearing goggles and a ridiculous tweed cap. He rolled the noisy vehicle through the front gates and up to the house, where Rose was now standing on the porch, watching resignedly. Harry abruptly braked the motorcar and then took several moments figuring out how to shut the racket down. He smiled at Rose.

"Well?"

"You couldn't have found a fancier one?" she asked.

Harry laughed. "Nope. Nor a better one neither. This is the brand new Cadillac. Had her going twenty-five miles an hour coming out of Cut Bank. Imagine that! We could be in Helena in just four hours."

"Except I have no desire to go to Helena. Fast or slow."

Climbing out of the seat, Harry ignored her negative tone. "And look here. Gas lights. I'll take you on a midnight drive, Rose."

"You go tearing around the range with that noisy contraption after dark and you'll have a cattle stampede on your hands, certain as sunrise. And take those goggles off. You look like a frog."

Harry removed the goggles but not the grin. "Let's go for a drive. We'll go into town for dinner at the Belmont."

"I'm cooking a roast for dinner," Rose said. "And putting in my vegetable garden."

"That why you're dressed like a muleskinner?" Harry asked. "You know I don't like you wearing my trousers. It's not ladylike."

"I'm digging in the dirt, not waltzing with President Taft. I might just as well wear your pants; they don't fit you anymore."

As Harry looked down at his considerable girth, Rose relented a bit. She wasn't determined to hurt him; it was just that she was not overly enthusiastic about the motorcar. There were a lot of things about the new century she was not impressed by, although she was quite content with some advances, such as the fact that she could fill a tub with hot water whenever she desired. But she could live without the noise, and the general sense that life was improving with each new development or invention.

"We can go for a drive later," she said. "If you leave the silly hat in the house."

Harry smiled as he climbed back into the motorcar. He fired the thing up again and jerked away, leaving Rose to breathe in the acrid exhaust. Watching him, she sighed.

Three

OPPORTUNITY, IN SPITE OF THE ENCOURAGING nature of its name, wasn't much of a town, just a whistle stop on the rail line forty miles south of Deer Lodge. Nate took the morning train, a steam locomotive pulling two passenger cars, two freighters, and a caboose. They chugged out of the station at ten o'clock and in minutes were clear of the town. Nate sat on the west side of the car, looking out the window to the passing country. He could see the John Long Mountains in the distance, their slopes peppered with stands of pine and fir. There had been rain recently, and the creeks and streams were running full, flowing south, parallel to the tracks, sometimes tumbling east beneath the wooden trestles of the rail line. Nate found the view outside the Pullman window to be familiar and somewhat reassuring. The town he had just left was as foreign as any he could have imagined. It was louder and brighter and the people moved faster than he recalled. They even talked quicker, like chattering squirrels. The pace of the world had increased, like a horse that had been spurred into a gallop that never ended.

But outside the train, where the country ran on forever, things remained the same. Mankind couldn't change a mountain or a river. Maybe someday he would be able to, Nate admitted, but not now and not in his lifetime. It made him content to think that there were things outside the influence of man.

It was just past noon when the train pulled into Opportunity. The depot was at the north edge of the village, along a rock-strewn road that ran parallel to the tracks. A man in a duster and brown derby, leaning against a one-horse buggy, offered a lift into town for a dollar. Nate declined and walked the quarter mile or so along the road to the main street, the new boots squeezing his toes like they were apples in a cider press. He passed a livery and a general store and a mortician's enterprise that served double duty, according to the sign out front, as the local newspaper office.

There was one hotel in town, with a saloon on the ground floor and rooms above. A saloon was a good place to get a drink and, as a rule, just as good for obtaining information. Nate was in the market for both. The bartender, a pock-faced mutterer with oily hair and dirty fingernails, served the drink. Or drinks, as it turned out, as Nate had three shots of second-rate rye before he found out what he wanted to know, the information coming from a swamper, who stumbled out of a back room, corn broom in hand and a look about him that suggested he'd just gotten up from a nap.

Willard's house was at the end of a narrow lane a mile out of town, a sagging bungalow with peeling paint, set back in a copse of thin aspens a hundred yards or so from the dirt road. There were more weeds than flowers in a garden out front, and broken shutters on the house. To the right and behind was a small barn, with a pole corral attached where a swayback sorrel stood, looking over the top rail at Nate's approach. A dozen red hens ran in and out of the barnyard, pecking in the dirt. Beside the barn was a leaning woodshed of gray board and cedar shingles. A kid of maybe fourteen or fifteen was out front of the shed, splitting kindling with an axe. Nate stopped short when he saw the youngster, taking a moment to consider his presence before walking over. His knee, where the knife had gone in twenty years earlier, was bothering him some from the long walk.

"Howdy," he said.

The kid was a cringer for certain. Dirty blond hair and brown freckles, peach fuzz on his upper lip so inconsequential that a cat could have licked it off. He was skinny and scarred up and looked like he'd had a rough go of it so far in life. It sure as hell wouldn't be getting any less rough. Not in this man's yard. This man's employ.

"Willard around?" Nate asked.

The kid jerked his head toward the house. He apparently didn't have much talk in him. Maybe it had been encouraged out of him.

"He alone in there?"

The kid nodded and looked down at the pile of kindling at his feet. There was a considerable amount there, and Nate could see maybe five times that stacked inside the shed, alongside a half dozen cord of firewood. The kid wore patched overalls and no shirt, in spite of the cool day. His shoes hardly qualified as footwear, scuffed void of all color, no laces, tongues lolling out like that of a pair of tired hounds. Nate saw now that the boy had a droopy eye, the lid hanging at the corner, a triangle of fresh scar tissue just above. Somebody had taken a stick to the kid, or a poker. Nate could guess who.

"You be the hired hand, I expect," Nate said.

Another nod.

"You ain't a mute, are you?"

"No, sir," the kid said. A long pause. "Ain't exactly hired neither."

"What's that?"

The kid glanced toward the house before answering. "Ain't hired. My pap owes boss man some money from a card game. I'm working it off."

That's the way it would be with Willard. And working for free wouldn't be the worst of it. Not by a damn sight.

"How long you been working it off?"

"Some months now," the kid replied.

Must have been quite a card game, Nate thought, turning to look toward the silent house. "What's he doing in there?"

"Maybe taking a nap. Tends to do that of an afternoon."

Nate's eyes remained on the front door as he wondered what to do about the kid. After a few moments, he took four bits from his pants and offered it over. "Do me a favor, boy, and run down to the telegraph office. There'll be a wire coming for me. Wait on it and fetch it here."

The kid looked at the coin like it was a gold piece, but he never made a move for it. "I can't be going nowhere. Boss man have my hide."

"I will square things with him," Nate said as he reached forward to drop the coin in the boy's breast pocket. "Now you get. And you wait for that wire."

Every move the kid made was slow and deliberate, like he worried over it being the wrong one. He'd probably had that beaten into him, too. Now he leaned the axe handle against the chopping block and then—after one more nervous glance toward the house—started for town. When he reached the dirt road, he stopped.

"I need your name for the telegraph."

Nate, watching the house, didn't turn. "William H. Bonney," he said.

Willard was fat when Nate last saw him, and he'd grown fatter in the five years since. He was sleeping on a davenport when Nate walked in, legs splayed, one arm across his eyes, his breathing labored. He wore just an undershirt and black striped pants that looked as if they were at one time part of a morning suit. Now they were stained, unbuttoned at the waist. Across the room was a small dining room table, with four chairs. There was a Bible on the table, along with some periodicals.

Nate walked past the sleeping man and into the kitchen at the back of the house. The stove there was black and silver, splattered with the remains of countless meals. A burled maple ice box stood against the wall. In a little room off the kitchen, there was a pallet on the floor, with a dirty sheet and an ancient cavalry blanket on it. The kid's bunk. Nate went back into the main room, past the sleeping man, who had begun to snore, and down a narrow hallway. There were two bedrooms there, one obviously belonging to Willard, the other a guest room, with a four poster bed and a maple dresser and a clean chamber pot. A room apparently too nice for the help.

Nate walked back into the living room and listened to the guttural sounds coming from the man on the couch. Nate hadn't been sure he'd even find him in Opportunity. He'd gotten the information a few years earlier, from a guard who'd kept in touch with Willard for a time. But the guard had left the prison since, discharged as had been Willard, and the information was dated.

Nate moved over and jabbed the toe of his new boot sharply into Willard's ribs. As the man came out of his slumber, Nate retreated to pull out a chair and sit at the dining room table, facing the fat man. Willard sat up, his thin hair every which way, eyes blinking. He looked at Nate, then his gaze went to the front door, as if questioning how Nate came to be there.

"Who the hell are you?" he asked.

Nate put his hands flat on the table and said nothing as he watched slow recognition come to Willard's eyes.

"Cooper—ain't it Cooper?" He took a couple of shallow breaths as he tried to figure out what was going on. "So they let you out, did they?"

Nate was silent as Willard got to his feet and walked over to look out the front window. "Where's that boy at?"

"I sent him into town."

Willard turned. "Why would you do that?"

By way of reply Nate removed the new Stetson and placed it carefully on the table. He leaned back and hooked his thumbs in his vest, like a banker or lawyer, presiding over a meeting of sorts. Willard watched him suspiciously for a moment before making his way to a sideboard where he poured whiskey into a dirty tumbler. He looked at Nate over the rim of the glass as he drank it off. He poured again.

"I don't recall inviting you into my house, but I'll offer you a drink. Whilst you tell me the reason for your being here."

Nate shook his head, his eyes steady on the man.

"Take the cure, did you?" Willard asked. "Seems to me you were one of them that was always making homemade hooch, out of rotten apples or chokeberries or whatever you could get your hands on. You and that sorry bunch of wop sodbusters from down south." He drank again, growing impatient with Nate's silence. "How long you been out?"

"Two days," Nate said.

"Two days," Willard repeated. "And first thing you do is take it upon yourself to track me down. Ain't that peculiar?"

Nate shrugged, his fingers drumming lightly on the tabletop.

"Who told you how to find me—that sonofabitch Conley?" Willard asked. He took another drink, growing more antsy. "And why are you even here, anyway? I don't recall us being any kind of friends."

Nate watched the man's face grow redder and redder.

"What are you doing in my house, goddamn it? Walk in here and set there with that stupid look on your face, don't say nothing. I never had no truck with you, all the time I was there. Who do you think you are?"

"Who do you think you are?" Nate asked.

"I'm the goddamn owner of this house."

"No," Nate said. "I truly would like to know. Who do you think you are? Is there any remorse in you? All those boys, don't you ever step back and think about what you did? Don't it give you pause when you are alone at night, considering all the things a man considers in his dark hours?"

"I don't know what you're talking about. I never did nothing."

Nate gestured toward the kitchen. "You did, and you're doing it yet. Got that boy sleeping on a wood pallet like a dog. Except those times, I'm guessing, when you take him into your bed. That's a step up for you. Back in Deer Lodge, it was the laundry, wasn't it? Or the stable. Some dirty place for your dirty business."

"You get the hell out of here," Willard said. His eyes shifted to the front door and quickly back. Nate saw now there was a shotgun leaning there, in the shadow of the corner, an old hammerlock double barrel. It would be loaded, against prowlers or skunks, or foxes after those hens.

Now Nate picked up the Bible and held it in his hand without opening it, like a man swearing his testimony in court. "You got religion, Willard?"

"What if I do?"

Nate leaned forward to place the Bible in the center of the table. "How you figure to square it? When you arrive at those gates, how do you intend to explain yourself?"

"I got nothing to square."

"No? You figure that fucking children ain't going to count against you?"

"I never touched any of them boys. That was all lies, made up by them against me. Lies Conley believed. Cost me my job."

Nate fingered the brim of the new Stetson, turning it on the table top. "You remember that Polish kid, Petey?"

"No."

"Yeah, you do. Boy climbed up the guard tower. At first they thought he was climbing the wall to escape. You recall—the guards yelling at him, all of them holding rifles, itching to shoot. Warden held them off. That boy got to the top of the fence and just kept climbing up the tower. Kept climbing 'til he got as high as he could get and jumped off." Nate looked up from the hat. "Because of what you done to him."

"That's bullshit."

Nate shook his head. "No, it's not bullshit. You know it took that boy four days to die. I sat with him. You never came around. Guess you had no use for him, not then anyway. You used him before that though, didn't you?"

"No, I did not."

"Do you think you can lie your way into heaven?" Nate asked. He waited for an answer he didn't expect. "You know why that boy was in Deer Lodge? Probably not; you wouldn't care about that. His father was a drunkard, died from wood alcohol poisoning in Miles City. That left the boy and his mama and a passel of brothers and sisters. The boy stole a bag of flour and a side of bacon from a general store. Looking to feed his family. Judge sent him off to Deer Lodge for a year to teach him a lesson. Well, he got quite a lesson there, didn't he?"

"Get the hell out of my house," Willard said. He was shaking now, with anger or fear. He had moved another step toward the hammerlock shotgun.

"I got to know Petey," Nate said. "He helped mend harness and I taught him to make a horsehair rope. He told me he wanted to be a cowpuncher when he got out. I discouraged him some, said there were easier ways to earn your keep. He was a good boy. I believe he'd of been a good man." Nate paused. "Given the chance."

"I'm telling you I never touched him," Willard said, his voice rising. "What's your game, Cooper? You after money? You sonofabitch, you try something smart with me and I'll call the law and have you back in Deer Lodge come nightfall. I ain't about to be bullyragged by an old man."

Nate got to his feet, picked the Stetson up, ran his fingers along the crease and put the hat on his head. He could hear Willard's breath coming quickly. "I guess I am an old man. I don't know what I got ahead of me. Maybe not much. And I got my own fair share of sins behind me, enough that I got no illusions about those gates you dream of. But I have one thing. I told that boy Petey, before he died, I told him I would come see you, if ever I got the chance."

"Well, you spoke your piece, now be gone," Willard said, panic setting in. He glanced toward the yard. "Why'd you send that boy to town anyway?"

"He'll need an alibi," Nate said. "I reckon sitting in a telegraph office all day will do the trick."

When the fat man had his hands on the shotgun, Nate pulled the .38 from his coat and fired once. The slug went in behind the ear and Willard fell heavily into the wall, sliding to the floor on his side, his bulk blocking the doorway. After a moment he rolled over onto his back, his eyes wide open and looking up at the ceiling, toward the heaven he'd convinced himself he deserved.

Nate left the revolver on the table and went out the back way. He walked the dirt road into town, had a sandwich in a diner and took the afternoon train north, arriving in Deer Lodge as the sun was going down. He drank a couple of glasses of draught ale in the Great Western Hotel and had a conversation with a man who was selling magazine subscriptions. He was out of Denver and young, maybe twenty-five or so. He told Nate that he was a natural born salesman and intended to be a millionaire by the time he was thirty.

"And what is your line of work?" the man asked Nate when he finally quit talking about himself.

"I don't have one at the present time," Nate replied. "I had but one little job to take care of, and I did that today."

"And what job was that?"

Nate finished the ale and got to his feet. "Oh, I took the train down south a bit and shot a man dead in his living room."

The salesman stared. "Come on, you're pulling my leg."

"Of course I am," Nate said and left.

Four

IT BEING FRIDAY, THE SENATE ADJOURNED at noon. Many of the members headed back to their districts for the weekend, although a good number, especially those from the farther reaches of the state, remained in town. There was always a shindig of some description going on someplace and senators and legislators were usually welcome, regardless of party affiliation. Helena might be a partisan town from Monday to Friday, but on weekends it was belly up to the bar.

Clayton stood outside the senate building for half an hour, talking to Bill Ferguson and Andy Duncan about the highway act, each of them telling the other what he thought he wanted to hear before walking to his office in the common building. Nancy was at her desk, typing something on the Underwood. She wore a dark blue dress, buttoned down the front, the tailoring of which displayed her figure nicely. There was a thin haze of smoke in the air, and the window was open. She would have heard Clayton coming down the hallway and either butted the cigarette or tossed it out the window before he arrived. She smiled up at him as he entered, looking over the tinted glasses on her nose.

"How did it go?"

"As expected," Clayton replied. "Ben Stoddard and that bunch, if they moved any slower they'd be going backward. Every comma, every period, must be debated over, dissected, eviscerated. Good thing for Moses those boys weren't around in his day. He'd have been lucky to get down one commandment, never mind ten."

Nancy smiled at him brightly. Her blonde hair, blonder this week than last it seemed, was tied in a French braid that came over her left should to rest on her impressive breast. Clayton took a step toward the window and had a look outside.

"Look at this. Somebody threw a perfectly good cigarette onto the lawn."

Nancy immediately went back to her typing. Clayton headed for the inner office, stopping in the doorway.

"You're never going to find a husband if you continue those nasty habits," he said.

"Did I say I was looking for a husband?"

"I just assumed. A woman your age."

"I'm surprised you would do that."

"Do what?"

"Assume things you don't know, a smart man like you. And besides—why is it all right for you to smoke a cigarette but it's not for me?"

"It's not ladylike," Clayton told her. He left the door open as he crossed the room to sit at his desk. He glanced at the correspondence there. "Did I know that Park Watson died?"

"You sent a card," Nancy said, meaning that she sent the card.

"I should send flowers too."

"You did that as well."

"How did he die?"

"I believe he told a lady friend she wasn't allowed to smoke cigarettes and she shot him."

Clayton smiled toward the outer office, where Nancy was typing away as she cracked wise. "You are in a mood, Miss Swenson."

"You bring it out in me, sir," Nancy said. "Are you heading for the ranch?"

"Yes," Clayton replied. "I'm taking the three o'clock train."

"Is Mrs. Covington going as well?"

Clayton hesitated. It seemed that Nancy was slowly becoming more interested in his personal affairs. She had been his secretary for a little over a year. Her predecessor, Mrs. Myrtle Birch, had been extremely interested in Clayton's non-political dealings and it had led to her dismissal. But Myrtle Birch was a doughty type, in her sixties, with a mustache that rivalled Teddy Roosevelt's. Miss Swenson was a different creature.

"No, she'll be staying in the city."

"Does she not like it at the ranch?" Nancy said.

"It's not that. She has many interests here in Helena."

"I love it up there myself. I think often of the time I went, when you were campaigning. The air seemed so fresh there. I liked seeing your cattle, all spread out on the green grass. And your cowboys. Just like the days of the wild west. Even the Indians I liked seeing. In spite of their appearance, there is still something—I don't know—noble about them."

"Is there?"

"Yes." Nancy rolled the paper up from the typewriter to read it. "What happened to them anyway?"

"Who?" Clayton asked.

"The Indians," Nancy replied. "In school back east we would read all about the noble savage. One time the whole class went to see Buffalo Bill's western show. Sitting Bull himself was there! What a specimen he was, fearful even to look at. But those Indians in the north country seem to be a sorry bunch. What happened to them?"

"What happened is that they cannot grasp the concept of progress," Clayton said. "They are Neanderthals living in the age of enlightenment. Lord knows we have tried to help them, but they won't be helped. Their life as they knew it is gone and now the only thing they are good at is getting in the way. They were in the way of the settlers, of the miners, and then the railroad. Now they're in the way of civilization in general."

"How do they live?"

"Handouts," Clayton said. "With them, the sun rose and set on the buffalo herds. Well, the buffalo are gone. We've been giving them food and clothing for forty years. My father, in particular, tried to help them. He was there when the treaty of 1855 was ratified, with old Lame Bull. Maybe it was a mistake, giving them welfare. Maybe we should have left them to fade away."

"Is that what will happen to them?" Nancy asked.

"It might be for the best," Clayton said. "Better that than they breed with white people, which is already happening. That just creates a mongrel strain that nobody wants. Better they go the way of the buffalo."

"That's too bad," Nancy said, fingering the braid that came over her shoulder. She was finished talking about the Indians though. There was nothing she could do about their situation. "I must say that I most certainly liked your ranch though."

The steer hung from a ponderosa pine in a clearing a mile east of the reservation. The animal had been skinned out and gutted. The Blackfoot who had done the work wore dirty deerskin leggings and a navy wool coat. Now he was kneeling by a small fire on a flat rock, roasting something on a stick. The tenderloins, Garner surmised. There was a skinny pony, wearing a blanket and a rope bridle, standing hipshot at the back of the clearing.

Garner was sitting his horse in a heavy cottonwood thicket down the slope, a quarter mile away, looking at the scene above him through a brass spyglass that he'd taken off a drunken swabbie in a San Francisco alley one night twenty years earlier. Garner knew the Indian by sight, if not by name. He'd seen him in town, like the rest of them, always with their hands out. Wanting tobacco, wanting sugar, wanting whiskey. Stealing when the begging didn't pan out.

Garner fished the makings from his breast pocket and rolled a cigarette. Before he lit it, he wet a finger and tested the wind. He doubted the man kneeling by the fire up the slope could pick up the smell of a cigarette at that distance, but you never could tell with an Indian. The breeze was slight and in Garner's face, so he lit up and smoked while he watched the rustler at his lunch.

The steer was a healthy animal, probably a two-year-old. Garner wondered how the Indian intended to tote the meat off. The skinny pony might be up to carrying a quarter at best, and even with that, the Indian would have to walk alongside. Maybe the man had a cabin or a lean-to nearby, somewhere hidden where he could hang the rest of the carcass. Take it back to the reservation piecemeal. At this point, of course, it really didn't matter what the Indian's intentions were. His plans were in the wind.

When he had finished the cigarette, Garner butted it against the saddle horn and climbed down from the big gelding, pulling the fifty caliber Sharps from the scabbard. He slid a shell into the chamber and found a low hanging branch to rest the barrel on. In the clearing above, the Indian finished his meal and as he stood to scatter the fire Garner drew a bead and shot him in the small of the back. The heavy slug hit the Indian with such force that he pitched forward ten or twelve feet.

By the time Garner mounted the horse and rode up to the clearing, the Indian had done all the twitching and convulsing he was ever going to do. Garner took a switch to the pony, sending the animal off at a gallop, heading back to the reservation. Garner looped his rope around the Indian's ankles and tied it off to the saddle. He dragged the body down the slope, through Thompson Creek, and out onto the grassland. There he untied the man and stripped him of his clothes. He left him there, naked and dead, in the high prairie grass. It would be a contest as to what got to him first—the coyotes or the buzzards.

Heading back to the ranch, Garner spotted half a dozen hands, driving forty or fifty heifers up to the summer graze. Old Fields was on the drag, poking along on the jughead gray he favored. Garner rode over to cut him off.

"Had to shoot a lame steer up there a ways," he said, jerking his thumb over his shoulder. "I skinned it out and hung it from a pine tree, about a mile above Thompson Creek. Take a team and a wagon and fetch it back. Murphy can butcher it for the crew."

Fields was nearing the end of his usefulness as a hand and he was reluctant to take on any chores he perceived to be extra duty. He looked at the sky. "Be dark by the time I hitch a team and get there and back. Might just as soon wait 'til morning."

"By morning the wolves will have it. Do it now."

Still the old cowboy balked. "Would made more sense to drive it down to the ranch to kill it."

"I told you the animal was lame," Garner said. "And I don't need you to tell me what makes sense and what don't. Get to it."

Garner reined the gelding around and rode off before Fields could offer further complaint. He skirted the herd of heifers and approached the ranch house from the south. As he rode into the yard, he spotted Clayton, standing on the porch, a glass in his hand. Garner pulled the Sharps rifle from the scabbard before unsaddling the horse and turning it loose in the corral. He headed for the house, the carbine in the crook of his arm.

"Hello, Ed," Clayton said. "How are things?"

"Could be worse."

"How you coming with the gather?"

"Pretty fair," Garner said. "There's still a wild bunch scattered up top we need to flush out."

"No problems?"

"I wouldn't say that," Garner replied. "There's a grizzly making a nuisance of himself. I got bad news—he took down your English bull last week, up above the tree line. Looks like they had a regular battle. The bull was still alive when the hands found him but couldn't be saved. The bear got away, but the track showed he was bleeding pretty good. Three days later he killed and ate a heifer, so he's still in business. I'm gonna have to take a couple days, see if I can track him."

Clayton looked past Garner toward the mountains, where the incident took place. "I paid a lot of money for that bull."

"I know it, boss." Garner waited a moment. "We're going to need some new blood for breeding. Those heifers on that west range are all the same line as that roan bull."

Clayton exhaled. "Let me see what I can find on the market. Goddamn grizzly. Four thousand head out there and he's got to kill that particular animal. Money down the drain."

"I was thinking that very thing," Garner said.

"Are we losing any other stock? Any two-legged bears taking advantage?"

"Now and again," Garner said. "Matter of fact, I had a situation today." He pointed his chin west.

"These people are slow to learn," Clayton said, shaking his head. "I've hired some extra help to deal with the problem. Be here first of the week."

"I don't need any help on that front," Garner said. He looked down at the ground, clearly put out.

"We need to make a statement to these people," Clayton told him. "What happened today?"

"I took care of it." He shifted the Sharps from his left hand to his right. "Proper like."

Five

AFTER WAKING UP IN THE BOARDINGHOUSE on the second morning there, Nate sat on the edge of the bed and examined the blisters on top of his feet. He realized he had done nothing but walk everywhere he'd had to go since getting out of prison. Nate had never been a fan of walking. He never knew a cowpuncher worth his sand who was. Walking was for farmers or drummers or railroad workers. And if Nate was not in favor of walking under ordinary circumstances, he certainly wasn't in favor of walking in brand new, too-tight, blister-causing Frye boots.

He took breakfast in the dining room and afterward paid Mrs. McKee twenty-five cents for a tub. Nate sat in the parlor, drinking coffee and reading the weekly Deer Lodge newspaper while a colored boy traveled up and down the stairs with buckets of water, heated on the gas stove in the kitchen. If Nate were in charge of the boardinghouse, he'd have installed the tub on the ground floor. He suspected the colored boy, sweating like a coal miner, would vote in favor of such a plan.

Once it was filled, Nate took a long soak in the copper tub. The warm water loosened his stiff knee and relieved the tension from his bunched back muscles as well. Climbing out, he got dressed, pulled the new boots on and got back in, standing in the warm water until the leather was completely saturated. When he left the boardinghouse, his wet footprints could be seen crossing Mrs. McKee's faded Persian carpet. Nate wore the wet boots all that day and throughout the night, sleeping atop the bedspread so as not to dirty the sheets. By morning the boots were dry and fit perfectly. Mrs. McKee kept a honey pail half full of rendered bacon fat on the back of her cook stove. Using a rag, Nate greased the boots to lubricate and waterproof the leather. Other than the fact that he was followed by half the cats in Deer Lodge for the rest of the day, he was pleased with the effort.

Now that he could walk in comfort, that afternoon he made the two-mile trek to the Kohrs ranch, on the flat plain northwest of the city. Nate had been there once before, delivering a string of ponies for a rancher outside of Bynum, up in Teton County. At that time he had met Conrad Kohrs, and even had a drink of whiskey with the man. Kohrs had been the first large scale rancher in Powell County, and one of the first in the state. He had arrived in the territory as a miner and, when he didn't find gold, he had gotten rich by selling beef to those who did.

The ranch had grown even bigger in the thirty years since Nate had been there, the corrals and outbuildings now spreading across ten acres or more. There were thousands of short-horned cattle grazing along the banks of the Clark Fork, and a few hundred horses in paddocks nearer the house. A couple dozen hands could be seen across the great expanse of the ranch, riding among the herds. Nate found the foreman by the bunkhouse, smoking a pipe and writing in a ledger of sorts while he sat in the seat of an unhitched buckboard.

"The old man's up in Helena," he said when Nate asked after Conrad Kohrs.

"When is he due back?" Nate asked.

"No telling," the foreman said. He took a moment, looking Nate over. "You know he's a senator?"

"A senator?" Nate repeated.

"That's right."

"Hell, he was the biggest cattleman in the territory. That's a step backward, ain't it—becoming a politician?"

"I reckon you can foster your own opinion on that," the foreman said. He went back to his writing. "Something I can help you with?"

"Looking for work," Nate said.

The foreman glanced over. "What kind of work?"

"What kind do you think?" Nate asked. "This is a cattle ranch, ain't it?"

The foreman finished his tallying and closed the ledger. "It is, and we're about to start the gather. How are you with chuck? Cookie needs somebody to help him out."

"I'm looking for work as a hand," Nate said. "I ain't driving no chuck wagon. Your boss knows me. I brung a string of thirty-seven horses down from up north, ran 'em right in that corral behind the house. Set on the porch later and shared a jar with Mr. Kohrs."

"And when was this?"

"Spring of eighteen and eighty-one," Nate said.

"That's thirty years ago. You figure that's going to earn you a job today? I'd say your best years are behind you."

"Maybe you'd have a job for me if I wasn't wearing this suit," Nate suggested.

"If you recall, I just offered you a job," the foreman replied. "Driving chuck wagon. You were wearing the suit when I offered."

"I'm no damn cook."

"Suit yourself." The foreman climbed down from the buckboard.

"I'll do just that," Nate told him. "There's plenty of outfits around can use a man like me."

It turned out that there weren't. There was a mercantile in town that did a steady business with both farmers and ranchers and, with the proprietor's permission, Nate passed three days sitting on a chair out in front of the place, asking if any of the customers were hiring. It was the spring of the year, which meant there was stock to gather, newborns to brand, bull calves to castrate. Farmers were working ground and planting and digging ditches for irrigation. It was soon evident after a time that a good number of outfits were hiring. They just weren't interested in hiring Nate. Whether it was because of his age or the fact that he'd just walked out of Deer Lodge prison was hard to say. And even harder as none of them would give him the time of day.

On the third day, the proprietor told Nate a rancher named Ehler had sent word that he was taking on hands and that anyone looking for work was to gather at the mercantile after noon. Ehler came into town in a long freighter pulled by two brindle mules; he was there to pick up supplies as well. He was a short, round man, wearing a flat-brimmed hat and smoking a stubby cigar. He had a loud voice and came off bigger than he was.

There were ten or twelve men out front when Ehler arrived, and he promptly hired eight of them, including a Mexican and a colored. He hired them without speaking, standing up in the freighter and pointing at this one or that, as if they were good enough to hire but not worthy of any conversation with the man doing the hiring. When he finished with the pointing, he climbed down from the wagon and started into the store. Nate intercepted him on the plank sidewalk.

"I'm looking for work," he said.

Ehler removed the cigar from his mouth and looked at Nate, his eyes flicking over the rough serge suit. "You're not what I'm looking for," he said in his auctioneer's voice.

"You're taking on hands," Nate pointed out.

"I'm looking for young men," Ehler said. "This is hard work." He walked into the store.

Nate followed. "I brought five herds up from Texas," he said. "In the early days. Never lost more than a dozen or so head a drive. I don't shy from hard work."

Ehler glanced at the proprietor, rolling his eyes. "Whatever you did that earned you that suit, I suspect you'd do again if you got the chance. There's a livery across the way might hire you to shovel out the stalls."

"I ain't shoveling horseshit," Nate said. "Try me for a week. I don't cut it, you don't have to pay me a nickel."

"I told you I want young men." Ehler moved away.

"That Mexican you just hired ain't but a few years younger than me," Nate said. He was feeling less cordial by the minute. "And what about yourself? You working the gather?"

"Of course I'm working it," Ehler snorted. "It's my concern."

"I'd outwork you, six days to Sunday."

Ehler turned to the owner again. "Tim, if this old bird don't stop pestering me, I'm gonna introduce him to the back of my hand. What are you letting him hang around for?"

The proprietor had been generous with Nate, giving him permission to approach his customers. Now he looked apologetic, glancing from Ehler to Nate and finally shrugging his shoulders, as if asking Nate to get him out of a fix with the little rancher. Nate nodded then looked over at Ehler.

"I'll be on the veranda out front," he said. "You won't have any trouble finding me if you still feel like introducing me to the back of your hand."

"Don't push your luck, old-timer."

"It's not my luck I'm worried about," Nate told him.

Six

THE BUYER CAME OUT TO THE ranch Saturday afternoon, driving a one-horse buggy he rented at the livery in town. Harry was off to town for the day, picking up supplies and a quantity of rope for the gather, so Rose showed the man what stock was available for sale. His name was McCrae, and he was a burly Scot, wearing a fedora and a tweed suit, the vest of which strained its buttons against the man's stomach. The man was young, in his twenties yet, and said he was working for his uncle, who had extensive holdings in Wyoming. Something about him suggested the uncle was the one with the money.

The young horses were pastured along the creek a mile south of the ranch buildings. There was no true road running there, and no bridge over the creek. They'd have to go by horseback, which wasn't a problem, other than the fact it was soon apparent that young McCrae had spent very little time astride a horse. Rose saddled her mare and picked out an older gelding for the Scot, one of her favorites from years gone by. The man stood by helplessly while she saddled both mounts. It was an inauspicious beginning to a business relationship as Rose had little use for a man who wasn't somewhat capable. Maybe the young Scot's talents lay in other areas.

The horses were stretched out along the creek for a mile or more, pulling at the spring grass. They were all yearlings or two-year-olds, and not a one was so much as green broke as yet. McCrae looked them over for a time from atop the docile gelding. Never once did he suggest that he'd like a closer look. Rose kept thinking he might climb down to check some teeth, or look at some hooves, but he never did. After a while he nodded to her, as if agreeing on something unspoken, and they headed back.

When they got to the house, Rose offered the man a drink while they talked business, but he flatly declined, saying he was not fond of spirits. Rose had never met a Scot who wouldn't take a drink. McCrae's tone suggested that he didn't approve of others partaking either, so Rose made a point of pouring herself a couple of fingers of rye in front of the man. They came to an agreement on the stock shortly thereafter, and he bid her goodbye.

When Harry came home it was late afternoon. He left the unloading of the goods to one of the hands and proceeded to convince Rose that they should take the automobile into town for dinner. It was her first time in the motorcar and nothing of the experience came as a surprise to her. It ran in spurts and sputters and in negotiating the ruts in the dirt road, it bounced her around considerably. She'd had smoother rides in a buckboard over corduroy roads. She held her tongue though; it was evident that Harry liked the automobile as much as she did not.

They ate in the dining room of the Belmont Hotel. The place was busy, the Saturday night crowd, and they passed a good deal of time visiting with people before finally making their way to their table. People that Harry knew, for the most part. He spent more time in town than did Rose these days. When things settled down Rose ordered the local trout while Harry decided on a steak that probably came from their own ranch, as they had been supplying the hotel with beef for years.

"You're paying money for beef you raised," Rose told him. "We could have stayed home and I would have cooked you a steak."

"But you wanted to ride in my automobile," Harry said.

Rose snorted.

"So what did the Englishman have to say?" Harry asked.

"He's a Scotsman," Rose said. "And a teetotaler to boot. He says he'll take fifty of those two-year-olds."

Harry made a face like he had a tooth bothering him. "Do we really want to get rid of that many?"

"We're horse rich these days," Rose replied. "We need to sell some stock or hire more hands to break them. That will cost us."

"Has the man got the money?"

"Seems like a situation where the uncle has the money. The nephew is a dude. I put him on old Buster to ride out to the creek pasture and you'd of thought I'd tied the man to a whirlwind. Horse broke into a lope on the way back to the barn and he grabbed the saddle horn with both hands and damn near started crying."

"You give him a price?" Harry asked.

"I told him a hundred a head," Rose said. "He never batted an eye."

"Uncle must have deep pockets." Harry thought a moment longer. "What the hell. We'll have that many and more again next year."

"You wouldn't take the man for a horse trader," Rose said. "I asked him when he wanted to make his picks and he told me to make 'em. He said he figured I knew more about horses than he did."

"Then he's not stupid," Harry said.

"I'm going to reserve judgment on that," Rose said. "I never knew a man didn't want to choose."

Harry took a drink of whiskey. "What the hell is an Englishman going to do with a herd of half-wild horses anyway?"

"I told you he's a Scotsman," Rose said. "Who knows? Maybe he's got a market for them someplace back east. Doesn't concern me, one way or the other, what he does with them. Once his draft clears at the bank."

The food arrived. While they were eating Rose saw Harry look up toward the front door. "Your brother," he said.

Rose glanced over to see Clayton standing inside the entrance, surveying the room. Just as he spotted them, Sheriff Henry Pearce appeared from somewhere, sidling up to Clayton like the sneak he was. He leaned in close to say something, but Clayton waved him off like he was shooing a fly. He walked over to the table.

"I see a brand new Cadillac motorcar tied to the hitching post out front," he said. "Now why do I think it belongs to you, Harry?"

"Because you know I'm a man of taste, Clayton," Harry replied. "Have a seat."

Clayton pulled over a chair and sat. He smiled across the table. "How's Rose?"

Rose nodded. "Clayton."

"You eaten yet?" Harry asked.

"I had something over at the diner," Clayton said. He removed his hat and smoothed his hair with his palm. He had thick black hair, shiny with oil, and he was inordinately proud of it. He looked for a place for the hat and finally put it on a chair behind him.

"I need a favor," he said. "Grizzly got hold of my good English bull last week. Maimed him so bad my foreman had to put him down. I'm looking for a new bull but I have heifers to cover now. I need new blood. I was wondering if you still had that old Hereford."

"Ivanhoe," Harry said. "He's still around. Wanders up and down the creek bank. You're welcome to him. He's like me—still got a little pride in his stride."

"Christ sakes," Rose said.

Harry smiled at her. "You're welcome to him, Clay."

"I'll pay you."

Harry dismissed the suggestion with a shake of his head. "I'll have him up at the barn for you."

Rose finished her trout and set her utensils aside. "I didn't realize you were all that involved out at the ranch these days, Clayton. What with your important responsibilities down in Helena."

"I run the ranch," Clayton replied. "Always have."

"You were never one to shovel horse shit," Rose said. "Yet I suspect there's no shortage of it down at the capitol." She smiled as she took a sip of wine. "The irony."

Clayton indicated the glass. "How many of those have you had?"

"Just the one," Rose said. "So you're running the ranch and the state, too. Must be quite a load to bear."

Clayton smiled back. "But I can bear it. Being civic-minded isn't a crime, you know. Where would we be without statesmen?"

"You're a statesman now?" Rose asked in mock surprise. "How does that work? Do you get a little pin and a secret handshake?"

"All right, you two," Harry said. "That's about enough."

Clayton kept his eyes on Rose a second longer. "Maybe even more than enough." He turned to Harry. "So how do you like the Cadillac?"

"Finest automobile out there," Harry said. "Thirty horsepower, Clayton. *Thirty.*"

"I'm sure it's a nice machine," Clayton said. "We'll have to compare. I've ordered the new Hupmobile. Be here in a few weeks."

"Shit," Harry said. "Johnny-come-lately. Cadillac's been making motorcars for ten years."

Clayton shrugged and reached for his hat. Standing, he smoothed his hair again before putting the hat on. Not that it had gotten mussed any, sitting there, trading conversation. "I'll send my man over for that bull this week. Much appreciated."

He nodded at Rose and walked away. Harry watched him before turning to Rose.

"Kind of hard on your brother, aren't you?" he asked.

"Am I?"

"Yeah," Harry said. "I thought that might change over the years."

"Maybe it will," Rose said, looking across the room at Clayton. "But I doubt it."

When Clayton walked out of the Belmont, Sheriff Pearce was standing there on the sidewalk, smoking a cigarette and waiting for him. The rotund little sheriff was antsy, quite obviously aggravated about something. Aggravated enough to lie in wait on a Saturday night, at a time he was usually in his cups over in the Bighorn Saloon.

"What bug has crawled up your ass tonight, Henry?" Clayton asked.

"I got problems with the Blackfoot," Pearce said.

"What did they steal now?"

"Ain't that kind of a problem," Henry said. "Two of them came to see me today. Well, three of them, all told. One was stretched across the back of a mule, covered in a blanket. He had a hole in him big enough to drive an oxcart through. I know the man by sight, goes by the name Johnny Little Bear. Other two said his pony came back to the reservation alone, so they went looking for him, took his dog along. Dog found the body."

"Where?"

"On the range, in the tall grass below Thompson Creek. Looked like he'd been dragged there. His ankles were bad rope burned and he was naked as a newborn. Now, I don't know if he'd been dragged and shot, or the other way around. Don't make a lot of difference."

While he listened, Clayton was admiring Harry's shiny black Cadillac. Now he stepped down from the sidewalk for a closer inspection. "And this is my concern why?"

"That's your range, Clay."

Clayton leaned into the motorcar to have a look at the dashboard. "Then the question we need to ask here is what was this Indian doing on my land, Henry? Maybe something he shouldn't have been doing?"

"Maybe he was," Henry said. "I know you've had problems with rustling. If that was the case, then it should have been reported to me. Looks like somebody took it upon himself to execute the man. There's such a thing as due process."

Clayton slid onto the leather seat of the new automobile. He put both hands on the steering wheel, moved it back and forth.

"I'm glad we're having this conversation, Henry. I have a problem of my own right now. A grizzly bear killed a prize bull I had imported from Chichester, England. A bull I paid five thousand dollars for, and the shipping to boot. I guess I need you to swear out a warrant for that grizzly, and then you can head on up there and arrest him. Put him in cuffs, lock him in jail, and see he gets a fair trial. What you call due process."

"Now you're making a joke."

"Am I?" Clayton asked. He stepped out of the vehicle. "You explain to me the difference. I got a bear killing my livestock, or a greasy damn Indian doing the same thing. Explain to me the difference between the two."

"You know the difference," Henry said.

"I don't know anything about it," Clayton said. "And neither do you. Besides, how do you know it wasn't another Indian who shot this Johnny Blackfoot? Maybe he was prodding another man's squaw. You ever think of that?"

"That was the case, I doubt the other two would have brought him in," Henry said. "They'd of kept it on the reservation. This is the third dead Indian in less than a year, Clay. And it makes it a half dozen since you hired Ed Garner away from the Johnson outfit a couple years back."

"Watch it, Henry," Clayton said sharply. "You're treading on some very thin ice. And you're beginning to get on my nerves."

Henry Pearce backed off. "I'm just saying that it makes me look bad, what with the election coming up next year. Indians riding into town with dead Indians in tow makes me look bad. Makes the whole damn town look bad. It's 1910, for God's sakes."

"What would you like me to do, Henry?" Clayton asked. "What would you like me to do about this situation that seems to have absolutely nothing to do with me?"

The sheriff looked away, sulking a bit now. "I realize that these things happen. And I ain't pointing fingers. I guess I'd like it a lot better if the body didn't turn up afterward. If there's no body, there's no questions. That's all I ask. Makes me look a little better in the public eye, Clay."

Clayton smiled. "Well, let's try for that then, Henry. Let us all try to do whatever we can to cast you in the best possible light. How's that sound?"

Henry looked past Clayton toward the Bighorn Saloon, the place he wanted to be. The place he would be in short order. He nodded but none too happily.

"One last thing," Clayton said. "That grizzly I mentioned. Do you intend to arrest him or can I tell my men to take care of that situation themselves?"

"You do what you got to do," Henry Pearce said and walked away.

Seven

B<small>Y WEEK'S END</small> N<small>ATE WAS THOROUGHLY</small> discouraged of any notion of finding work in the Deer Lodge area. He had even sunk so low as to ask a couple of farmers if they had anything for him. It seemed he was looked upon as either an old man or an ex-con and neither was worthy of hiring. By nine o'clock that evening he was sitting in at a poker game in the back room of the New Baltimore Hotel. There was a pool table in the room, and Nate had been there earlier on, drinking beer and playing eight ball alone. He'd been a fair hand on the felt at one time. Coming up the trail it seemed as if every town had at least one table and some had several. Nate's game was rusty, but he kept at it, out of boredom more than anything. At a nickel a glass, the beer was cheap.

The five boys had come in while he was shooting, loud and full of themselves, already into the beer or the rye. They immediately set up a table, one of them produced a deck and in short order they had a game going. They were typical youngsters—full of piss and vinegar, and convinced they were the first young men ever to set out primed to take on the world. A couple of them fancied themselves cowboys, with wide-brimmed hats and loud bandanas. One—a pimply-faced youth—had a Birdseye Colt stuck in his belt.

As the poker game continued they began a bantering exchange with Nate, who was practicing bank shots on the table. They talked down to him somewhat, mocking him, as boys will do with an old-timer, trying to impress each other more than anything else. Nate let them have their fun and it wasn't long before he found himself invited into the game. Maybe they thought he would be an easy mark. The leader of the crew seemed to be a boy named Kershaw, a gangly kid of twenty-one or so. He wore a new high-crowned hat and a tooled leather belt with a buckle the size of a saucer. He'd just signed on with a local ranch and was acting the cock of the walk.

They might have been tomcats, but not a one was any hell as a poker player. They bet when they should've folded, and bet even bigger when they were called. They cursed and threw cards when they lost, as if the gods were against them, not their lack of skill. They didn't stay mad for long though; they were out for fun and a few dollars was the price of it. Kershaw was probably the worst player of the lot, but he was on a run of cards and kept winning in spite of his ineptitude, convincing himself in the process that he was a sharp. All of that worked to Nate's advantage; he picked his spots and by eleven o'clock was up over thirty dollars. He kept at the beer and after a time he got to telling stories.

"Now let me get this straight," Kershaw was saying. He had the cards in one hand, already shuffled, and now was pausing in the act of dealing. "You're telling me you were playing poker with Wild Bill Hickok when he got shot."

Nate drank from his glass of beer and wiped his mustache with the back of his hand. "That's what I'm telling you, son."

Kershaw shot the others a look, the look saying—*hey boys, this will be fun.* "You want to pull my other leg while you're at it?"

Nate tapped his forefinger on the table top. "I was settin' right across from Bill. Working on a heart flush, if memory serves. When it bust, I tossed my cards and at that moment young McCall walked in and put a bullet in Bill's brainpan before a man could blink an eye. Quick as that, like a cat grabbing a mouse."

The pimply-faced boy with the Colt in his belt leaned forward. "And what did you do, old-timer?"

"Nothing," Nate said. "The deed was done."

"Why didn't you shoot McCall?" This from another boy, this one with a shock of white hair.

"I would have," Nate said. "I would have done for him like he done for Bill, but as luck had it I wasn't heeled. I had taken my forty-four into the gunsmith's that very afternoon for repairs." Nate watched as the boys exchanged amused glances. "You gonna deal them cards or just sit there?"

Kershaw smiled as he began to deal. "So tell me—what was Wild Bill holding when he died? I always heard it was two pair. Kings and sevens."

"Aces and eights," Nate said, gathering his cards. "Any damn schoolboy knows that."

"I heard kings," Kershaw said.

"Well, you weren't there," Nate said, looking at his hand. "Open for a dollar."

The boys all called and Kershaw cleared his throat. "Did I ever tell you boys about the time I rode up San Juan Hill with Teddy Roosevelt?"

There was general laughter around the table.

"That's interesting," Nate said. "Sounds like you've led quite a life. Although I suspect you were still shitting your pants when Roosevelt made that ride. I'll take one card."

Kershaw dealt the draws, with everyone but Nate taking three cards. The boys weren't much on folding a bad hand. There was no fun to be had in sitting idle.

"Raise five dollars," Nate said, sliding forward a pair of two dollar bills and a silver dollar.

Four out of the five called him. Nate showed a king high heart flush.

"Lookit here," he said. "That very flush I was chasing in Deadwood that day." He raked in the money.

"Lucky sonofabitch," the boy with the Colt said.

Nate nodded and smiled as he stacked the bills in front of him. Kershaw pulled his new hat down, leaned backward in his chair, and stuck his thumbs in his fancy belt. Nineteen or twenty and he was already an old hand, at least in his mind. He knew all the moves; he'd probably been practicing them in front of a mirror for years. He would get knocked down a peg or two when he showed up at his new job, green as grass and looking like he stepped out of the Sears and Roebuck catalogue, but for tonight he was top dog.

"What next?" he asked of Nate. "I suspect you were involved in that business with the Earps and Doc Holliday down in Tombstone too, weren't you?"

"No, sir," Nate said. "But I saw Wyatt Earp once. In a saloon in Wichita."

"That a fact?" Kershaw glanced around the table. "And I just bet you had a conversation with him, too."

Nate gathered his money and got to his feet. "No, I did not. He was passed out drunk on a faro table." He smiled. "There wouldn't be a sporting house in this town, would there?"

"A sporting house?" the redhead snorted. "Listen to that. Still fancy the ladies, do you?"

Nate tucked the money—their money—in his vest pocket. "I still got the inclination. And now, thanks to you fool young huckleberries, I got the cash."

There was no sporting house in Deer Lodge, as it turned out. Nate ended up in the Great Western Hotel, drinking beer with the bartender. Around closing time, the man told him about a woman who lived just beyond the railway station who took on customers. He allowed that Nate could use his name to get in the door.

The woman was neither lovely nor particularly friendly. In his relationships with whores in the past, Nate had always liked to strike up some sort of amiable conversation before getting down to the exercise at hand. The fact was that he liked women in general. This woman, who said her name was Dot, wasn't much of a talker. She was heavy-set, with graying hair and huge, sagging breasts. No sooner had Nate paid her the seven dollars and mounted up and she was nagging at him to finish.

"You got a train to catch?" he joked.

She swore at him then and Nate decided he might just as well comply with her request. Walking back into town afterward, he further decided it had been the worst sexual experience he'd ever had. And that included those he'd had by himself in prison. But still it had been all right.

It was late when he arrived at the town square, the streets largely deserted. Nate found a bench facing west and sat down. The stone walls of the prison, just a block away, were visible beyond the electric streetlights. During his years inside those walls, Nate had yearned for many things. A cold beer and a thick beefsteak. A roll in the hay, a hand of cards. A chance to settle that bastard Willard's hash.

One week and he had filled those desires. Yet inside of him, nothing had changed. Being outside those walls wasn't all that different from being inside. He had always considered himself to be a man of purpose, however menial, and now he had none. And it was apparent that whatever purpose was left for him was not going to be found in or around Deer Lodge. Hell, he could barely strike up a decent conversation in the town.

The next morning he took breakfast in the dining room and then again asked Mrs. McKee for a bath. While he waited for the boy to tote the water, he walked over to Wilson's Haberdashery. There he bought heavy cotton work pants and a linen shirt and undershirt. Back at the boardinghouse he had a soak in the tub and afterward put on his new clothes. He hung the prison suit in the closet. He kept the vest.

He went down to the street and walked over to the mercantile, where he found the proprietor in the street out front, shoveling a fresh deposit of horseshit into a wheelbarrow. Nate asked the man one last time if he'd heard of anyone else hiring.

"Nothing today."

Nate hadn't expected to hear otherwise. As he stood there, he saw two of the boys from the poker game come out of a diner across the way, fresh from their breakfast. It was Kershaw and the blond. They spotted Nate and Kershaw yelled over.

"Hey, Wild Bill!"

The blond one laughed and drew an imaginary gun and pointed it at Nate. The proprietor watched them, perplexed. After a moment, Nate turned to the man.

"Where can I catch a stage coach to Cut Bank?"

"Stage coach? You got something against trains?"

"There's a train runs to Cut Bank?"

"Yes, sir. Once a day. There and back again."

Nate looked over at the two boys, lounging now in front of the diner, smoking cigarettes and grinning like they had the whole damned world figured out. Nate knew exactly how they felt. There had been a time when he'd had it figured out too.

"I got no interest in the back again," he said.

The train north didn't run; it crawled, stopping at every little town along the way. Nate bought a ticket for the coach. The seats were cramped, the leg room limited. Nate sat on the left side of the car so he could extend his right leg out into the aisle. The knee gave him trouble when it was immobile for too long. In truth, Nate was fortunate to still have the leg. The knife wound had been behind the knee, the homemade blade going in to sever the tendon. The prison doctor, a consumptive bone rack named Gray, had told Nate in no uncertain terms that the leg needed to come off. Nate had been in the prison for twelve years at that point and come to know the man as a lazy shirker with a fondness for laudanum, of which he had a steady supply. He would rather cut Nate's leg off than go to the effort of saving it. Nate had balked at the diagnosis.

"Sew that tendon back together," Nate had told him. "Any damn seamstress could do that."

"You'll lose that leg to infection either way," the doctor said. "You're stuck in here for life. You don't need two legs."

"I might take up flamenco dancing," Nate said.

"You are full of shit."

"So are you. And you ain't going to saw my leg off."

So the tendon was sewn, and afterward the leg turned purple. Nate was taken with a fever as the wound swelled and filled with pus. Nate drenched it with turpentine daily, and had the doctor lance the skin when needed, to keep the wound draining. The man continued to offer his expertise with the saw, but Nate would not hear of it. The color in the joint slowly returned to normal and the fever subsided, although it was six months before any weight could be put on the leg.

That wasn't the first time the knee had given Nate trouble. When he was new to the territory, he had taken a job breaking green horses for Parcell Covington's outfit, not far from the Canadian border. Covington had a split rail corral built beside the bunkhouse for that purpose. Nate was a fair hand with young stock and, for the most part, never had much trouble gentling a raw mount. One day though, when he was aboard a rank piebald colt, something over by the ranch house distracted him and while he was gawking in that direction the colt ran him hard into the railing, catching Nate's knee on one of the posts. The knee twisted like a piece of licorice and Nate was tossed backward from the saddle onto the hard ground. He pushed the knee cap back into place with the heel of his hand and wrapped it tight with a bandana but it never was the same after that.

And neither was Nate. That which had distracted him from the porch that morning was Covington's daughter Rose. She was, at the time, the prettiest girl Nate had ever seen. She remained so to this day.

Now, as the train rumbled north, Nate's back began to stiffen up. Like the knee joint, it could only stay in one position for so long. As the train was approaching Great Falls, the conductor entered the car to announce the station. He found Nate lying in the aisle on his back, his boots elevated on a threadbare pillow he'd found in the overhead compartment.

"Are you drunk, sir?" the conductor demanded.

"I am not."

"Then what are you doing?"

"Stretching my back."

"Well, stretch it somewheres else," the conductor said. "There's passengers gonna be walking here soon."

Nate got up and returned to his seat. His back felt better from the short time on the floor. It was a minor concern, along with all the other ailments he'd accumulated over the years. Arthritis in his hands, some loss of hearing, periodic bouts of hemorrhoids. He had one finger that was as crooked as a dog's hind leg. His memory was still pretty sharp though. There were a few names he'd managed to forget, but those were no accident. A few faces too.

But those he remembered, he remembered very well.

Eight

Late Sunday the cook Jonesy came down to the ranch with the chuck wagon to pick up supplies for the hands working the gather. He mentioned some of the men—the new crew hired on for the gather—had been complaining about their wages, claiming that Harry was paying less than the other ranches in the area. It was untrue, Jonesy knew, but the whiners were spreading discontent with the rest of the hands. Monday morning Harry said that he would go up and have a talk with the men.

"You're not going to try and drive that machine of yours up to the bench," Rose said. "You won't get two miles."

"I can still ride a horse," Harry told her.

They were eating breakfast in the kitchen. Rose had baked cornbread and fried up sowbelly and a half dozen pullet eggs. In April she'd gotten two dozen young hens freighted in from Wisconsin and they had just started to lay a week earlier.

"You want to come along?" he asked.

"No," she said. "I need to cut out those fifty head and get them in the corral. The Scotsman said he'd be back this week."

She was surprised Harry was heading out to the range. In recent years he'd grown more and more contented to leave the work to the crew. He handled the business end, buying and selling cattle. The horses he left mainly to Rose. She had considered asking him to help with the fifty head, but she knew he would have balked at that. He hadn't thrown a rope in years. As he was leaving, Rose told him to send young Donnelly back to the ranch when he ran across him.

"But don't tell him why," she said.

"Don't tell him why?"

"I'm going to have a little fun with the boy."

Harry shook his head, content to be ignorant of the details, and rode out of the yard on a large black gelding named Punch. He was a big man nowadays and so he needed a big horse. After doing the dishes, Rose made up a half dozen sandwiches for lunch and packed them, along with some cake, into saddlebags. She changed into pants and a work shirt and went out and roped Daisy, her buckskin mare. By the time she had her saddled and ready, Donnelly was riding in from the west. Even from a couple hundred yards away, she could see that he was tentative; he looked like a schoolboy trudging home with a poor report card. To encourage his concerns, she'd led the saddled mare into the barn, out of sight.

"I hope you're up for some more planting," she said as he drew near, and she watched as the boy's face fell. She waited a bit. "Well, are you?"

"You're the boss, Mrs. Longley," Donnelly said. He kept his eyes down, looking at the reins in his hands. "I mean, I hired on to cowboy. But whatever you choose for me to do, I guess I have to be all right with it." He sighed dramatically. "Like I said, you're the boss."

"That's right," she said seriously. "I am the boss, and I'll decide who does what around here." She played him a moment longer, enjoying it. "So today you and I are going over to the south slope and cut out fifty head of two-year-old horses that I sold to some Wyoming outfit. How does that suit you?"

Donnelly's face lit up like a harvest moon. "It suits me, ma'am," he blurted out. "It suits me fine."

She smiled back at him. "I thought it might."

They got some extra ropes and rawhide leads from the barn and headed out. The day was sunny and growing warmer; for the first time that year it actually felt as if spring had arrived. It had rained heavily the day before and the creek was over its banks. The herd of horses, a hundred and twenty or thirty strong, was on the far side of the stream, where the ground was slightly higher. As Rose and Donnelly waded their mounts through the creek, the young horses instinctively began moving away from them. Gaining the far bank, Rose reined in the buckskin as Donnelly came up beside her.

"We're going to have to take them on a lead line, a half dozen at a time," Rose said. "They're too wild to drive in a bunch, with just the two of us."

It took them most of the day to choose and gather the horses and deposit them in the ten acre pasture that was fenced off on the slope below the barn. Donnelly was a fair hand with a rope, so Rose let him handle that chore while she made the picks and ran the leads. The herd, wary of the two riders, kept stretching out along the creek and twice they had to head them and drive them back. At noon, they stopped and ate the lunch that Rose had packed. They unsaddled the horses and sat on the blankets in the shade of a large cottonwood tree. Donnelly removed his hat and placed it carefully on the grass. It was a Stetson, a good cowpuncher's hat; he'd bought it with his first month's pay, Rose recalled, throwing away the old derby he'd arrived wearing, an object of much ridicule during his first weeks at the ranch. His hair was black as ink and his eyes nearly as dark. He'd worn his hair long, like that of his ancestors, when he had first shown up at the front gate the previous summer, afoot and looking for work. Early this spring he had been shorn like a sheep, as were most of the young hands. Jonesy the cook did the barbering free of charge. Now the hair was growing back, already long enough to cover his forehead when he bent to his food.

"You handle that rope pretty good," Rose told the boy. "Where'd you learn?"

"Back home."

"Where was that again?"

"Above the Milk," Donnelly said. "My old man had a quarter section there."

"Had a quarter section?"

"He give it up. Never could make a living on it. Him and my mother moved to Big Sandy. The old man works odd jobs there and my mother takes in laundry."

"You're Indian on your mother's side then?"

"Yup," Donnelly said, reaching for a second sandwich. "She's half Crow. Her ma married a French trapper back in the beaver days."

"Was your mother from the reservation?" Rose asked.

Donnelly shook his head. "The tribe turned her mother out after she married the Frenchman. Not cuz of him being white. I hear he was none too honest."

Rose finished her sandwich and reached into the saddlebag for the cake, wrapped in waxed paper. "Who taught you to cowboy— your father?"

"No, ma'am. My grandfather, on my pa's side. He was from the Rio Grande country originally, and he came up the trail with Story, the first drive ever. You heard of that?"

"Yeah, I guess everybody's heard of Nelson Story," Rose said. She offered the cake over and the boy took a piece.

"Thank you," he said. "Well, my grandpa knew him personal, worked for him. He's the one taught me how to throw a loop. Most of the time all I was roping was the sheep my pa raised, or my little sister, but a loop is a loop, my grandpa used to say."

"I'll bet he's got some stories," Rose said. "I recall some of those old hands when I was growing up. I could listen to them all day. I suspect the truth got stretched a bit at times, especially if there was a jar or two involved."

His mouth full of cake, Donnelly nodded. "My grandpa seen some things," he said after swallowing. "My ma always said that somebody ought to write his stories down in a book. It would make my old man mad, her saying that."

"Why?"

"Seemed like he never liked her talking up his father over him, like she was sizing one against the other. He was mad a good deal of the time. Nothing ever went right for him, he always claimed. Used to give me the belt for stacking the firewood wrong. Give it to my ma, too."

Rose watched the boy as he licked the cake crumbs from his fingers. He didn't have any whine in him, he was just telling it. "Where's your grandfather now?"

"Oh, he died when I was fourteen," Donnelly said. "Some sort of cancer, started in his mouth, and went through him. We buried him on the farm there."

"When did you leave?"

"The day after the funeral."

After lunch, they saddled their mounts and went back to work. In all, they gathered sixty horses. Rose reasoned that she might as well bring in an extra ten, in case McCrae got choosy at the last minute. If not, she could start them on a lead. Eventually, after the gather, she'd have to bring in the whole herd to break them. Either that or sell more off, which she was more than willing to do at a hundred a head.

When they had the last of them in the corral, Rose walked to the house and returned with a clay jug of cold water and handed it up to Donnelly, who was sitting his horse along the rail fence of the pasture, leg hooked over the horn, watching the half-wild horses in the pen as they ran back and forth, confused by their sudden confinement and calling out to the rest of the herd a mile away, out of sight but not out of earshot. Walking down the hill, Rose thought that Donnelly looked like a cowpuncher in one of Charlie Russell's paintings, and she suspected that he knew that. It was nice, seeing a youngster with some pride in his work. Who he was.

He took a long drink of water before handing the crock back to Rose, who had a drink and then went about removing the saddle from the buckskin. Donnelly, with one eye on the agitated horses in the pasture, pulled his makings from his shirt pocket and rolled a cigarette. Like most kids wet behind the ears, he was a little on the transparent side.

"Something on your mind?" Rose asked, hoisting the saddle onto the railing.

The boy exhaled and blew smoke. "No, I guess not."

"Your no is pretty much the same as a yes," Rose told him. "Speak your piece."

"Just wondering," Donnelly said. "What kind of money you getting for them?"

"Hundred a head."

The boy whistled through his teeth. "That's dear."

"The going price," Rose said. She rubbed the mare down and began to brush her out. After a while she looked over the horse's withers at the boy where he sat smoking, still looking at the milling horses in the pasture. "Why do you ask?"

"I fancy that roan filly, is all," Donnelly said finally. "If I had the money, I'd offer on her."

"How much do you have?"

"Maybe twenty," the boy replied. He did some calculating in his head. "More like fifteen, the truth be known."

They were paying the boy fifty a month and found. Apparently he wasn't saving much of the fifty. None of them did, though, particularly the younger hands. Come Saturday night, they were off to town in a flash, hair slicked, clean shirts on, if one was available, heading for whatever meager entertainment a town like Cut Bank would offer boys of that age, mainly cards and cheap whiskey and possibly girls, although the young ladies of the community would be outnumbered ten to one by the cowboys. Rose had never heard of a cathouse in town, but it wasn't information that would be made available to her. She would be quite surprised if there weren't some women available someplace within riding distance. She'd never known a cowboy who couldn't turn up a soiled dove, so long as he had the inclination and a few dollars in his pocket. And usually those dollars were gone, when the hands dragged themselves back to the bunkhouse sometime on Sunday, or even Monday morning, looking hungover and bruised and plain worn out. Old Jonesy the cook would watch them from his chair outside the bunkhouse door, whittling a cottonwood branch down to nothing and smiling to himself. He'd seen young cowboys come and go and he allowed they were all the same after a Saturday in town, like somebody had thrown half a dozen tomcats in a burlap bag and left them there to scrap overnight.

Now Rose led the mare over to the corral, where they kept the saddle horses, and turned her loose inside. When she returned, she looked at the filly the boy had mentioned, and saw the filly looking back at her, ears forward. She had a handsome head, and sharp inquisitive eyes. She was big across the chest; she would fill out nicely. Donnelly had a good eye and a natural way with horses. Rose had hired him on a whim the day he'd shown up, thinking there was something earnest about him, something that reminded her of other young cowboys from the old days, youngsters looking to prove themselves but without being showy about it. He hadn't disappointed her.

"You willing to work it off?" she asked him.

"Yes, ma'am," the boy replied at once. "Why, I'll even work in that garden of yours."

"Easy now," Rose said.

"Fifty a month," he said, rising to it now. "I can pay it off in two months."

"Just settle down," Rose advised him. "You pay fifty a month, you're not going to have any cigarette money or go to town money, or even a dime for cards in the bunkhouse. You can pay it off gradual, ten or twenty at a time. She's not going anywhere. And you can start working with her anytime you please. As of today, she's your horse."

"Thank you, ma'am. I do appreciate it."

"What are you going to do with her?" Rose asked, still watching the filly. "You have all the horses you want to ride right here. Or are you looking to race her?"

"Oh, she's not for me."

Rose turned. "Who is she for?"

"I'm gonna make a present of her," Donnelly said. It took him a little longer to allow the rest of it out, as if letting slip a secret. "For a girl."

"Your girl?"

"Well, ma'am, that's something I can't really say. I'm hoping."

Rose fetched the jug from where she'd set it on the ground and had another drink of water. She tried to think of a local girl young Donnelly might have encountered. Maybe one of the girls in town. Maybe even one still in school. She guessed Donnelly wasn't any more than nineteen or twenty himself. She wiped her mouth. "Would this girl have a name?"

"Libby Thompson is her name," the boy said. "She's from over Pondera County."

Rose knew the girl, or at least knew of her. Libby Thompson was probably the prettiest girl in Pondera County, and one of the prettiest in any of the counties in the state. Her father, Oliver Thompson, was wealthy, and had gotten that way in the cattle business. He'd shown up after the big freeze-up of '86 and had made his start by buying up half-starved stock left behind by the men made bankrupt by that horrible winter. Oliver had arrived at the right time, with enough cash in his pockets to tempt desperate sellers. Although to hear him tell it, he had pretty much invented the cattle industry in Montana, even though he had come on the scene twenty years after Nelson Story had driven those thousand head of longhorns up from Texas. Rose knew him well enough to dislike him to a large degree. He was a stupid man who was convinced he was smarter than everybody else, a poor combination in Rose's eyes. He was also a bully who rarely had a good word to say about anybody. And Rose would bet every one of the herd they'd just gathered that Oliver Thompson would suffer apoplexy if he even suspected that a young Indian boy had set his cap for his daughter. The fact that Donnelly was only part Indian would not have made any difference. Not only that, but the boy looked Indian. The native blood was strong. It was an odd combination; in every other way he acted and talked like any other wet behind the ears young cowpuncher.

"How did you meet Libby?" Rose asked.

"I saw her at the fair last fall down to Conrad."

"And you talked to her?"

"Yes, ma'am."

"So you have actually met the girl?"

"Sure I met her. I wouldn't buy a horse for a woman I never met."

Rose put the jug down. "You've been keeping time with her ever since the fall then?"

"Not exactly," the boy admitted.

"When did you last see her?"

"Yesterday."

"Yesterday?" Rose was surprised. "Where would you see her yesterday?"

"At her ranch," Donnelly said.

"The Thompson ranch is forty miles from here."

"Yes, ma'am. I know how far it is."

Rose thought it might be time for her to stop interrogating the boy. His affairs were none of her concern. And she might have, had not the specter of Oliver Thompson hovered over the entire conversation.

"So you're welcome at the Thompson place?"

Donnelly removed his hat and, hanging it on the saddle horn, he gave his scalp a vigorous scratching with both hands.

"That's where it gets tricky," he said. "I'd rather you didn't repeat none of this to Libby's father."

"I won't be talking to Libby's father."

"I'm welcome at the Thompson ranch provided he don't see me," Donnelly said. "So we sort of meet in a stand of pine trees, by a creek, a good piece north of the house."

Rose smiled.

"I say something funny?" the boy asked.

"No," she replied. "I was just reminded of something. Did you ever hear of déjà vu?"

"I struggle enough with the English language."

"Maybe I'll explain it another time," Rose said. "I'd better let you get back to the gather."

When she picked up the jug and headed toward the house, something occurred to her. She turned back. "How did you ride down to Pondera County when we're in the middle of a round up?"

"The rain stopped us yesterday," the boy reminded her. "Couldn't brand anything, the fires wouldn't burn. Foreman give us the day off."

"You rode forty miles in the pouring rain?"

"Yes, ma'am. There and back."

"And she was waiting for you by that creek?"

"Yes, ma'am."

"In the rain?"

"Yes, ma'am."

You are in trouble, Rose thought. Both of you. But she wasn't going to tell the boy that. She would let the two of them figure things out on their own. Along with the pain, there was considerable pleasure to be found on the way to figuring such things out. That was one more instance of déjà vu.

Nine

AFTER YOUNG DONNELLY LEFT, ROSE WENT into the house and had a bath. She lingered in the tub for a long time, adding more hot water when it was needed, thankful for the miracles of modern plumbing. She had a recent copy of the *Saturday Evening Post* with her, but she found she couldn't get interested in any of the articles. Her mind was on the boy and the Thompson girl. She wondered how long they thought they could keep things from Oliver Thompson. The man was obstreperous by nature, and a royal pain to be around, but he wasn't completely obtuse. Even if he was, he would surely take notice when his daughter came home in possession of a pretty roan filly.

She heard the singing as she was getting dressed. She cocked her head at the sound, wondering just what she was hearing, before walking across the hall into the front bedroom to look out the window there. He was standing outside the front gates, looking up at the woodwork above his head, where the HRH brand had been fashioned from sections of lodge pole pine. He looked different and yet exactly the same. As lean as he ever was, with the same drooping mustache, now shot with gray. He wore work clothes, and a high crowned Stetson that appeared to be brand new. And he was singing, something he could never do very well, although he had always feigned ignorance of the fact.

I ride an old paint, I lead an old dan,
I'm goin' to Montana for to throw the houlihan . . .

Rose finished dressing quickly and ran downstairs and outside in her bare feet. Still chasing the verses of the song, he watched her as she approached.

They feed in the coulees, they water in the draw,
Their tails are all matted, their backs are all raw . . .

She stopped twenty feet shy of him. He removed his hat and smiled as he quit the song, that smile she knew better than nearly any other she'd known. There had been times when she couldn't get the memory of that smile out of her head, and other times when she had almost forgotten it. Almost but never quite.

"Well," she said now. "It's quite apparent that the state of Montana doesn't provide singing lessons to its guests."

Then she went to him, put her arms around him, kissed him on the cheek and hugged him, then kissed him again. She felt the tears on her own cheeks as she stepped back.

"Stop that now," Nate said. "By God, I'll start singing again."

They sat on the porch and drank bourbon, a bottle from Kentucky Rose had been saving for a special occasion she could not have named, right up until it arrived. She told him about the ranch for a bit, letting him get settled, before asking about the circumstances that led to his parole. Nate watched the young horses milling in the far corral as he told the story.

"The boy was sixteen or so," he was saying. "Got caught stealing a mule from a farmer over on the Musselshell. Judge gave him five years, which seemed pretty stern for borrowing a pack animal. Boy didn't take much to being locked up. Got hold of a knife somewhere and took the prison cook hostage, right there in the kitchen. Said he wanted a couple of horses and safe passage into the mountains. Said he'd set the cook free in a day or so, providing he wasn't followed."

"Indian boy?" Rose asked.

Nate nodded. "Well, they told him he could have what he wanted. They even got the horses ready. But they weren't about to let that boy ride off and set an example for anybody who could fashion a blade out of a bed spring. The warden there, a man named Conley, came to see me. Pretty good man. He knew I could talk some Blackfoot and he asked if I would have a word with the boy, sort of a last resort before they shot him out of the saddle. I went down to the kitchen and talked to him through the door, explaining what was in store for him. Took some persuading, but he finally give me the knife."

"You were the hero," Rose suggested.

"I wasn't nothing of the kind," Nate said. "But I couldn't see the value of another dead Indian, especially a boy. Anyway, a week or so later, the powers-that-be decided to cut me loose. I suppose they're of a mind that I'm all bark and no bite these days."

Nate glanced over at Rose as he finished the story. He was sitting half facing her, his legs crossed, the rock glass of whiskey propped on his knee.

Rose indicated his leg. "Where'd you get the limp?"

Nate hesitated while he decided what to tell her. "I can't recall now, it was so long ago. Might of slipped on some ice in the yard one morning."

"That's your story, is it?"

Nate smiled. "I might do better, after a little more of this mash."

"You should have sent a wire you were coming," Rose said. "I could have picked you up at the station. It's a long walk from town. And I don't ever recall you being any fan of walking."

Nate gestured toward the road. "I got a lift from a farmer and his wife, in a buckboard full of squawking geese. The wife was jab-bering away in Bohunk, louder than the fowl. I only walked the last couple of miles. I didn't mind—it was good to see this country again." He took a sip. "And it's good to see you too, Rose. You haven't changed one bit, you know that?"

"So your eyesight is going too, on top of everything else?" she said.

"My eyes are just fine," Nate told her. "You never could take a compliment."

"I guess I'm out of practice in that regard," Rose said. "But I know how old I am, Nate Cooper. I'm a little sketchy on just how it happened. Seems as if I went to bed one night when I was thirty years old and woke up the next morning and I was fifty."

Nate smiled again before nodding toward the ranch surrounding them. "Looks like you and Harry have done real fine."

"We have," Rose said. "And we did it on our own."

"You mean without any help from your old man?"

"That's right," Rose replied. "I never spoke to him, not once, after what he did. Clayton ended up with the ranch."

"Clayton." Nate laughed. "That little snot. I hear he's a politician these days. We would get a newspaper from time to time inside the walls, brought in by one of the guards or whatever. I read that Clayton got himself elected senator and I thought, well, that's just the ticket for him. Right about where he ought to be." He looked over. "I don't mean any offense. He's still your brother."

"You want to offend me, you'd better come up with something better than Clayton," Rose said. She saw that Nate's glass was nearly empty and she reached over with the bottle and poured a couple inches.

"How do you know that Harry won't spend the night with the gather?" Nate said.

"There's no chance of that," Rose said. "Harry's gotten used to a feather bed and all the other comforts of life. He hasn't slept on the ground in fifteen years and he won't tonight. You watch—first thing he's going to want to do is show you his new motorcar. It's in the shed over there, if you're interested."

"I seen my share of them already," Nate said. "I find them hard on the ears, and I'm half deaf." He took a sip of bourbon. "What do you have in that far corral—two-year-olds?"

Rose nodded. "Ready to ship out. Sold them to a Scotsman from Wyoming."

"Good-looking string," Nate said.

"We raise good horseflesh here. I just brought them up from the south pasture today. Me and a youngster named Donnelly. The boy's a quarter Crow, signed on with us last summer. He's bound to cowboy, that one. I've been having some fun with him, had him cultivating my vegetable garden the other day. I swear—it was like putting a bull terrier in a baby carriage."

Nate shook his head. "Those youngsters ain't too fond of scratching in the dirt."

"Said the kettle to the pot." Rose got to her feet. "Young or old, I never knew a cowboy willing to get off his horse for anything, unless there was a drink of liquor to be had. Or maybe a tumble with a willing woman."

Nate smiled. "You need to get off your horse to partake of those?"

Rose admonished him with a wagging forefinger. "I'm going to check on that chicken in the oven. When was the last time you had home cooking?"

"Oh, I was a few days at a boardinghouse in Deer Lodge," Nate said. "Colored woman there could fry an egg. She made good biscuits, too."

Rose stopped in the open doorway. "A few days. How long have you been out?"

"Week or two."

"What took you so long to get here?"

Nate shrugged. "Well, I had a couple errands to tend to, and then I looked for ranch work around Deer Lodge, but nobody's hiring a limping ex-con with hearing problems and a fresh-out-of-prison suit."

Nate looked out over the plains, grimacing inside and wishing he could take back what he just spoke. He wasn't looking for sympathy from anyone, and especially not from Rose. In the doorway, she watched his profile a moment before going inside.

Nate lifted the glass to his mouth and took a sip of the good whiskey, letting it lie there on his tongue for a while. He never remembered liquor tasting this good. Maybe he'd never had anything of this quality before. In the early days they could buy rye in Miles City for two dollars a gallon; he suspected the Kentucky bourbon in his glass fetched a higher price than that.

As he lowered the glass something on the horizon caught his eye and soon he realized he was looking at a man approaching on horseback, a half mile away, making his way down the slope. Nate watched him a while then turned toward the door.

"Better peel another potato," he called. "You got company coming."

"It's probably just Harry," Rose said from inside.

Nate squinted into the setting sun, waiting for the rider to come into view. "No, it's a chubby fella with a face full of whiskers," he said.

Rose walked out onto the porch, wearing an apron now. "That would be Harry."

The rider—Harry—was now just a few hundred yards away and Nate could recognize his old partner, hidden behind the flesh and the beard.

"I'll be damned," Nate said. "He's turned into Santy Claus."

Rose sat down again and reached for her glass. "I told you he's gotten used to good living. I put him on a diet once and he gained ten pounds, sneaking off to the diner in Cut Bank every day."

"Well, it's a good thing he didn't see me show up like I did," Nate said. "I'd never live it down. It's a shameful thing, Rose . . . a cowboy afoot."

"Well, I can't fix all the troubles in the world but I can fix that," Rose said. "You see that chestnut mare in the front corral? The one with her head over the rail?"

Nate looked where she was pointing. The mare in question was standing sideways to them, watching over the top rail to something in the distance. "What about her?"

"She's yours, Nate. Call it a coming home present." She mocked him a bit. "To avoid you suffering any further shame, going afoot."

"I didn't come here for charity."

"Oh, stop it."

"I mean it, Rose."

"For Christ sakes, I hope one day to meet a man who's not addled with pride. You can work it off, if it makes you feel better. Not the first time today I've sold a horse for a dollar down. But she's your horse and she needs work. She reminds me of you, Nate. Look at her, staring off in the distance, like there's something better over the next rise."

"That's the way I am?"

"The way you were," Rose said. "I remember dancing with you, and you sweet talking me, and all the while sneaking glances at the other girls in the hall. You remember that, Nate Cooper?"

Nate smiled, his eyes on Harry. "Pick up the pace, old pal."

Rose laughed. A few minutes later Harry rode up to the barn and climbed down from the horse, looking over at the porch, where they sat. He glanced over once or twice more as he pulled the saddle and blanket from the animal. He carried the tack inside and came back to give the big gelding a quick brushing before turning it out with the rest of the saddle horses.

He was halfway across the yard before he finally realized who it was sitting on the porch. His pace quickened at once. Smiling broadly, he came up the steps two at a time.

"Well, I'll be hung for a horse thief!" he shouted.

Nate stood. "I'm surprised you never were, Harry." He extended his hand but Harry ignored it and gathered Nate into a bear hug.

"Goddamn it, Nate," he said stepping back. "Goddamn it." There were tears in his eyes.

Nate was uncomfortable with the display. To deflect it, he patted Harry on his belly. "It appears you haven't missed a meal since I left, Harry, that's plain to see. And it looks like you own half the stock in northern Montana."

Harry could do nothing but shake his head and smile. "Goddamn," he said.

They had dinner in the large dining room that overlooked the ranch's southern exposure. There was chicken and mashed potatoes and gravy and biscuits. Greens that Rose said came from Chicago on the train. Harry got into the bourbon before they sat down to eat, and insisted on opening two bottles of wine with the meal. He drank more than he ate, and as he drank he gave Nate the history of the ranch, even though Nate had already heard much of the story from Rose. Harry's telling didn't quite synchronize with hers, but it was close enough. Nate knew how certain embellishments could over the years become fact, especially in the mind of the man doing the embellishing.

At nine o'clock, they were still at the table. Rose had cleared the dishes and Harry had produced several bottles of brandy from a walnut sideboard against the wall. He was schooling Nate in the history of each, and getting even drunker in the process.

"Now this here," he said, selecting another bottle. "This here is a mighty refined liqueur. All the way from France. Wrap your lip around that, Nate." He poured into a snifter and passed it over.

"That's real nice," Nate said after taking a sip. "Keep in mind I been drinking dishwater coffee and sour buttermilk these many years. Any hooch I saw was of an inferior grade. There was one old-timer in there claimed he could make alcohol by soaking stale bread in kerosene."

"How did that taste?" Harry asked.

"Like somebody soaked stale bread in kerosene."

Rose watched Harry's eyes, saw the lids getting heavy. "I think I'll make a pot of coffee," she suggested.

"A man drinks coffee in the morning," Harry said.

Rose stared at him, but he wouldn't look back. She turned to Nate. "I feel guilty that we didn't get down to Deer Lodge to visit you more often. We let the years slip by and there is no excuse for it."

"Keep in mind I asked you not to," Nate said. "You had a ranch to run. And besides—the times you did come, it was always damned hard watching you leave. Knowing you could and I couldn't. So it was for the best."

"Water under the bridge," Harry mumbled. He poured again for both Nate and himself. Rose had quit drinking when she saw that Harry would not. "You *cannot* dwell on the past, Nate," Harry added.

"I don't intend to," Nate said.

"What would you like to do?" Rose asked.

"First off, get a job," Nate said. "Then—"

"You don't need a goddamn job!" Harry said. "You're gonna stay right here. You and me were always partners, and still would be, it wasn't for that business out on the reservation."

"I already told Rose I'm not in the market for charity," Nate said.

"And I ain't offering it," Harry told him. "Tell him, Rose. We need a good man with stock, to start. Christ, we got enough horses to run five ranches. Selling 'em off, we got so many nags."

Harry was drunk enough that Nate didn't care to pursue the matter right then. "We can talk about it another time. Who knows—I just might decide to become a banker, or a politician. Wear a suit and tie every day and a flower in my lapel."

"I'd pay money to see that," Harry said, leaning back in his chair. He took more brandy.

Nate looked at Rose. "You say that bunch in the corral is going to Wyoming."

Rose nodded.

"When?"

"This week, or so he said."

"They broke to saddle?"

"Hell no," Rose said. "Most never had a rope on them until today."

"How's he going to get them to Wyoming?"

Rose shrugged. "Not my concern."

At that moment Harry began to snore. They looked over at the sound. His head was on his chest and the snifter in his hand was tilted forward. Rose reached for it.

"He used to pull that trick on me all the time," Nate said. "I would have a good argument going and that sonofabitch would fall asleep right in the middle. Like he did it on purpose. That would ire me to no end. I'm a tough man to beat in an argument, Rose. Even tougher if I happen to be right."

"You're stubborn, is what you mean," Rose said.

"Well, yeah," Nate admitted. "I don't trust a man who doesn't have a stubbornness to him. You can't count on him when the chips are down."

Rose looked unhappily at Harry for a moment. Nate watched her in the soft light. Of course he'd been fibbing earlier when he'd said she hadn't aged. She was older. How could it be otherwise? There were lines on her face and crow's feet around her eyes. But she wasn't much older, not to look at, and she was still beautiful. Her thick brown hair showed only a little gray and her figure, the figure Nate had once known very well, was the same. Her lips, her breasts, her attitude—all were full and desirable. And always had been.

Nate decided to change the subject; he ran his hand over the linen tablecloth. "Long while since I've seen a tablecloth. Never really gave it any thought 'til now."

Now Rose turned to him. "What else did you miss in there, Nate?"

"Too many things to list, Rose," Nate replied, his fingers still moving absently on the linen, as if appraising its quality. "Too many to list."

Ten

CLAYTON ORIGINALLY HAD PLANNED TO TAKE the evening train back to Helena on Sunday night. Instead he stayed at the ranch until mid-week. The senate was back in session, but he'd had enough of the foot-dragging and whining and pork barrel bargaining over the designation of the new highway commission. He decided to stage a one-man boycott of the debate. Monday morning he sent a wire to the capitol saying he was in the midst of the spring round-up and that he wouldn't be back for a few days. The highway bill was his and he demanded that discussion be tabled until his return.

He spent most of the three days sequestered in the large stone ranch house, sleeping and eating and catching up on his reading. He intended at some point on riding out to the gather but, with the weather cold and wet, he never got around to it. It had been years since he had actually been involved in the day-to-day operation of the ranch and even back then he'd done more watching than helping. He'd never learned to throw a rope and he wasn't of a mind to get down in the dirt with a branding iron. That's what hired hands were for.

There was no telephone at the ranch; the lines hadn't extended that far yet. He took the rig into Cut Bank on Tuesday afternoon and found several wires waiting for him at the depot. Most were from fellow senators and almost all were of the conciliatory nature. To these Clayton sent no replies. There was also a wire from Governor Toole, requesting a meeting with Clayton at his convenience. Someone, probably Nancy, had told the governor Clayton was at the ranch. Clayton sent a wire reply, saying they could meet on Thursday. He had a few drinks and dinner at the Belmont and went back to the ranch.

The two new men he'd hired—Ballinger and Munson—showed up late Tuesday afternoon. They had been due there Monday morning. When Clayton returned from town, Ed Garner came up to the house to tell him of their arrival.

"What am I supposed to do with them?" he asked. "We got all the hands we need working the gather."

"Young Ballinger claims to be a top notch bronc buster," Clayton said. "You can start him on those young horses."

It was obvious Garner was unhappy about the new hires. "And the big one?"

"He can help the little one for now," Clayton said. He watched Garner's sour expression. "I didn't hire these two to punch cattle, Ed. It's occurred to me that you're stretched pretty thin these days, with everything that's going on. Particularly with the stock we've been losing. These new men have come recommended. They have special talents in that area. I think you can work together with them on that."

"They showed up two days late and just in time for supper," Ed pointed out.

"Well, I guess we take the good with the bad, dealing with these types of individuals," Clayton said. "Anything else?"

If Garner had anything else, he kept it to himself. He had already shown the two men the bunkhouse. The cook was with the crew, so they had to rustle something up for themselves. The little one, Ballinger, was a talker, and he let slip that he was quite a hand with the pots and pans. Wiry and thin, he was maybe twenty-five at most, a supposed bronc buster and cook, and who knew what else? Garner wouldn't believe any of it until he saw it. Munson, the other one, was tall and muscled heavily. He was pushing fifty years old, Garner guessed, and he looked to have some hard bark on him. He didn't seem to be listening when the little one was yapping. Garner told them to fend for themselves then saddled up and rode out to the range east of the foothills, where the men were still working the gather.

Wednesday morning Clayton came out of the house shortly before noon, dressed in his traveling clothes. Young Ballinger was in the pole corral in the yard, attempting to saddle a green filly. The big one Munson was sitting on the back of a buckboard a few feet away, drinking coffee and watching with disinterest. He wore dirty brown pants and a corduroy coat. The youngster in the corral was dressed all in black, including a low-cut gambler's hat and a leather vest festooned with silver conchos. He looked like somebody's idea of a gambler on a riverboat.

He had somehow managed to slip a rope hackamore on the filly, but she was having none of his further plans, sidestepping away from the saddle he offered her and kicking out at him whenever he got close. After a few futile minutes Ballinger retreated. Dropping the saddle in the dirt by the gate he rolled a cigarette and lit it, watching the filly as he smoked. After a time he stuck the smoke between his teeth and took up the saddle to try again. The horse moved away and he ended up following her around the corral like a spurned suitor.

As Clayton watched from the porch, Garner rode into the yard astride the huge brown gelding he usually rode. Taking in the scene, he looked in disgust at the idler Munson before dismounting and going through the corral gate. Without pause, he grabbed the filly's mane roughly in one hand and kneed the animal so hard in the ribcage, it brought her to her knees.

"Bring the saddle," he barked at Ballinger.

Ballinger did as he was told. Twisting the filly's ear, Garner slammed the saddle on the animal. When the cinch was jerked tight, Garner himself got on the horse, yanking her head up cruelly and raking her flanks with his spurs. He rode the little filly around the corral for two or three minutes, keeping a hard rein on her the whole time, before jerking her to a stop. He got down and handed the reins to Ballinger and walked off without a word. The filly's mouth was bleeding freely from the bit, the bright blood dripping into the dust at her feet. Ballinger stood there with no idea what to do next. Munson, other than to toss his coffee dregs aside, still hadn't moved.

Clayton came down off the porch, carrying his valise. Garner approached him.

"So that's your bronc buster?"

Clayton smiled. "We've got men on the crew who can break a horse, Ed."

"So long as you know what you're getting, boss."

"I told you yesterday," Clayton said. "These men have a special skill set."

"Then why are we allowing them to fumble around with the horses?"

Clayton looked at the two men in question. Ballinger was removing the saddle from the skittish filly, whose flanks were also running blood, while Munson was rolling a Bull Durham.

"Good point," Clayton said. "You know what to do with them. Call them range detectives, if you like. Or regulators. And keep in mind what Henry Pearce said."

"What was that?"

Clayton turned to him. "A lack of evidence represents a lack of misdoing."

"Right," Garner said, realizing too late the criticism was directed at him. He indicated the valise. "You're off then?"

"Taking the afternoon train. By the way, did you send someone over to Harry Longley's ranch for that Hereford bull yet?"

"Not yet," Garner said. He looked at the two men loafing by the corral. "Might that be a job those two could handle?"

"No," Clayton decided after a moment. "We don't need them showing up at my sister's door. Send one of the hands."

Garner nodded.

"And what about that grizzly?" Clayton asked.

"One of the men spotted it up above Turtle Creek two days ago," Garner said. "I'll get him, once the gather's done."

"Skin him out with the head on," Clayton said. "Get old Murphy to tan the hide, he's good at it. I'm going to take it down to the capitol and put it on my office floor."

Where you'll tell people you shot the animal yourself, Garner thought. Thought it but didn't say it. What did he care about the lies of politicians?

"You sure about that?" he asked instead. "Them fancy folks down in the city just might shit their pants, they come across a big bear like that."

"They just might," Clayton said.

Garner nodded toward the two men by the corral. "You want to have a word with them before you go? I'll hitch up the rig."

Clayton considered it before shaking his head. "No. I don't need to talk to them ever. I hired them through an intermediary. I'm confident he would have explained the situation to them. Mr. Munson was in his employ under similar circumstances in North Dakota."

Garner stood there, saying nothing. He wasn't happy that it was left to him to deal with the two regulators, if that's what they were to be called. It was typical of Clayton—wanting to keep certain things at arm's length. For his part, Clayton was getting tired of his foreman's reticent attitude.

"You can hitch up that rig," he said. "I have a train to catch."

Eleven

WHEN NATE OPENED HIS EYES, THE wind-up alarm clock on the table beside the bed showed ten minutes before six. He sat up, his head fuzzy from the liquor Harry had insisted on pouring the night before. Not that Harry was completely to blame; Nate hadn't done a whole lot of resisting. At least for one night, it felt like old times.

The bedroom window faced west and although the sun was up, the yard and the barn and the corrals were still in shadow. The house was as quiet as the morning. Nate got out of bed and dressed in the half light. There was a bathroom, with running water and a shiny porcelain tub, across the hallway from the bedroom but he didn't go in, not wanting to awaken anybody else. He went downstairs. In the kitchen he found a part loaf of bread in a tin box and cut a thick slice from it. He slathered the bread with honey from a Mason jar and walked outside, eating as he crossed the yard.

Leaving the bread atop a fence post, he had a piss in the shadow of the barn wall, glancing toward the house as he unbuttoned his pants. Coming back around, he finished his breakfast as he quietly approached the front corral, where most of the saddle horses were sleeping. The chestnut mare, however, was not. She was watching

Nate as he walked across the yard, her ears forward, eyes sharp as a hawk's. When he got to the railing, she moved warily toward him. He licked the honey from his fingers and put his hand out. Her ears went back and she jerked her head away. Nate stood still and in a moment she came forward again, lifting her nose over the top rail to breathe of him. They stayed like that for a full minute or longer, Nate giving her time. When he ran the heel of his hand up and down the mare's forehead, she let him.

There was a tack room in the corner of the barn and inside there were any number of saddles and bridles and hackamores. Harnesses and ropes and martingales hung from wooden pegs. There were farrier tools spread on a bench built into the wall. Nate picked out a well-travelled saddle, high in the cantle and horn, and a stitched bridle with a mild bit and braided rawhide reins.

He saddled the mare at a hitching post outside the corral. She was fussy about it, side-stepping on him and blowing her stomach up against the cinch. When Nate pulled on the strap, she turned on him with her teeth. He cuffed her sharply across the nose and she settled. He adjusted the stirrups and climbed into the saddle, feeling his knee creak with the effort. He turned the green mare one way and then the other to see how she responded to the bit. As he rode out of the yard, he glanced toward the house and spotted Rose standing in a window upstairs, watching. Nate waved and kicked the horse into a lope.

He had no destination in mind, just the westward range in general. He pointed the chestnut toward the tree line in the distance, where the top of the valley leveled out on a high bench running east and west. The climb was steep, and he was obligated to switch the mare back and forth on the ascent. She was blowing heavily when they rode into the tall black pines along the crest and Nate got down from her and loosened the cinch and led her for a bit before stopping to look back over the valley below. Back at the corral, he'd swung into the saddle like a man easing into his favorite parlor chair. Dismounting now, however, he felt pain in his muscles and creaks in his already stiffening joints, a combination of his years and the fact he hadn't be on a horse in near three decades. He might be inclined later that night to take advantage of Rose's fancy bathtub.

The sun was full up now and he could see for miles, past the ranch house and the out-buildings and the corrals where the horses were now stirring. He could see the road leading into Cut Bank and even the roofs of the taller buildings in the town. In the valley running west, maybe two or three miles away, he spotted the herd belonging to Rose and Harry. The camp was up and moving. Smoke rose from a fire near the chuck wagon, and more smoke from another fire, this one farther out, past the milling herd. The second fire was for the branding crew, Nate guessed. They'd have kept the coals going overnight.

After a time he mounted the mare again and continued west, keeping to the ridge, moving at a walk now while he studied the country he used to know so well. The day began to warm. As he drew nearer the camp he could see the cowboys down below, finished with their breakfast, saddling up and heading out. There would be jokes flying, and insults too, as they rode off. Who was the better cowboy, who was the best mounted, what somebody was going to do to somebody's sister come Saturday night. Nate remembered it well, both the give and the take. He was of a mind to ride down to the fire for a cup of coffee, but he was a stranger here these days; it was hard to say if he would be welcome. Back in his time a rider was always offered a cup if he happened by, but maybe things had changed since then. He kept hearing that it was a new world. Was it so new that a man couldn't expect a cup of coffee at a campfire though? He didn't know and he decided he could wait a little longer to find out.

So he remained on the ridge, a mile or so above. He rode past the camp and then past the herd as well, pushing on into the foothills. The mare was solid beneath him. He was getting used to her gait, the way she responded to the reins on her neck. He suspected she was getting used to him too. She was raw but intelligent and aware, stopping often to sniff the air. What she could smell that Nate couldn't was impossible to say. Wolves, or maybe even a bear. Maybe just other horses—the remuda back at the camp or those ridden by the hands working the round up. Maybe her nose told her of the wood smoke from the branding fires, or water nearby. There could be wild horses in the foothills farther west. Did she smell them, did she sense her kinship to them? Was her nose so keen it could breach the past?

His head, fuzzy from the previous night's alcohol, began to clear as he rode past the Covington ranch. He spotted the barns and house from the bench. The place looked more prosperous than ever, the stone ranch house added onto, with porches built along the south and west walls and what appeared to be a bell tower. There were new barns and expanded corrals. The stars and stripes fluttered from a high pole in the yard, a suitable adornment for a state senator, Nate thought.

He kept moving. By late morning he was in the foothills, where he presently found himself approaching Turtle Creek, a fast running stream with a gravel bottom and firm grassy banks. It occurred to him he had been bound for the creek all along, without knowing it. He pointed the mare south and began the climb to the plateau where the water first gushed out of the rocks.

The line shack was still there, although just barely. Half the roof was collapsed and the front door was held in place by a couple of bent nails, the leather hinges rotted away. The old corral, off to the rear of the cabin, was mostly gone, the rails broken or hauled away for some other use. Nate dismounted by the old gate and pulled the saddle from the mare. There was plush grass in and around the corral; he tied her off and let her graze as he walked to the shack and moved the door out of the way to go inside. The potbelly stove was there yet, and the bunk. Across the room were two chairs, the backs missing, and a rough plank table. There was even an old coffee pot, maybe the pot Nate had used when he'd passed the summer there in the employ of Parcell Covington. He wished he had brought along some beans to brew.

After a time, he sat outside in the sun with his memories. The line shack was the one place he'd returned to, over and over, during his years at Deer Lodge. The one thing they couldn't take from him, the only thing he could claim ownership to in that place. But remembering was a hard task sometimes. Even good memories came with sadness and regret. There were times over the years when Nate hadn't been up to it, times when he refused his mind entry to this place. Sometimes denying a memory was easier than giving in to it.

But remembering was easy today. Nate couldn't say why for sure. Maybe it was simply because he was finally here, in a place he'd long suspected he would never see again. Or maybe it was because he had the day before spent time with the one he remembered the best when he thought about the shack. It was something he needed to stop thinking about, now that he was back.

After a half hour, he mounted up. Riding back toward the ranch, he took a different trail, keeping to the south. By midday he was on a high hog's back above a wide valley and moving due east. As he rode, the ridge dropped away, and another valley intersected the first at an angle, coming from the southeast. At the bottom of the intersection was a narrow stream, no more than fifteen feet wide. It came out of a stand of cottonwoods and was running fast from the rains, snaking along the valley floor through the buffalo grass. Nate angled the mare down the slope, stopping on the mossy bank where both he and the horse drank from the swift current. The water was icy cold, numbing his teeth. Straightening up, he heard a shrill voice coming from off to the left, where the creek curved into the trees. Afoot now, he led the mare along the creek flat toward the sound.

The voice quit for a moment and then started up again as Nate entered the trees. It seemed to be coming from a youngster, and one whose vocabulary consisted mainly of curse words. When

Nate walked out of the cottonwoods, he came upon the boy, who was on a mud flat on the far side of the creek, squared off against a large Hereford cow. The animal had somehow allowed the young cowboy to lasso it with a rawhide lariat, but that was the extent of the cow's cooperation. She was standing wide-legged, her hooves dug in, and she was staring at the boy with mayhem in her eyes. Behind her, a dozen feet away, was a calf that could not have been two weeks old.

The youngster was as thin as a rake handle and fuzzy-cheeked. The coat he wore was at least two sizes too big for him. He was dismounted from his horse, a bay gelding now wandering away, looking for graze, and he was holding tight to the lariat while he cussed out the cow. It was a standoff and one that the boy, who might have weighed a hundred and forty pounds, was not going to win, no matter how many names he could think of to call the cow.

"Hello," Nate shouted over after listening for a while longer.

The sound of Nate's voice silenced the boy in mid-curse and he whirled round to see who was coming up behind him. He was immediately embarrassed by his situation.

"What do you want?" he demanded.

"Nothing," Nate said.

"Then keep moving," the youngster advised him. "I got no time for idle talk."

"I can see you're busy," Nate said. "What do you intend to do with that cow?"

"Taking her back to the herd, if it's any of your business."

"It's not," Nate said. "Where's the herd?"

The boy switched hands on the lariat, the better to jab a thumb vaguely to the north. "Back that way a piece. You happy now?"

"I was happy before," Nate told him.

"Then keep moving. I got work to do."

Nate nodded. Climbing aboard the mare, he looked at the bay horse, now picking at some green shoots further along the creek bed. "You realize that cow is not going back to the herd just because you managed to land your loop on her and are now calling her names."

"What do you know about it?" the boy asked.

"I know a little," Nate said. "I might have an idea."

"Go to hell. I'm doing all right on my own."

"You're doing all right if your intention is to stand out here until you are old and gray," Nate said.

The boy, loath to ask, bit his bottom lip. "What's your big idea?"

Nate urged the mare through the creek and up the bank on the other side. He moved to the bay gelding, where he'd seen a short lead coiled on the saddle horn. Taking the rope, he walked the mare over to the newborn calf and dropped a loop around its neck. Then he rode to where the boy was standing and offered over the rope.

"You lead the calf back to the herd and that cow will follow along like you was Moses himself. She'll be cursing you like you've been cursing her every step of the way, but she'll follow you, guaranteed."

The boy gave the matter some thought and then took the rope from Nate without a word. Nate waited until the youngster was mounted and leading the calf away before he turned to push the mare through the creek. He rode into the trees and up the slope once more, heading east again.

When he got to the top, he looked back to see the boy and the calf moving out onto the range, heading for a large herd that Nate now saw farther to the north, where the valley opened up. The cow was following the calf, bellowing her displeasure. As Nate watched, the boy glanced up, his eyes searching the ridge until they rested on Nate and the mare. Even from that distance, Nate could sense the stubborn set to the youngster. Finally the young cowboy touched his finger and thumb to the brim of his hat. With that, he went on his way.

The sun was high and Nate's stomach began to rumble as he rode on. He remembered a flat plain a few miles to the south, where a young German couple had been homesteading a section of land in the time Nate had been riding herd for the Covington outfit. Nate had been friendly with the couple. He had helped the husband put up a lean-to for his milk cow, and even taught them a little English, at least the language as Nate knew it.

The section was originally without a source of water and the last time Nate had been to the farm, the man had finished digging a well and had spent most of the couple's remaining grubstake on a windmill. If there was one thing Montana offered in great abundance, it was wind. Nate had been standing in the yard when the first gush of water came up out of the ground, the blades overhead whirring, the drive rod thumping, gearbox meshing smoothly. The water spilled along a wooden spout to a trough built of sycamore, the seams caulked with pine gum. The German couple stood by, smiling proudly at their accomplishment and what it meant to their little spread. Until that day, the man had been hauling barrels of water from a spring on the Covington ranch. Purcell Covington had been charging the man twenty-five cents a barrel.

Now Nate rode the mare onto a high flat above the plain where the homestead sat. Below him was the farm, or what was left of it anyway. The place was deserted, the house empty, the windows gone, no doubt taken by someone to be used elsewhere. The lean-to that Nate had helped to erect had fallen in, the rafter poles broken, cedar shingles scattered on the ground. The windmill still turned, but Nate could see that the drive rod was gone and most likely the gearbox as well, salvaged as had been the windows. A chicken house had been built on the property, a few yards from the lean-to, and it was still intact but listing, a piece of burlap tacked over the door. The house itself had gained a small addition since Nate had last seen it, a narrow extension across the back. There must have been children, he thought.

So what had happened? Where had the dreams gone? It occurred to Nate that everything required for success had been there. There was good land and water. There was ambition and backbone, an immigrant couple with the tenacious nature required to overcome what the country would throw at them. And yet, looking down at what remained of their dreams, it seemed they had failed. The wind would eventually blow the house down. The windmill would topple; the chicken house would sink into the ground.

Montana was a sonofabitch in a fight. And she didn't always fight fair.

Riding down the hill toward the ranch an hour later, Nate could see Rose, standing alongside the corral where the young horses milled. She had a clipboard in her hand and she was writing something as Nate trotted over. Looking up at his approach, she removed the wire rimmed glasses she wore and reached for a cup of coffee perched atop a fence post.

"Afternoon," she said before taking a drink.

"Afternoon."

"How are the two of you getting along?"

"Pretty fair," Nate said, patting the chestnut on the neck. "Once she figured out who was boss."

"Just wait until she discovers your great humility."

Nate merely nodded, not taking the bait.

"Where did you ride to?" she asked.

Nate pointed his chin. "West. Crossed your brother's spread."

"I bet you weren't invited to tea."

"Nor breakfast neither," Nate said. "I kept to the high bench and rode all the way to the foothills." He paused. "Funny how the memory works. I would have sworn I could draw you a map of this country, with every creek and gulley exactly where I recalled. But things weren't where they used to be."

"You figure somebody moved the creeks and gullies?" Rose asked.

Nate smiled. "I reckon not. I did find the old line shack on Turtle Creek. Right where it always was."

Rose busied herself with her notes.

"I do believe you're blushing," Nate said.

"I am not," Rose said.

"Maybe you got yourself a sudden sunburn then," Nate said, letting her off the hook. He looked at the bunch in the corral. "What are you writing?"

"I need to describe each for the bill of sale," Rose said.

"When did you start wearing eyeglasses?"

"When I discovered I had to hold the newspaper three feet from my face to read it," Rose replied. "It's called getting on in years, Mr. Cooper."

"I wouldn't know about that," Nate said. "I feel the same as I did when I was twenty. Riding past your herd this morning, I had half a notion to go down there and show those young bucks how to bulldog a calf."

"Go ahead," Rose told him. "You end up breaking a hip and it won't be me nursing you back to health."

"Who's breaking a hip?" It was Harry asking the question, having just walked around the corner of the barn, leading the black gelding he'd been riding the day before.

"Nobody," Rose said. "Not if I have any say in matters."

Nate started to climb down from the mare.

"You might as well stay up there," Harry told him. "You and me are riding up to Muskrat Creek, try and locate Ivanhoe."

"You have a hand named Ivanhoe?" Nate asked. "And worse than that, he's lost?"

"Ivanhoe is my old bull," Harry said. "I promised the loan of him to Clayton. Grizzly got his good bull and he's got heifers in season." Harry turned to Rose. "You coming along for a ride?"

"I have work to do," she told him.

"Suit yourself." Harry winked at Nate. "Hard to believe that any woman would deny herself the pleasure of our company."

"Go, before I start to cry," Rose said.

It was five miles to Muskrat Creek, a shallow, meandering stream that marked the eastern boundary of the ranch. There were a few hundred yearling steers on the range there, scattered along the plain, grazing on the spring buffalo grass. When they finally came across the old bull named Ivanhoe, he was lying down near the creek, chewing contentedly. The animal was close to twenty years old, grown heavy and set in his ways, and it took some convincing to get him on his feet and headed back toward the ranch. Once moving, though, he plodded along steadily, if not quickly. Nate and Harry followed behind, watching the huge swinging testicles of the bull as he ambled through the heavy grass.

"Look at that fat old bugger," Nate said as they descended the slope. "I'd make pot roast out of him before I'd lend him out to Clayton Covington."

"First of all," Harry said. "If you were to cook up any part of that bull, the *gravy* would be too tough to cut with a knife. Secondly, don't come down too hard on Clayton. He was never much of a hand, but he's represented us well in Helena. And remember—our problems were with his old man, not him."

"I always figured he was cut from the same cloth," Nate said.

"I'm not so sure about that," Harry said. "Rose might agree with you. I do know he's well thought of down at the capitol. He's the one behind the new highway act. We need highways and roads. Bridges too. How many rivers did we cross in our day, never knowing if we'd make it to the other side?"

Nate didn't comment and Harry was happy to move past the topic. He pulled a silver flask from his vest pocket, took a drink, and passed it over. He indicated a spot in the creek where the water pooled up.

"We fished for catfish in that mouse hole, our first year in the territory," he said. "You recall?"

Nate drank and wiped his mouth. "I do. We ate our fill of catfish back then. Not by choice neither."

"I still like a plate of it," Harry said. "But you're right—we were poor as Job's turkey in those days." He took the flask back. "And look at us now. Drinking twelve-year-old bourbon, having a lazy day. A gypsy with a crystal ball couldn't have dared to tell us our futures back then."

"I had my fortune told once," Nate said. "Old woman in a medicine show told me I was to be rich one day. Cost me a dollar to hear it. I found out later she told every damn cowboy that came into her tent the same thing. If anybody was getting rich, it was that old woman. She had chin whiskers and a nose as big as a potato."

Harry had another measure of whiskey before tucking the flask in his pocket. He seemed to have something he wanted to say but was having trouble getting to it. Looping the reins over the saddle horn, he took a curved pipe and a pouch from his coat, tapped the pipe in the palm of his hand three or four times to empty it and began to pack the bowl. He glanced over at Nate.

"Sometimes it's just dumb luck, the way things happen," he said. "Like the winter of '86. Temperatures thirty below, snow up to the eaves. Half the ranches in Montana and Wyoming went tits up. Cattle died by the thousands, out on the range, piled one atop another like cordwood. Rose and I were just starting out, didn't have but a hundred head of cows. Ironic thing was, having a small herd is what saved us. We never lost a single cow. It was a backward wind that winter, hard out of the east, and we stacked the herd in the lee of the barn and kept them from straying. Cut shag bark from dead cottonwoods to feed 'em when the hay ran out. Boiled snow for drinking water. Spent all our long days looking after that herd. It was just the two of us; we didn't have a nickel to pay a hand, let alone thirty a month. Living in that log shack that's the smokehouse now, burning buffalo chips in the fireplace. We didn't know which we would do first—starve to death or freeze to death. But we made it through."

"You did better than make it, from what I see," Nate said.

Harry nodded quickly, wanting to get it out. "That's the thing, Nate. You and me come out here together. That business out at the reservation: that coulda been me as easy as you. Like God was flippin' a coin. And if it had of been me, then maybe all this would be yours. The ranch and the stock, even old Ivanhoe there." He shrugged his shoulders, hesitating for a bit. "And Rose, too, for that matter."

"I ain't so sure about any of that," Nate said. "I was never any kind of a businessman. If I made twenty dollars I always seemed to spend twenty-five. As for Rose, that woman has always loved you."

"There was a time when she shone for the both of us and you damn well know it," Harry said. He lit the pipe; the wind was up and it took three matches to get the bowl burning. He puffed away for a bit. "Whatever the case, we both made it through alive. Who'd have thought that thirty years ago, when we came out of the Dakotas? But we did it, whether through shit luck or good management or fate, whatever you want to call it."

"We're both still breathing," Nate allowed. "But that's just about where our similarities end."

"What I have is yours," Harry said. "I've built a good life and you're welcome to it. Like I said, our paths could easy have been reversed. Why not enjoy the good life? I don't remember you ever shying away from the finer things. Who knows how many years we got left?"

"Christ, Harry," Nate replied. "You're talking like I'm the same as that old bull there. You fixing to turn me out to pasture, too?"

"If you care to recall, I'm not turning him out to pasture. I'm sending him over to Covington's to meet a bunch of pretty young heifers."

Nate smiled. "If you put it that way."

Harry's pipe went out and he took a moment to light it again. Once he succeeded, he pointed the stem at Ivanhoe. "Now that I think about it—that old critter is stubborn and cantankerous and he's got a pair of balls as big as the moon. Maybe you and him are the same after all."

Twelve

CLAYTON MET WITH GOVERNOR TOOLE LATE Friday afternoon in Clayton's office. They had spoken by telephone earlier, after the senate had recessed for the weekend. Clayton offered to walk across the capitol grounds to the governor's office, but Toole had insisted on coming over.

Clayton had returned to work Thursday morning, when the debate on the highway bill resumed. In his absence, Bill Ferguson decided that the impasse over the budget could be solved by asking for federal money to make up the difference. Clayton's position was that they could ask, and then wait for six or eight months for an answer that would, in all likelihood, be no.

"It's a good idea," he told Ferguson after the morning session. "It just won't work."

Unfortunately the notion got enough support that the request went forward. Discouraged, Clayton walked back to his office and spent the afternoon answering mail. Nancy had asked if she could go home early, as she was taking the train to Missoula for the weekend to visit friends.

"It's a wild town," Clayton had told her. "Careful you don't get yourself into trouble there."

"If I was inclined to get myself in trouble, I'd stay right here in Helena with you," Nancy had replied. And she had smiled at him, standing in the doorway, with her hip against the jamb.

Clayton was going to ask what she meant by that, but he decided there was no need. He had a pretty fair idea. He told her to have a good time.

"If I was going to have a good time—" she began and left it at that.

Clayton heard the governor's heavy footsteps on the stairs shortly past five o'clock. He got to his feet and met the old man in the doorway. After climbing the single flight of stairs Toole was wheezing like a leaky bellows. Clayton ushered him into a leather chair and then sat across from him.

"How did it go today?" Toole asked.

"Different violins, same old song," Clayton said. "It's always the same question. Where are we going to get the money? Do we raise taxes, steal from Peter to pay Paul, sell the Rocky Mountains to France or Russia?" He shook his head in discouragement. "The latest suggestion is that we ask Washington to finance our highway system. The theory is that the government's coffers are overfilled with money from the new income tax."

"Even if that is true, it doesn't mean the administration is keen to use that money to build roads here," Toole said. "Mr. Roosevelt might have at least considered the notion. He's always had an affinity for our state. But Taft won't go for it."

"I know that and you know that," Clayton said. "But there are a couple dozen dunderheads over there on the floor who don't." He raised his palms. "And so we will now make our way down that blind alley for a few months."

Toole, exhaling heavily at the futility of the notion, reached into his pocket for a tailor made. His pallor was bad, and his hands shook slightly as he lit the cigarette with a gold-plated lighter.

"This is going to be a long-term proposition," Clayton added. "We might have to wait for another presidential election. I hear rumors that Teddy wants his job back."

Toole snorted. "I suppose hunting big game in Africa doesn't compete with the blood sport in Washington."

"I guess not," Clayton said. "Either way, it looks as if we're in for a long haul."

"You are," the governor said.

"What's that?"

"You are," Toole repeated. "But not me. My congestive system continues to confound the medical profession. However, they all seem to agree that a dry and warm climate is a tonic I would be foolhardy to refuse. They're not saying it will cure me, mind you. But neither are they saying it will not."

"Doctors," Clayton said. "They like to hedge their bets."

"They do."

Clayton watched the old man draw on the cigarette. "What does this mean—you're taking a vacation?"

Toole shook his head. "I'm stepping down, Clayton. I can't climb the front steps to the capitol building without stopping to rest halfway. It's time. I wanted to hold on until November, but I can't."

It seemed the old man might start to cry. Clayton waited before speaking, letting the moment pass. "I am truly sorry to hear that, Joseph," he said then. "There are healthy men on that senate floor who can't hold a candle to you when it comes to legislating and negotiation and . . . just plain horse sense. Where's the justice in that?"

"It's not for us to decide what is just and what isn't," Toole said. "We just carry the water around here." He came half out of the chair to flick the ash from the cigarette into an ashtray on the desk. "Now as you know, the lieutenant governor will take over for me. But only until the election in November. At that point, I'm going to endorse you for governor, Clayton. If you want the job."

Clayton's mind had already moved to November. He was now required to look surprised. "Well now," he began. "I don't know what to say. Other than I am honored."

"You could say you still keep a bottle in the bottom drawer of that desk," Toole said. "We could drink on it to seal the deal."

Clayton moved around to fetch the bottle and two glasses. He poured and the two men sat in the leather chairs and, although such words were not spoken, toasted the demise of the governor's career. After the first glass, Clayton poured a second. He noticed that Toole's hands shook less now.

"Who knows about this?" he asked.

"My wife and my daughter," Toole said. "And now you. This is one thing I've managed to keep from those mongrel picklocks of the press." He sipped from the glass. "But I intend to make the announcement of my resignation tomorrow. It might be a good thing if you were there beside me. I'm speaking of the subliminal effect, Clayton."

"Of course," Clayton said. "But only if you wish it so. This will be your moment, Joseph, not mine. Is there anything else I can do?"

"As a matter of fact, there is one thing I would like, Clayton. Chalk it up to an old man's vanity, if you please. But this interstate highway project. It would mean a lot to my family, and to me, if my name could be attached to it in some small manner."

Clayton's mind went into gear. "I think the main thoroughfare running north and south should be called the Joseph K. Toole Highway, and I've already recommended that," he lied.

The old man smiled. "I am overwhelmed." He drank off the rye and got to his feet. Clayton walked him to the outer door and watched as he made his way down the stairs. He wasn't huffing or wheezing now. But then going down was easy.

Going up was the tough part.

Thirteen

LATE THAT AFTERNOON, NATE TOOK A ride into Cut Bank. He and Harry had deposited Ivanhoe in a run alongside the barn, where the old bull turned a couple circles before lying down in the dirt and falling asleep. Harry said that one of Clayton's hands would be coming over to drive the animal to the Covington range, ten miles to the west.

"He'd better bring some grub along for the ride," Nate had said. "It'll take that bull all day to amble that distance."

"I expect he'll send old Fields, he's a plodder himself," Harry had said. "Come on, I want to show you something."

That something was Harry's new motorcar. He opened the shed and, after some cranking, fired the machine up and backed it out onto the lane. Harry sat there behind the wheel, looking very serious, as he adjusted various levers and switches. The engine rumbled and coughed and leveled out. Harry, his hand resting on a brass knob protruding from the dashboard, smiled at Nate.

"This here advances the spark," he said. "That fires the cylinders. Internal combustion, is what it's called."

Nate regarded the motorcar suspiciously. "What's it run on?"

"Gasoline," Harry replied. "Like kerosene, you could say. But more refined."

Nate indicated the horse he had been riding all day, now unsaddled in the corral, picking at some hay. "That mare will run all day on grass and oats."

"There's nothing wrong with progress," Harry said. "You're looking at the future. There will come a time when horses will be obsolete."

Nate scoffed. "You telling me you're going to throw a loop from that thing. You're going to chase mavericks up and down switchbacks and into the underbrush in that overgrown sewing machine? I kindly doubt it, Harry."

"All in due time," Harry said. "The world is moving fast. When we came here thirty years ago, if somebody had told us you could talk to somebody fifty miles away through a wire, or light a room with electricity, we'd of told them they was daft. Yet here we are. And that man Edison back in New Jersey is inventing something new every day. He probably invented something this morning." Harry thought a moment. "I don't know, maybe a gadget that puts your boots on for you."

"I can pull my own damn boots on," Nate told him.

"That was just an example. Why don't you climb aboard? I have to drive to Shelby to the bank. This machine will go twenty-five miles an hour."

"I believe I'll pass."

"You afraid of the future, Nate?"

It took Nate a while to respond. "I wouldn't say I'm afraid of her," he said finally. "It's just that so far she don't look all that pretty to me."

The shadows from the buildings were growing long as he jogged into town on the chestnut mare. Rather than tie her to a hitching rail, he paid twenty-five cents to put her up at the livery. The owner was a man of sixty-five or seventy, with a crooked back that wouldn't allow him to straighten. For the two bits he allowed he would water the horse and throw her a pitchfork of hay. He kept his hay stored in the mow overhead, he told Nate, not outside in the elements like the other livery in town. He was still going on about it when Nate left him.

Nate wandered out onto Main Street. Coming in on the train the day before, he hadn't dawdled, wanting to reach the ranch before nightfall. Thirty years earlier, the town hadn't been much more than a trading post, with more tents than buildings. Now the main thoroughfare was lined with commercial ventures—two banks, a library, bakery, a half dozen hotels and saloons. A haberdashery and millinery standing side by side. The sheriff's office and jail was a stone building, two stories high, with barred windows and a sign out front identifying one Henry Pearce as high sheriff. As Nate walked by, he could see a man inside he assumed to be Pearce, around his own age with a paunchy middle, sitting at a desk, talking to an old man who was leaning on a push broom.

Across from the train station was the schoolhouse and beside that was a large frame building bearing the name Gill's General Store. There were a number of wares on display—picks and shovels and barrels and the like—on a veranda that ran across the front and down one side. The building itself was a hundred feet wide and half that again long, featuring plate glass windows in the fore and a loading dock behind, where some larger farm implements were displayed.

In front of the store a half dozen Indians loitered, sitting on the sidewalk or leaning against the wall. Some appeared to be drunk, or addled in a fashion. They were mainly dirty in their appearance, wearing faded cotton shirts and pants with the knees wore out. When Nate walked over to enter the store, he was stopped by one of the Indians, a man of maybe twenty-five, wearing a stained Stetson with holes in the crown and an eagle feather in the band.

"Gimme dollar," the man demanded, slurring his words.

"I don't think I will," Nate said and went inside.

The place sold everything from clothes to toys to rifles to soda pop. Nate wandered around a bit before buying a bag of licorice candy. Rose had always had a sweet tooth for licorice. The man behind the counter gave him change from a dollar. He was a short man, barely five feet tall, with a head of curly black hair, combed straight up, as if in an effort to reward himself with greater stature.

"You Gill?" Nate asked.

"No, sir," the man replied. "Mr. Gill is not here right now."

"You got some Indians begging out front," Nate said.

"We are well aware of that," the little man said. "If you have some ideas on getting shed of them, we'd be more than anxious to hear them."

"Where are they from?"

"Off the reservation."

"Blackfoot?"

"I'm not an expert at identifying Indians."

"They got nothing better to do?" Nate asked. "I don't recall the Blackfoot stooping to begging for coins."

"I can't imagine where you've been then, sir. There's not a day goes by we don't have them loitering about. You'll note that the smaller implements out front are chained to the wall. Otherwise they have a habit of disappearing."

Nate tucked the licorice in his vest and walked outside. The Indian in the Stetson was now leaning against the newel post. He looked over, curling his lip. "Where's my dollar?"

"You from the agency, son?" Nate asked.

"Gimme four bits."

"You're not gonna get a nickel from me."

The Indian lunged forward to throw a wild punch in Nate's direction. Nate easily ducked the blow and then drove the heel of his hand into the man's breastbone, knocking him into the dusty street.

Stepping down from the porch, he walked around the man and headed over to the Bighorn Saloon. The place was more than half full. Nate sat at a corner table and drank a beer. He thought he might see someone he recognized. The men standing around, talking and drinking, were mostly merchants or businessmen, it seemed. They wore suits and ties and talked loudly, and they were for the most part two or three decades younger than Nate. Nate thought he might run across a cowpuncher or two, maybe some-body from the old days he could reminisce with, but he expected those hands were all gone, either drifted or dead.

He had a second beer after the first. The paunchy sheriff he'd seen earlier—Pearce, if the sign on the jail was correct—came in, and walked directly to a stool at the far end of the bar. The bartender brought him a glass half full of whiskey without being asked. The sheriff took to the drink like a thirsty man.

A couple of the businessmen started up a game of eight ball. Neither one could sink a rock in a lake. Nate considered challeng-ing them to a game, but instead he finished his beer and left. He walked to the livery and got the chestnut mare from the man with the crooked back and headed south to the ranch. He'd had enough of civilization for one day.

The next morning he was up again with the sun. His back muscles were as stiff as a new collar as he dressed in the half-light before heading downstairs. There was a fresh loaf in the bread box, and honey in the pot. The chestnut mare was more agreeable to the tightening of the cinch than the previous morning. Nate rode out of the yard as the shadows began to shorten, and the songbirds started their day.

He kicked the mare into a lope and headed west, the rising sun on his back. He reckoned it was twenty miles or more to the Blackfoot reservation. Some of the ranches on the way had put up fencing, so Nate took to the county road, which ran in a very general sense in that direction, dipping and curving along the way to accommodate the various homesteads in between. The last ranch he passed before he arrived at the dirt road leading to the reservation belonged to Clayton Covington. Beyond that was open range.

Where the grassland met the beginning of the tree line, a clear stream ran down from the foothills and flowed parallel to the road. Nate stopped to water the mare and give her a breather. He loosened the cinch while she drank and let her graze in the wheatgrass there for a quarter hour.

He'd been climbing steadily the last few miles and now he looked back over the ground he'd covered. In the distance he could see the Covington spread. Nate was familiar with the house and had even been inside a few times, back when he'd worked for Parcell, his first year in the territory. Those days there had been just the house and a small barn and whatever range the old man had put claim to. Between the spot where Nate stood and the ranch buildings there were numerous herds of cattle, a few thousand in number, he would guess. Farther south, where the ranch ran up against the foothills, he could see a chuck wagon and remuda, and a couple dozen riders with a herd. Covington hands, working the round up. Nate wondered if Clayton was among them. He doubted it.

Back in the saddle, he moved along the dirt road, following the narrow stream. A couple of miles on, he came to another ranch, this one smaller in scale. The house was built along the creek, a sturdy log building with a cedar roof and shutters painted yellow. There were corrals extending to the south, with a couple dozen horses inside, and beyond that a herd of shorthorn cattle, maybe two hundred in all. An Indian was busy shoeing a horse in the yard while a woman—quite likely his wife—was hanging wash on a line. When the Indian looked up, Nate waved, but the man went back to his work without response.

A half hour later Nate came to a sign nailed to a pair of ponderosa pine trees, the lettering faded and the face of the sign pocked by dozens of bullet holes.

MONTANA BLACKFOOT RESERVE

As Nate passed beneath the sign, he saw two women, dressed in deer hide dresses, picking Saskatoon berries on the far side of the creek. They stopped in their work to look at him as he rode by. When he lifted his hand, they did not wave back but continued to stare, their faces expressionless.

The agency store was still standing on the high side of a curve in the road where it led onto the reservation. Somebody had built a lean-to alongside it at some point, under which a quantity of cordwood was stacked. The split shingle roof was patched with pieces of tin here and there. A rusty stovepipe protruded from one wall, then elbowed upward, above the eaves of the old building. Behind the store several Indians were playing a game of wheel and arrow and betting on it. Nate knew the game; he had played it in the years past, when the stakes had been pennies.

Alongside the dirt road, beyond the trading post, were a few shacks, made of rough planking, and a couple dozen teepees. Several fires were burning in the cool of the day. A dozen or more dogs ran about, some barking at Nate's arrival. One came too close to the mare and she lashed out with a rear hoof, catching it solidly in the rib cage. The mutt sulked away, whimpering, and the others kept their distance. There were a number of Indians in and around the shacks and tents. Most of them were on their feet, watching Nate, although some were sitting or lying on the ground. An older man was scraping an elk hide, pegged between two trees. If he noticed Nate's arrival, he never showed it.

Most of the shacks and teepees had makeshift corrals in behind, built of cottonwood or pine saplings, lashed together with raw-hide rope. Each corral held a horse or pony, the occasional mule. There were several small vegetable gardens as well, freshly tilled, the recent planting marked with stakes and string.

The barking of the dogs is what drew the attention of Ulysses Elkhorn, who now stepped out of the old store. He stood on the sagging porch and had a long and critical look at Nate, who reined the mare to a stop on the dusty road a few yards away. Ulysses wore his hair long, as most Indians still did, and he was dressed in plain black pants and a red cotton shirt. White man's clothes. He was tall and barrel-chested and had an arrogant cast to his eye.

"Howdy," Nate said.

"What do you want?"

The mare began to move and Nate reined her in. "Passing through."

"This isn't a place you pass through," the Indian said. His voice was as flat and cold as his eyes. He turned his head, glancing in the direction Nate had ridden in from, looking for more riders. A vivid red scar ran from his nose across his cheekbone to his ear. "You came here on purpose."

"I do most things on purpose," Nate told him.

Ulysses turned to him. "And what is your purpose here, old man?"

Nate glanced about. Several other Indians were now watching him. "Would Little Bull be around?" he asked.

"Never heard of him," Ulysses said.

"Never heard of him," Nate repeated. "He was a Blackfoot chief."

"I don't think so."

"Hell, I knew the man," Nate told him.

Now Ulysses smiled. "I think you are a dreamer. When was this?"

"When I knew him?" Nate asked. "Winter of '79. I stayed in his father's lodge, down on Muskrat Creek. His father was White Bull. I spent the better part of two months in their camp, me and my partner Harry Longley. Don't tell me I'm dreaming it."

"White Bull," Ulysses said, turning now to look at Nate. "He's dead. All those Indians are dead now. Ghosts. They never got to be old, like you."

Nate regarded the churlish Indian for a time, then turned in the saddle to have another look at the surroundings.

"This place is a shithole," he said. "What happened?"

"What did you say?" Ulysses demanded.

"I said this place is a shithole," Nate repeated. "I spent time here, back when this reservation was new and you were still pissing your buckskins. I don't see much improvement to show for thirty years. If anything, it's gone the other way."

"Who are you to talk like this?"

"I talk any way I please," Nate said. "And I told you—I had friends here."

"Maybe you did," the Indian said. "But no more."

The women Nate had seen earlier had returned from their berry picking and now they were standing along the lane, tin pails in hand, watching the conversation. As Nate glanced at them, something occurred to him. He looked back at Ulysses. "Where are the children? I don't see a one."

"You ask a lot of questions," Ulysses said and then he paused. "The children are at the white school. They go there to become little Christians. Then they come back here to the reservation, with their hair cut, and their stories of Jesus and how he will save them in the next world. Instead of starving like little Indians, they can starve as little white people."

Nate's eyes went past the man on the porch, into the open doorway of the old store. He could see the counter there, along with some bags of grain and a few air tights on a shelf behind. The last time Nate had been inside the building, he'd been looking down the barrel of a ten gauge shotgun. He'd been a half second or so from the world that Jesus was apparently now promising the Indian children. Nate could still recall the terror gripping him at that moment, the panic as he reached for the Colt in his belt. Nearly thirty years on, it was as fresh in his mind as last night's supper.

"Well, you've seen the poor Indians," Ulysses said. "Keep riding, old man."

Fourteen

Rose was carrying water to the vegetable garden, a bucket in each hand, when she noticed the buggy approaching along the county road. By the dapple gray pacer pulling the rig, she knew Abigail Jones was about to arrive for one of her visits. For a fleeting moment Rose had a desire to duck into the barn and hide there until Abigail, after knocking on the front door of the house and yelling yoo-hoo a dozen times, concluded that Rose was not at home and went on her way. She could stop at the Butlers or the Parsons; maybe they had time for her jabbering today. Rose chided herself for the notion; she should be happy for company. But she had lots to do, and Abigail's visits were rarely short, and just as rarely entertaining.

They sat on the side porch and drank tea. Abigail had baked scones that morning and arrived with a dozen of them in a box. The afternoon was sunny; the thermometer on the wall behind where they sat read seventy degrees, the warmest day of the year thus far. A good day to be planting or cleaning or tending to any number of chores on Rose's list. Instead, she sipped tea and nibbled at a pastry as hard as a pine knot.

"And he spent every cent of it gambling," Abigail was saying. "According to Irma Johnston, whose word I wouldn't ordinarily trust if she was swearing on a stack of Gideon Bibles. But I've heard from other sources that Ralph is a gambler. Reverend Fletcher confided that his wife had spoken to him about it."

"Isn't the good Reverend required to keep such things to himself?" Rose asked.

"He told only me," Abigail said. "He knows I am the soul of discretion."

"Of course."

"I also heard that he had another woman, somewhere in Oregon."

"The Reverend?"

"No!" Abigail exclaimed. "Land sakes. I'm talking about Ralph."

Rose nodded, looking at the young horses in the front corral, and thinking that she should have heard from the Scotsman McCrae by now. She tried to recall just who Ralph was. Abigail had run through quite a roster of people since she'd arrived, many of whom Rose didn't know, or had never heard of. This disreputable Ralph character, gambler and womanizer, was one of them.

"There are worse things to be," she said.

"Than what?" Abigail asked.

"Than a gambler," Rose replied. "I try to give everyone the benefit of the doubt. And I never talk about people when they aren't around to defend themselves. I know you are the same way."

"Absolutely."

Rose smiled, hoping that the suggestion would stop Abigail's gossiping. If she stopped gossiping she would be required to stop talking, which might very well send her on her way. As she looked at the younger woman, she saw Abigail's eyes narrow as she spotted something out past the barn. Rose turned to see Nate approaching on the mare. He'd left at sunrise and been gone the better part of the day.

"Looks like company," Abigail said. "One of the hands?"

"No," Rose said. "A guest."

"Oh." Abigail straightened in the chair; her hand went immediately to her hair, patting it into place.

When Nate spotted the two women on the porch he rode over to say hello. Rose watched his eyes as he took in the robust feminine creature that was Abigail Jones—her lustrous red hair, her ample bosom, her full lips. And Abigail returned the gaze, switching from town chinwagger to blushing coquette in a blink of her blue eyes.

Rose made the proper introductions, still watching Nate.

"So nice to meet you, Mr. Cooper," Abigail gushed.

"And I am always delighted to meet a beautiful woman," Nate replied. He was standing at the bottom of the steps now, holding his hat in his right hand.

Rose rolled her eyes. Nate was careful not to look her way.

"You're just talking nonsense now, I swear," Abigail responded, casting her gaze downward. "Rose tells me you're visiting?"

"Yes, ma'am."

"Would you have tea with us?" Abigail asked. "I baked these scones just this morning."

"I would love to," Nate replied.

While he tied the mare's reins to the hitching post in front of the porch, Rose drew another chair near. She had never known Nate Cooper to drink a drop of tea, but she poured a cup for him anyway, handing it over as he settled between the two women. He still would not meet Rose's eye. When Abigail offered the plate of scones, Nate took one.

"Why, thank you. I've been in the saddle since daybreak without so much as a bite."

"Where are you from, Mr. Cooper?"

"I was born in Missouri," Nate told her. "But I left there when I was just a pup. I used to cowboy in these parts, way back when."

"And where have you been of late?"

Rose interjected. "Mr. Cooper has been down south for the past few years."

Nate attempted to bite into the scone. "Fact of the matter is, I've spent the last twenty-eight years in the Montana State Prison."

"Oh my," Abigail said. She busied herself with her tea cup. "Why . . . um . . . what was your offense, if I may ask?"

Nate looked quizzically at the scone a moment longer before setting it aside. "I shot a man named Dudley."

"Oh, dear. Was he badly hurt?"

"Bad enough that they buried him."

"The man Dudley was a despicable criminal," Rose said. "He was a swindler and a bully and a cheat. He should have been tried and hung for his crimes."

"Goodness gracious," Abigail said.

Nate glanced at Rose and then away. He took a sip of tea before turning to Abigail. "And what about you—are you a ranch woman yourself?"

"I was," Abigail replied. "I was indeed. But my husband died in a blizzard seven winters ago, while out looking for some lost sheep. I sold the ranch. I now have a little house in town." She paused and then added, "On Fremont Street."

"Sounds lovely," Nate said.

Rose made a noise in her throat. Nate ignored her.

"Well, it seems you are a bit of a Robin Hood character, Mr. Cooper," Abigail said. "Right out of the storybooks."

"I wouldn't say that."

"But I would." Abigail turned to Rose. "You never told me, Rose, that you had such a fascinating friend."

Rose gave Nate a long look. "It must have slipped my mind."

"Now *that* seems impossible," Abigail said, beaming at Nate.

Abigail left shortly thereafter, although somewhat reluctantly, saying she needed to be on the road in order to reach town before darkness settled in. She insisted that Rose keep the rest of the scones and maintained her flirtatious demeanor as Nate helped her into the buggy. Rose stood on the porch, arms crossed, watching the two of them in their dance.

"I look forward to hearing more of your stories, Mr. Cooper," Abigail said. "Bye . . . for now."

"Good-bye for now," Nate repeated.

Abigail gave the reins a flick and the little pacer started. Nate stood waving like a man on a train platform. Rose was silent until the rig had passed through the front gates and was on the road to town.

"You have no shame," she said.

"What do you mean?" Nate asked, still watching the departing buggy.

"I mean you have no shame. I swear, if I wasn't sitting here, you'd have climbed atop the woman right here on the damn veranda. You've always been the biggest flirt I ever saw."

Nate turned. "Are you saying the woman wasn't flirting with me every bit as hard?"

"I've seen Abigail Jones flirt with the mannequins in Gill's mercantile," Rose said. "So don't get too full of yourself."

"Christ almighty."

Rose looked at the setting sun, half hidden by the roof of the barn. "Well, the day's pretty much shot. You want a drink of bourbon or would Robin Hood prefer more tea?"

"I vote for the whiskey," Nate said. He indicated the table. "As far as them biscuits go, you can save them for stoning a leper if you come across one."

Rose carried the tray with the tea and scones inside while Nate walked the mare to the barn and unsaddled her. After brushing her out, he turned her loose in the corral, where she promptly flopped on her side in the dirt and rolled over twice. When he got back to the house, Rose was on the porch once more, with bourbon and glasses.

"Where's Harry off to now?" Nate asked as he settled into a chair, glass in hand.

"Took his motorcar to town," Rose said. "Some buyer from Chicago is set up in the hotel there."

"Buyer for what?"

"Beef."

Nate took a sip, allowing the whiskey to set on his tongue a moment. "How many head you got on the place, Rose?"

"We'll have a proper count in a few days," she replied. "Somewhere around forty-eight hundred, I expect."

Nate shook his head at the number. "And Clayton? I was past his spread again today. Looks like he's running a big bunch too."

"He is," Rose said. "I don't know how big and I don't care." She had a drink before turning to give Nate a look. "Why would you ride over to Clay's place? What's your interest in his spread?"

"I don't have any," Nate said. "I was passing by."

Rose didn't say anything else for a time. She ran her forefinger around the rim of her glass while she came to her conclusions. "So you rode to the reservation."

Nate nodded, looking across the yard to the corrals. "I thought that Scotchman was coming for those horses."

"So did I," Rose said. "What were you doing at the reservation?"

"Just having a look-see. Had a conversation with a surly buck who acted like he wanted to carve me up with a skinning knife." He had a sip. "That's a sad state of affairs up there, Rose."

"Yes, it is," she agreed. "I haven't been there for years. Hiding my head in the sand, I guess. We do hire Indians from time to time. When it comes to the work, they're no better or worse than the other hands. Socially is another thing. They seem caught between the two worlds and not all that comfortable in either. Some of them take to drink and they don't handle spirits well." She gave Nate a look. "Although that's not an unusual thing for a cowboy of any stripe, I could add."

Nate smiled as he allowed the comment to pass him by.

"Some leave the reservation and do all right," Rose went on. "There's a number that own ranches of their own."

"I saw a place today," Nate said. "Little spread along Grand Creek, a few miles west of your brother's place. Yellow shutters on the house. Looks like they're running a couple hundred head."

"The ranch belongs to Mike and Sue Beartooth," Rose said. "Mike's made a go of it but he had to leave the Blackfoot ways behind to do it. He's fine with that, calls himself a modern Indian. But there are those at the reservation who aren't. They don't want to be modern Indians and they resent the notion that they should be."

"There was a boy in Deer Lodge from the reservation," he said. "The boy I told you about, the one who took the cook hostage. He was no modern Indian, had trouble written all over him. Now that I been there, I can understand why. Those people don't have a pot to piss in."

"Is that language necessary?"

"When describing that situation, I believe it is," Nate replied.

"And nobody does nothing about it?"

"What would you suggest?" she asked.

"I got no notion," Nate admitted.

"They get government assistance," Rose said. "What they are allocated and what they receive might be two different things. You, of all people, know about that."

"Whatever it is, I'd say it's stretched mighty thin," Nate said. "What does Harry say about it?"

"About the Indians? Harry doesn't say anything."

Nate emptied his glass. "Now that surprises me."

Rose sat looking at the horses across the way for a long time, her eyes fixed. Finally, she sipped the smooth bourbon, and afterward touched her lips lightly with the back of her hand.

"A lot of things change in thirty years," she said.

Fifteen

GARNER LED THE WAY INTO THE narrow box canyon, with Munson and Ballinger following. It was nearly noon and they'd been riding since daybreak. At the back of the canyon, where a winding trail could be seen leading into the trees, was a small corral, built of green cut saplings and brush. A stream narrow enough to step over trickled out of the rocks and passed within ten feet of the enclosure. Garner rode the big gelding to the water and let the animal drink. The two men trailing him did the same. The day was growing warm and the animals were thirsty. It was the third such pen they'd come upon that morning.

"This one is new," Garner said, indicating the corral. "Wasn't here a month ago."

"Don't see no shit," Munson said. He'd dismounted and walked over to have a closer look inside the enclosure. "Hasn't been used."

"Not yet," Garner said. "They'll wait 'til the gather's over, and the count's done. Then they'll pick off a few steers, stash them here, and butcher them one at a time. Either that or sell them off."

"Sell them to who?" Munson asked.

"There's some small outfits down south that'll buy stolen beef," Garner said.

"What about the brands?" Munson asked. "They doctor them?"

Garner shook his head. "Some of these places are so out of the way that nobody's ever going to show up checking brands. Not on one or two head. They figure to butcher them in the fall anyway. They can keep 'em out of sight for a few months."

Now Ballinger walked over, in his banty strut. He was wearing a Colt .44 in a fancy rig around his waist, tied down to his leg, like a gunman in a dime novel. Garner didn't know why he needed the sidearm. The work they had hired on for required a long gun.

"It's Indians doing this?" the little man asked.

"Maybe," Garner said. "We're no more than five miles off the reservation, so it fits. But it could be white men. There's always been rustlers on the range." He hesitated before turning to the pair. "Red men, white men—a rustler's a rustler. They all get the same treatment, we catch 'em in the act. Locking 'em up for a year or two in a jail cell ain't exactly what I call a cure."

Ballinger turned to flash a grin at Munson, who ignored him and addressed Garner.

"So we got three of these little hideaways spread out over, what, twenty miles or so," he said. "How do we work this?"

"Simple," Garner said. "You keep tabs on them. Check 'em each and every one, once a day. When you find some stolen stock inside, you lay up and wait for the perpetrators to show."

"Perpetrators." Ballinger laughed. "That's a fancy word for thieving Indians."

"You can call them whatever you want," Garner said. "So long as they get discouraged proper. Now are we clear that there be no evidence left behind?"

Munson nodded.

"Good," Garner said. "Sheriff Henry Pearce gets some funny ideas about his job sometimes. We don't need him calling in the state police. When it comes to rustlers running off Covington stock, we *are* the police." With that, Garner walked over to the gelding and pulled himself into the saddle. "I got a grizzly to track.

One of the hands came across a big pile of bear shit on a flat rock along Dutchman's Creek last night. Grizzly thinks he's smart, shitting out a Covington heifer right in front of us."

"That's what the buffalo gun is for?" Ballinger asked.

"Yeah," Garner replied. "Among other things."

As he rode off, Ballinger walked over to sit down on a mound of dirt left by whoever had done the digging to put up the corral. He took his makings from his leather vest and rolled a cigarette.

"Roll me one of them," Munson told him.

"Roll your own."

"I'm out."

"Why would you come out here with no tobacco?" Ballinger asked.

"Because that hardass had us in the saddle before the sun was up," Munson said. "I wanted to ride into town today. I need tobacco and whiskey."

Ballinger finished the cigarette and flipped it over. Munson missed the toss and had to pick it up from the dirt.

"We can still go to town," Ballinger said, rolling another. "Way I see it, we already made our rounds. And I figure we've seen the last of mister big shot grizzly hunter for the day."

"I expect so," Munson said.

"You get the feeling that sonofabitch is looking down on us?" Ballinger asked. He spit loose tobacco on the ground. "Like we ain't quite good enough to make his string?"

"Seems that way," Munson said.

"Like he don't need us at all."

Munson shrugged. "I don't care what he thinks, long as I get paid."

Ballinger nodded. "For all we know, there ain't no rustlers anyway. We'll get paid for doing nothing."

Munson nodded to the corral behind where Ballinger sat. "That pen didn't build itself. Somebody's fixing to steal some stock, sooner or later."

"That's all right, too," Ballinger said. "I'm looking forward to dishing out some law and order, old time fashion. Hell—I'll be the new Wyatt Earp."

As he spoke, he stood up, putting the cigarette in his mouth and letting it dangle. Eyes narrowed, he considered for a moment a skinny pine tree thirty or forty feet away. Going into a crouch, he snaked the Colt revolver from the rig on his hip and fired three shots into the pine. At the sound of the first shot, the two horses by the stream threw their heads in the air and galloped out of the canyon, tails up, dust flying from their hooves. They were out of sight within a minute, heading back for the ranch.

"You goddam idiot," Munson said. He butted his cigarette in the dirt and began to walk.

On Monday morning, Joseph Kemp Toole told an assembled group of friends and colleagues and members of the fifth estate that he would be stepping down as governor of Montana, effective end of day. Toole's wife stood to his left as he spoke, and his daughter beside her mother. Senator Clayton Covington, introduced by Toole as "my dear friend," stood to the governor's right. Lieutenant Governor Norris was on hand to accept the reins of office, which he would hold until the fall election. The reporters present, sensing a scandal that didn't exist, pressed the governor for reasons behind the announcement and he finally told them that it was health-related. Some were still unconvinced but by then he no longer cared. He and his family had left. The whole affair took less than thirty minutes.

Clayton was back in his own office by eleven o'clock, where Nancy was at work, having returned from Missoula on the morning train.

"Gosh," she said when he told her about Toole's resignation. "Did you know in advance?"

"I did."

"So now we have no governor?"

"Ed Norris is the governor," Clayton said. "For now. There will be an election in November."

She smiled knowingly at him. "And then who will be the governor?"

"I have no idea," Clayton said. "That's why we have elections. How was your adventure in Missoula?"

"It was fine," she said.

"Just fine? Not an enthusiastic endorsement of the town."

Nancy sighed. "Oh, I attended several social affairs. But I must say that I get bored quickly of miners and cowboys and roughriders. I need intellectual stimulation, not some crude man who wants to prove that he can lift me over his head."

"Sounds like a stellar crowd you were with," Clayton said.

"Hooligans," she said.

Clayton started for the inner office but paused in the doorway. "I almost forgot. I need for you to go into my original proposal for the highway act and insert an addendum that I am advocating that we call the north/south corridor the Joseph K. Toole Highway."

"All right."

"Be sure to make it retroactive, Nancy."

"I understand."

Clayton lingered a bit longer. "Nancy, I wonder if you would have time to have dinner with me one night this week?"

Her face brightened. "Why, yes. Yes, I would."

"I'd like to discuss this upcoming election with you."

"With regards to—?"

"Where I might fit in," Clayton replied. "Where you might as well."

Now she smiled. "I look forward to it."

Sixteen

IN THE MIDDLE OF THE DAY, under a cloudless blue sky, Nate rode into the town of Cut Bank. There had been no rain for a week and the road was dry, although deeply rutted from passing wagons and freighters. Nate kept to the grass on the high side of the roadway; as he neared town he loped past several buckboards being pulled by draft horses or mules. Ranchers and farmers heading in for supplies. Most called out howdy to him and he hurrahed them right back.

He again left his horse at the livery and walked along Main Street to Fran's Fine Diner, where he had a plate of fried chicken and roasted potatoes. After a slice of peach pie for dessert, he dawdled a while over a cup of coffee before ambling out onto the plank sidewalk where he stood for a time, picking his teeth. There seemed to be some commotion down at the train station, so he walked over to have a look.

A pair of young cowboys was attempting to load eight green colts onto a train. It was apparent the animals had never before been in a cattle car, or possibly any enclosure with a roof overhead, and they were expending considerable energy in an effort to forestall such a development. After watching for a bit, Nate pitched in to help and finally he and the cowboys succeeded in loading the horses into the car, only after blindfolding them, one at a time, with the shirt off the back of one of the wranglers. The blindfold came at Nate's suggestion.

The youngsters, grateful for the assistance, offered to buy Nate a beer for services rendered. They crossed the street to the Bighorn Saloon. One of the wranglers, a hefty boy named Mulgrew, allowed that he was a fair hand on the felt and challenged Nate to a game of eight ball. They played five games for two bits a piece, with Nate winning four of the five. As they played, he drank three more glasses of beer, courtesy of the cowboys. Thus fortified, he asked if any of them could direct him to Fremont Street.

When Abigail Jones answered the door, she had her hair tucked under a handkerchief and was carrying a feather duster. Seeing Nate Cooper on her doorstep, she squealed at first in delight and then mortification that he should see her in such a state. After ushering him into the front room, she hurried off to rearrange her appearance.

"I'll just be a minute," she declared. "Now don't you run away."

Nate removed his hat and sat down on a red velvet davenport. The house was small and immaculate, with flowers in vases and doilies on the arms of chairs. Brightly colored paper and painted wainscoting covered the walls. There was a burled maple staircase leading to the second floor, to where Abigail had recently disappeared. A record machine on a sideboard was playing a waltz.

Nate sat there for a time, listening to the music and the sounds coming periodically from upstairs. First the gurgle of running water, and then hurried footsteps back and forth. After a while, he realized he had an urgent need to use the privy, courtesy of the four glasses of beer he'd consumed at the saloon. There was obviously an indoor privy on the second floor, as he'd heard the pipes, but that was not an option. He got to his feet and walked about the house, through the parlor and into the kitchen at the rear. He saw nothing that would pass for a chamber pot, nor had he expected to. Finally, he stepped out the back door and relieved himself in some rose bushes there, the young buds just beginning to show. He was mindful of the thorns.

He made it back into the front room, and his seat on the davenport, before Abigail returned from her business upstairs. In fact, Nate sat there for nearly a half hour before she finally came down, having changed from the faded blue dress she'd been wearing to a pink frock, cut low in the front and cinched at the waist. Her hair had been brushed and puffed up somewhat and she smelled of lilac water. She descended the stairs like an actress in a play, one hand on the bannister and the other placed dramatically at her throat.

"What a wonderful surprise, Mr. Cooper," she said breathlessly.

"Well, I happened to be in town," Nate said. "And I thought I'd take a bold chance and stop by. I had no trouble finding Fremont Street and then an old codger down the way, cutting grass with a push machine, told me which house was yours."

"Mr. Vandervleet," Abigail said. "He has earned himself a peck on the cheek."

She stepped down from the staircase and crossed to the phonograph, which had stopped playing twenty minutes earlier, and began a vigorous cranking of the handle on the side of the box.

"That's a fancy music machine," Nate said.

"It's called a Victrola," Abigail told him as the waltz began again. "We are listening to Mr. Schubert. Do you like Mr. Schubert?"

"He's as good as the next fella, I reckon," Nate said. "Tends toward the maudlin, don't he?"

Abigail merely smiled in reply. "Can I offer you tea, Mr. Cooper?"

"Tea would be fine." Nate hesitated a moment. "Or whatever you have."

"Oh," Abigail said. "Well . . . I do keep a bottle of sherry on hand. For colds or chilblains or whatever."

"Sherry it is then," Nate said. "I mean, if that's your preference."

"You just wait here," Abigail said and she went off through the house.

Nate was left alone with Schubert once more. Looking into the parlor, he noticed some paintings on the wall he had missed earlier. He got up to have a look. There were some portraits of stiff-looking gentlemen in high collars, strangers who, for all Nate knew, might have been bankers or lawyers or horse thieves. A few frames of flowers. On an opposite wall were a half dozen paintings of the plains—Indians on horseback, a bronc buster at his work, a stampede complete with wild-eyed cattle and rearing horses.

Abigail returned with a decanter and two tiny glass flutes. She set the glassware on a small corner table and proceeded to fill the glasses, which held no more than a couple of ounces each. She handed one to Nate.

"Well, here's to new friends," she said.

"Here, here," Nate replied and he downed his glass.

Abigail, in the act of taking a small sip, noticed and then drained hers as well. Nate put his empty glass down beside the bottle in anticipation of more.

"You were admiring my paintings," Abigail said, missing the cue.

"I was looking at these here," Nate said, indicating the western scenes.

"Those plains pieces are among my favorites," Abigail said. "They're by an artist from Boston. Never been west of the Mississippi."

"What would he know about Montana then?"

"Oh, he read extensively about the area before ever putting brush to canvas," Abigail said. "He's a well-known expert on the west."

"How can he be any kind of expert if he's never been here?" Nate leaned closer to examine the depiction of the bronc buster. "I don't believe I've ever seen a horse with eyes popping out like that. Looks like he stumbled across a nest of rattlesnakes."

"That's his interpretation, Mr. Cooper. It's an artist's responsibility to be true to his muse."

"His what?"

"His muse," she replied. "Whatever it is that inspires him."

She stepped closer to the paintings, and to Nate. As he breathed of her perfume and stole a peak at her cleavage, she rested her hand on his arm. She indicated the print of the stampede.

"I particularly love this piece. The juxtaposition of beauty and savagery, it just . . . moves me in ways I can barely understand myself." She moved her hand along Nate's forearm, caressing it. "I must confess, Mr. Cooper, that I've always been drawn . . . to the rough-hewn . . . the primitive."

She turned her head to look up at him, her blue eyes shining. Nate leaned down and kissed her fully on the mouth. She pulled back.

"Mr. Cooper!" she exclaimed.

Nate froze. And then she threw her arms around his neck and kissed him hungrily on the lips, her tongue flicking wildly inside his mouth. In a moment they were headed upstairs and into a well-lit bedroom, where they got undressed as quickly as her complicated underthings would allow. A minute later, Nate was on his back and she was astride him, bucking as wildly as the bronco in the painting downstairs.

"Mr. Cooper! Mr. Cooper!" she exclaimed. And then, "Ooh . . . Mr. Cooper."

They had a lively hour and a half, with some rests in between, and managed three energetic couplings, a performance which Nate, when he had time to think back on it, considered well above average for a man his age. Abigail's enthusiasm and expertise were a great help. Afterward, they lay beneath a colorful quilt in the feather bed, lazing in the aftermath, while Abigail hummed contentedly.

"I can testify that twenty-eight years in confinement has done nothing to curtail your vim and vigor, Mr. Cooper," she murmured.

"That is gratifying to hear," Nate said.

"I am *so* happy you stopped by," she added. "I have been thinking about you ever since I left Rose's that day. I sensed something between us. Did you as well?"

"I showed up on your doorstep, didn't I?"

She squirmed happily in his arms, kissing him quickly on the cheek. Humming again, she ran her fingers over his mouth and then across his mustache. "We're going to have to get that mustache trimmed, my love," she said sleepily. "No, I think we should shave it off completely."

"I believe I'll keep my mustache," Nate said. "I've had it nigh on forty years."

"Well, we'll see," she said. "But a trim is definitely in order. You look like a desperado as it is."

"I thought you were the one who liked the rough and tumble," Nate reminded her.

"To a degree," she said. "But this is the twentieth century, my sweet. These are civilized times. You will soon learn that you have captured a refined woman."

Nate, having had all the action his peter could handle for one afternoon, was growing increasingly uncomfortable with Abigail's use of words like "my love" and "my sweet." Not only that, but to his mind he hadn't captured anything or anybody. And he wasn't in the market to do so. After a bit, they both drifted off.

She was sound asleep when he woke up sometime later. He lay there quietly for a moment before slipping out of bed. He gathered his clothes and his boots and crept down the stairs, where he got dressed in the parlor. Pulling on his boots, he glanced up at the paintings on the wall, put on canvas by some tinhorn from Boston. Standing up, he retrieved the bottle of sherry from the table and had a swig before leaving the house.

Back at the livery, he tossed two bits to the man with the crooked back and saddled the chestnut mare. Setting a fast pace, he headed south out of town.

Seventeen

THE HANDS FINISHED THE GATHER OVER the weekend. The extra men taken on were paid off and let go, while those that remained got back to the work on the ranch. There were tame horses to doctor and wild ones to break. New fences to build and old to mend. Blacksmithing and carpentry to tend to. Some of the cowboys were heading up to the summer range.

Young Donnelly was one of them. Nate had volunteered to help get the boy settled in the line shack above the pasture on Willow Creek, on the open range to the south of the ranch. It would be the boy's first time riding line and he could use some pointers. Tuesday morning he and Nate had their mounts saddled and ready and were loading the pack mule by the smoke house when Rose came out to see them off, carrying a basket covered in cloth.

"There's a fresh-baked pie in there," she said, handing the basket to Donnelly. "And a few other things you can use. Extra salt and pepper and preserves and such."

"Much appreciated, ma'am," Donnelly said.

"Where the hell is he going to carry a pie on horseback?" Nate asked.

"You shush," Rose told him. "I can remember you riding many a mile for a piece of my pie."

Nate shook his head. "Anything else? You got a feather bed you want us to tote up there? Maybe an embroidered pillow to go with it?"

"I don't have a feather bed," Rose said. "I hear Abigail Jones has one, though."

At that Nate spun on his heel and went into the smokehouse on the pretense of fetching something. When he returned emp-ty-handed, Rose had fastened the basket to the pack on the mule with a length of rope. She was smiling just slightly.

"We'd better get moving," Nate said, eager to get off the subject of feather beds and their owners. "It's all of twenty-five miles to Willow Creek."

Rose turned to Donnelly. "Mr. Cooper knows his way around this range. At least he used to, anyway. He was a line rider for my father many years ago."

Donnelly nodded. "He told me that."

"He'll help you to set up your camp," Rose went on. "You'll have to listen to his stories in the process, but that's just life. You have to take the good with the bad."

"You ought to bottle that sass and sell it at a carnival," Nate told her. He turned to the boy. "She's sure got you stuck out there in the boonies, son. Willow Creek, that's about as far as you can get from civilization."

"Actually, Tom here requested that particular pasture," Rose said, smiling at some secret between her and the boy. "Willow Creek is pretty far south. Matter of fact, it's not much more than fifteen or twenty miles to the Thompson ranch, if memory serves. Isn't that right, Tom?"

Donnelly blushed and made a show of checking the rigging on the pack mule. Nate looked from the boy to Rose, sensing the joke he wasn't allowed in on. He was not inclined to press her on it. She had been riding him about Abigail Jones since his midday visit to Fremont Street. Apparently Abigail wasn't one to keep her intimate affairs to herself. Not only that, but she'd sent a couple of messages out to the house, asking when Nate intended to come calling again. Abigail was one of the reasons Nate had volunteered to help Donnelly in transporting his traps to the summer range. But not the only reason.

"I was wondering," Donnelly was saying now. He paused, in his deliberate manner. "I was wondering, ma'am, if I might throw a lead on that filly and take her along with me. I was thinking I could work her a bit in my idle hours."

"I can't see any reason why not," Rose said. "She might just as well pasture there as here. Go fetch her."

Donnelly, anticipating Rose's reply, had a short lead ready on his saddle horn, coiled atop his lariat. He grabbed it now and headed for the front corral, where the filly was. Nate watched him stride across the yard before turning to Rose.

"What's this joke about the boy and the Thompson place?" he asked.

"Oh, come on," Rose said. "What do you think? You cowboys and your women."

Nate was saved from further ridicule by the arrival of Harry, who at that moment came over the rise in his motorcar and drove through the gates into the yard. The mule and the horses shied at the noise, throwing their heads in the air. Nate took hold of the mare's reins before she made a break for it. Rose grabbed the mule, which had begun to kick, as Harry rolled to a stop and shut the engine down.

"That damn machine," she said. "I'd like to send it up to pasture."

Harry climbed out but ignored her protest. Removing his goggles, he indicated the chestnut mare and looked to Nate. "Where you headed?"

"Willow Creek," Nate said.

"I thought you might come along with me today," Harry said. "I just have to fill the tank and then I'm headed up to Alberta to buy some of that good rye they make there."

"Canada and back in that contraption, I'd be stone deaf by nightfall," Nate told him. "Besides, I told young Donnelly I'd help get him settled."

Harry was disappointed. He regarded Nate a moment, as if considering whether or not he might change his mind. Realizing it was unlikely, he turned to Rose.

"Not me," she said before he could ask. "I got plenty to do without going on a whiskey run across the border with you. So now you're determined to scare the horses in two countries?"

"The hell with you both," Harry laughed. "Looks like I'm the only progressive one in this whole damn outfit."

"You figure that road to the border is passable in that thing?" Rose asked.

"I'm going to find out," Harry told her. "Been dry of late and I haven't been stuck yet. At least, not in a way where I haven't got unstuck."

Donnelly came across the yard then, leading the roan filly. He nodded to Harry and looked for a place to tie the horse to the mule.

"I'll lead her," Nate told him. "You bring the mule."

They mounted up and started out of the yard, heading up the slope to the southwest. Rose watched them for a while. Harry went into the shed and came out with a five-gallon can of gasoline.

"What's with Donnelly and that filly?" he asked, gesturing to the two men riding off.

"He's buying the horse," Rose said. "Working her off."

"We supply him with horses." Harry removed the fuel cap from the Cadillac.

"He's buying her for a young lady," Rose explained.

Harry made no comment as he poured the gasoline into the tank.

"You ever miss that part of it?" Rose said.

"What part?"

"Heading out like that," she said, pointing her chin toward the range. "Like going on an adventure."

"No, I don't," Harry replied. "Not one bit."

Rose watched the two men on horseback, her mind on the young love struck cowboy. "And what about the other part?"

"What do you mean?"

She hesitated as the riders she'd been watching crested a ridge and then were gone from sight. "Nothing, Harry," she said.

The line shack was on the south bank of the creek, on a flat above the stream in a stand of crooked willow trees. Just one room, with a tin roof and a plank door hung on leather hinges. A bunk built onto the wall, a table with four wooden chairs and a potbelly cook stove. Outside the cabin, the creek ran out of the willows and across a flat plateau and that's where the herd grazed, a few hundred steers and heifers and four young bulls to service the heifers, when they weren't fighting each other over the privilege.

It was mid-afternoon when Nate and Donnelly arrived at the pasture. The cattle were spread out and they rode through the herd before splashing into the creek and up onto the flat to the shack. There was a small corral built in the willow grove for the mounts. Donnelly loosed his saddle horse and the roan filly inside. Then he and Nate got down to the work of unloading the pack mule.

When they had the dry goods and utensils shelved in the shack, Nate took a walk along the creek while Donnelly stowed his personal belongings. He wandered a mile or so southeast, looking over the area. There were no fences that far south, just open range as far as he could see. To the southeast, he spotted a plank house and barn, the buildings surrounded by thirty or forty sheep. Beyond that, he knew, was the town of Conrad. It hadn't been much of a town back in Nate's day, but there had been a saloon there and a mercantile owned by a man named Anger. Nate had attempted to spark the man's daughter, a feisty girl called Priscilla, but the father was down on cowboys in general and on Nate in particular. He'd run Nate off one night with a shotgun before Nate had even gotten a kiss from the girl. Now Nate stood, gazing off in the direction of the town and wondering whatever might have happened to Priscilla. She probably married some damn clerk and put on a hundred pounds, sitting in a stuffed chair all the day long, eating bonbons. She should have kissed Nate when she had the chance. At least she'd have the memory. And so would he.

By the time Nate got back to the camp, Donnelly had lit the stove and brewed a pot. They pulled two chairs outside and sat in the shade, drinking the coffee and each eating a slice of the apple pie Rose had baked.

"So you're here for the summer," Nate remarked.

"Yes, sir."

"Well, I guess you know you won't be eating apple pie every day. I hope you brought a line. Beans and hardtack can get a little tired after a while. I'd wager there's trout in the creek. I came across a deep pool down there a piece. See—where that willow's bending over, like an old woman picking peas?"

Donnelly looked where Nate pointed. "I got a hook and line."

Nate tried the coffee and made a face. "Harry teach you how to make coffee?"

"I taught myself. Why?"

"This is near as bad as what he used to make," Nate said. "Next time try water instead of turpentine."

He made a point of taking another sip, to ease the criticism, before eating more of the delicious pie. Rose had always been a good cook, even going back to when she was a teenager, when Nate first knew her. She had learned from the housekeeper her father hired when her mother died. Nate glanced over at Donnelly, sitting there with his Stetson at his feet, his hair falling over his forehead as he dug into the pastry. He was greener than the pasture, Nate thought, but willing enough and not lacking in gumption.

"So you got a girl?"

"I believe so," Donnelly said. He waited a moment, having a sip from the tin cup. "Kind of hard to tell sometimes with women."

"It surely is," Nate agreed. "Get her to come visit you, if she can. I had a girl, used to come visit me when I was cowboying this range. She'd sneak away from her father on a Sunday and we'd spend the day together. She'd bring me strawberry preserves and fresh baked bread. You never had nothing so good."

"What was her name?"

Nate was not about to tell the boy that her name was Rose. He laughed. "You know, I don't recall. I had so many girls chasing me, I couldn't keep 'em all straight."

He finished the piece of pie and then walked over to the stream to give the plate and fork a rinse. Standing, he gestured to the herd where it was strung out along the creek bed.

"How many head they got grazing up here?"

"Not sure yet," Donnelly said. "That's my first job, making a count."

"Foreman doesn't know?"

"No, sir," Donnelly replied. "Last day of the gather, we split the herd and drove them wherever. He said it's the line rider's job to get a count and keep it."

Nate walked over to the mare, tethered along the cabin wall, and began to saddle her. "Well, get your bunk in order and you can make your count in the morning," he said. "Be an all day job, I reckon."

Donnelly stood and took the plates and cups inside. Nate could hear him, rattling pots and pans, stowing things away. When he came back out, Nate was in the saddle.

"I hope your girl comes to visit," he told the young cowboy. "Keep your powder dry."

Nate rode off, following the stream where it snaked along the plateau, dipping to the northwest. A mile along he turned and looked back. He was now out of sight of the line shack, and of young Donnelly as well. He took his rope from the saddle horn and trotted over to cut out two large steers from the bunch. He got them moving with a slap of the rope and headed them west.

Eighteen

The TWO BIG HEIFERS STOOD WITH their backs to the rock wall of the pen, looking at the men watching them. They were Durham cross, half wild, and it would have taken an effort to drive them into the enclosure. Coming up the trail to the pen, Garner had seen the tracks of five or six more cattle, and yet just the two animals stood in the corral. He concluded that the thieves might have cut out more than just the pair, but lost the rest along the way.

"Heifers," Munson said.

He and Ballinger were flanking Garner, sitting their horses. Garner, still after the grizzly, had come across the two hands an hour earlier, and decided to ride with them for a time. The heifers in the corral were the first sign of rustling they'd come across. Garner moved closer to the pen for a look at the brands on the animals.

"They Covington cows?" Munson asked.

"They are," Garner said. "And with calf, I expect."

"They ain't bound for the butcher then," Munson suggested.

"I expect not," Garner said. "Cow in calf is most likely gonna get sold to a farmer. A few months along, he's got himself a new unbranded calf and a heifer to butcher for the table."

"You figure it's Indians?" Ballinger asked. He was eager to shoot somebody but even more excited that it be an Indian. "We can't be far from the reservation."

"We're gonna find out," Garner replied. He looked around. "Nearest water I know is a little spring comes out of the rocks, about two miles north. Somebody's gonna be coming to water these two, if not today then tomorrow. Or maybe to move them out. Either way, they're coming back." He looked at Munson. "Hobble your horse up above in the pines, and hide him proper. You can lay wait in those rocks over there. Better bring your blanket, you might be here all night and you can't be lighting no fire."

Munson nodded. If he was unhappy with the prospect of spending a cold night, he made no complaint of it.

"What about me?" Ballinger asked.

"You're coming with me," Garner said. "We need to check those other pens. This could be all the same bunch, and they're just starting up now that the gather is done and they've no fear of running into hands. We need to nip this thing in the bud."

Ballinger, on one hand, would have just as soon stayed there, as he would be guaranteed some action when the thieves returned. On the other hand, he didn't like the cold and was not keen to spend the night in the rocks with just a blanket.

"Well, let's go," he said.

Leaving Munson behind, they rode down to the plain below and started south. Garner stayed ahead of the young man when he could. Ballinger was one to ramble on, usually about himself, a subject Garner had little interest in.

It was a good eight miles to the second pen. They were maybe halfway there, on a bald ridge, when they spotted a man on horseback in the distance. Garner stopped and reached for the brass spyglass in his saddlebag. He focused on the rider as Ballinger rode up beside him.

The man was mounted on a chestnut horse and pushing two big steers ahead of him, ambling along at a slow pace and heading due west. And he was all alone out there, in the middle of the range, middle of the day. What some might call in plain sight.

"What the hell?" Garner asked, as much to himself as anything.

"One of our hands?" Ballinger asked.

"No."

"He's thieving then," Ballinger said, growing agitated. "In broad goddamn daylight."

Garner kicked the gelding into a lope and Ballinger followed. Within five minutes they were abreast of Nate Cooper, who casually reined the chestnut to a halt as they rode up. Garner gave him a studied look before riding a circle around the two steers, which were still moving slowly through the wheatgrass. He saw that both wore the RHR brand of the Longley ranch.

As Garner examined the cattle, Nate sat the mare quietly, taking in the big bore Sharps in the man's scabbard before turning for a look at Ballinger, who was hanging back, cautious and fidgety. Letting the steers wander, Garner moved the gelding over and reined it to a halt in front of Nate.

"Howdy," Nate said.

"Where you headed?" Garner asked.

Nate nodded westward. "I'm headed that way."

"I didn't ask you what direction, old man," Garner said. "I can see what direction. Where you taking those steers?"

Now Ballinger urged his mount a couple of steps closer, along Nate's flank, his left hand on the reins, his right hanging down beside the revolver on his belt. Nate wrapped his own reins around the saddle horn and took the makings from his pocket. As he rolled the smoke, he watched the steers, which had stopped ambling and were now picking at some prairie wildflowers.

"The boss asked you a question," Ballinger said.

Nate lit the cigarette and wet the spent match before tossing it away. Blowing smoke, he regarded first Garner and then Ballinger. "I'd say you boys are pretty heavily armed for a couple of cowpunchers. Or did Butch Cassidy rob the Union Pacific again?"

"Are you deaf, old-timer?" Ballinger demanded. "The boss asked you a question."

"Fact is, I am a little deaf," Nate told him. "More in my left ear than my right."

"You sonofabitch," Ballinger barked.

Nate smiled. "I heard the man. I'm trying to decide what business it is of his—where I'm taking these steers."

"I'm Clay Covington's foreman," Garner said. "And you happen to be on Covington land."

"Well, I don't intend to hurt it none," Nate said. "I'm just riding across it."

"I hate a goddamn smart mouth," Ballinger snapped.

Nate turned to him. "Son, no offense intended, but you don't look like you're any kind of expert on what's smart and what ain't."

Ballinger glared at Garner, as if asking permission. "This sonofabitch," he began.

Garner held his hand out toward the little man before turning to Nate. "Does Harry Longley know you helped yourself to a couple of his steers?"

"You'd have to ask Harry that," Nate replied. "Besides, who said I took these steers? Maybe they were just crossing the range the same time as me. You ever think of that?"

"I'll tell you what I do think," Garner said. "I think it's a miracle you've lived so long, with that mouth of yours. What's your name, old-timer?"

"Nate Cooper is my name."

Garner was looking at the two steers when he heard the name. He hesitated before turning back to Nate. After a moment, he nodded slightly, as if agreeing to something.

"Well, Nate Cooper," he said. "We still have a problem with rustlers out here from time to time. But to tell you the truth, you don't look like a typical rustler. Typical rustler wears moccasins, if you get my drift. But we saw you from the ridge and thought we'd stop for a little talk."

"It's been an uncommon pleasure," Nate said.

Garner reined the gelding around and started off. Ballinger hung back before spurring his horse forward and riding a complete circle around Nate, staring at him the entire time. Nate didn't return the look but rather sat calmly, puffing on his cigarette. Finally Ballinger stopped directly in front of Nate, still glaring.

"Run along now, sonny," Nate told him. "Be careful you don't shoot your pecker off with that hog leg."

Ulysses Elkhorn was sitting on the sagging front porch of the store when Nate showed again, this time trailing two large Hereford steers. Ulysses, from inside the store, had seen him coming from a fair distance along the main road and had walked out to sit on the top step of the porch to wait. It was late afternoon. By the time Nate rode up to the store, the steers had wandered off to the side of the lane to graze at the sparse grass there.

The Indians scattered about the reservation were watching. A few walked closer, some regarding the healthy steers, others hoping to catch the conversation between Nate and Ulysses. Looking down the road to the village, Nate saw a young girl—a teenager— glance his way before hurrying into a teepee.

"What do you want now?" Ulysses asked.

Nate rode close to the porch before reining the mare to a stop. "Same as I wanted before," he said. "Nothing."

Ulysses looked past him, to the Herefords at their graze. "Do you think we will buy those steers from you?"

"Those steers aren't for sale."

"Then why did you bring them?"

Nate gestured toward the Indians watching the two men. "I got the idea that people here are hungry. Maybe this beef can help out a bit." He turned back to Ulysses. "But they will require butchering. Do you know how to butcher a steer or are you just good at sitting on your ass and yapping like a magpie?"

Ulysses stood. "I can butcher more than a steer. You have a big mouth for an old man."

"I been hearing that a lot today," Nate laughed. "I'm beginning to take it to heart."

"Why do you laugh?" Ulysses demanded. "Do you think this is a joke? I tell you not to come here and you come anyway." Then Ulysses' eyes went past Nate and he stopped.

"Nate Cooper," a voice said.

Nate turned in the saddle to see Standing Elk approaching along the dirt road, walking on creaky knees, bent slightly at the waist. His hair was long and completely gray. He smiled as he approached Nate; most of his teeth were missing and his eyes had grown rheumy.

"Nate Cooper," he said again. "My friend."

"Hello, Standing Elk," Nate said. "I'm glad to see you're still alive. I was beginning to feel plum unwelcome around here."

"You can kiss my ass," Ulysses said.

"No more from you," Standing Elk said sharply before adding something in Blackfoot that Nate didn't catch. The old man glared at Ulysses for a moment before turning back to Nate. "He has manners but he has left them somewhere. I hope he finds them soon. He is my son and I am not too old to cuff him on the ear."

Nate climbed down from the mare and extended his hand to the old man. "It's good to see you," he said. "You're the first friendly face I've seen here. I was starting to understand how Custer felt."

"It is good to see you, Nate Cooper."

Nate indicated the steers. "Some prime beef there, if you have a use for it."

Standing Elk turned and spoke Blackfoot to two women, watching from along the lane. They immediately picked up sticks and began to drive the Herefords away.

Nate and the old man sat on a rock ridge overlooking the plain to the east. When they left the village, Ulysses had followed them and now he was standing a hundred feet or so behind them, in the pine trees. Watching and listening.

In a clearing back in the village, the two steers now hung from a cottonwood limb. They'd already been gutted and the two women Nate had seen earlier were skinning them out.

Nate made two cigarettes and gave one to Standing Elk. The old man drew on his like it was a peace pipe, blowing the smoke into the air above his head without inhaling. He smoked the cigarette down to a nub before he said anything.

"Where did you get those steers, Nate Cooper?"

"They're a gift to the Blackfoot," Nate told him. "From Harry Longley."

"I remember Longley your friend," the old man said. "He does not come here anymore."

"Well, he's a busy man," Nate said. "Got a big ranch, a few thousand head of cattle. More horses than the U.S. Cavalry. And a brand new motorcar with coal oil lanterns and a circus horn."

Standing Elk smiled at this. Nate wondered if the old man had seen a motorcar. Of course, some of the Indians would have, the ones who worked at the various ranches around the state or traveled to town to beg in front of the mercantile. Standing Elk would not be one of those.

"And what do you have, Nate Cooper, after all these years?"

Nate shrugged as he stubbed his cigarette out on the rock beside him. "Not a lot," he admitted. "I got a good mare. And, I don't know, tobacco to smoke. Not much else, I suppose."

"You have nothing." Standing Elk smiled. "You are an Indian."

Nate shifted to have a look at the reservation behind them. The sparse garden plots, the skinny ponies. The hungry people now gathering in anticipation around the Longley steers. The beef wouldn't last long, once they started to parcel it out.

"I'll admit the farming doesn't seem to be working out for you," Nate said, turning back to the old man. "But why don't you raise cattle? Hell, it looks like everybody else is getting rich doing it."

"We have a few cows," Standing Elk said. "And some of the young men trade horses. But there is not much grass here. You need grass to raise horses and cows."

Standing up, Nate indicated the lush range, spread before them to the east. "What's wrong with that?"

"That's Covington land," Ulysses said. He had walked out of the trees to move closer. "Not part of the reservation. I thought you would know that, smart man that you are."

"I ain't half as smart as I think," Nate told him. "I guess that's the one thing you and me got in common."

"It was to be ours," Standing Elk said before Ulysses could respond. "The men said it was to be. But the sticks got moved."

Nate turned to him. "What sticks?"

"The treaty of 1885," Ulysses said. "The original boundary for the Blackfoot reservation was the bench above Grand Creek. The surveyors came and marked it. We would have had over six thousand acres of grassland. But then things changed. The surveyors came back and took it all away."

Nate looked again to the east. He'd forded the Grand earlier. It was a few miles away, a shallow stream running south to the Cut Bank River. "Did they give a reason?"

Standing Elk shook his head but said nothing, as if he despaired of the question or was past considering it. Possibly both. It was his son who finally replied.

"Are you asking if the white man gave a reason before he took our land?"

Nineteen

CLAYTON WAS BACK AT THE RANCH Friday evening, having left Helena shortly after noon. He'd had dinner with Nancy the night before, at a roadhouse ten miles east of the city on the old turnpike. Nancy was twenty-two years old and Clayton, after feeling her out for a time over oysters and wine, finally got around to asking what he would have to do to win the vote of people of her generation come October.

"But you are not up for re-election this October," Nancy had said.

"Call it a hypothetical question."

"We could do that," Nancy said smiling. "And since we're speaking in hypotheticals, why not go all the way and suggest that you could be running for governor this fall?"

"Let's do that," Clayton replied.

"At what point would we stop pretending?"

"I suppose now would be as good a time as any," Clayton said.

Nancy smiled again, pleased with both of them. "You would have no problem in that area," she said. "You're the youngest one out there and you look even younger than you are." She paused. "How old are you anyway?

"I will turn fifty next winter."

"You hold your years well, Senator," she told him. "Like I said, you're the youngest one out there. All you would need to do is get out the vote. Using your considerable charms."

Clayton was used to her flirtatious manner by now. He put it aside, at least for the time being. "And how do I do that?" he asked. "Young people are notorious for avoiding the voting booths."

"The best way would be to make me your campaign manager," Nancy said.

"You're a woman."

"Thank you for noticing."

Clayton smiled. "You don't even have a vote."

"That's something else we need to talk about," Nancy said. "But at another time. First we need to put you in the governor's mansion. I suppose it would cause a stir if you had a woman running your campaign. But you could name someone else and make me your behind the scenes campaign manager. I would report to you and you only."

"Why would you want to do that?"

"Because I would like to help you become governor," she said simply.

The ranch was quiet when he arrived there in the rig, having taken the afternoon train to Cut Bank. It was Friday, the gather was finished, so most of the hands would be in town, spending their wages. Clayton had eaten at the diner after getting off the train, talking to a few of the regulars there, answering questions about the proposed highway, which Clayton knew quite a bit about, and about the reasons behind the governor's resignation, about which Clayton claimed ignorance. It was still daylight when he got to the ranch. Inside the house he went around and lit the lamps, had a quick look at the mail that came to the Cut Bank address, then poured himself a glass half full of rye and went out on the porch to drink it. He wasn't there but five minutes when Ed Garner came out of the foreman's bungalow, built alongside the bunkhouse. He would have heard Clayton arrive and been waiting for him to settle in.

"Hello, Ed," Clayton said.

"Boss."

Clayton didn't offer his foreman a drink. He didn't want him getting the impression they were equals in any way. "You get that bear?"

"Not yet," Garner said. "Looks as if he's climbed higher up."

"He'll be back," Clayton said. "Like feeding a stray cat."

"I know it. I got time to find him now, with the gather done."

"You get a count?"

"Looks like fifty-six hundred plus."

"And we haven't lost any?"

"We came close," Garner said. "Somebody's been building hideaways in the foothills. We're keeping an eye on them. A couple of heifers showed up in one this week. I left that man Munson there to settle matters."

"Who took the heifers—Indians?"

"Not this time," Garner said. "Loafer from down south, always into something shady. I've seen him around. I figure he had himself a market for heifers in calf."

"Munson discouraged him from such activity?"

"Discouraged him permanent."

"Good," Clayton said. He had a drink. "We ever get that bull from Harry Longley?"

Garner nodded. "Got him up on that north section. Seems to be doing his job."

"Harry said he was still up to snuff," Clayton said. "But then I believe Harry figures he's still the man he once was. It's quite likely he's disillusioned on that count."

"Speaking of Harry Longley," Garner began and he told Clayton about his encounter with Nate Cooper on the range.

"And they were Longley steers?" Clayton asked when he'd heard the story.

"They were wearing his brand."

"What makes you think he was driving them to the reservation?"

"Nothing else out that way," Garner said. "Couple of small spreads further south, but he wasn't heading south. Wasn't acting like a typical rustler neither. Middle of the day, poking along."

"But you took him for one," Clayton said. "At first."

"At first," Garner agreed.

"Maybe you should have shot him then."

"I give it some thought," Garner replied. "And I might have, had it been Covington stock. But I had that damn Ballinger with me. He likes to flap his gums, that one. I put a hole in Cooper and he gets to blabbering about it in town, and then what? Next thing I know, I got Henry Pearce asking me questions. And maybe Harry Longley too."

Clayton had more rye, thinking about it.

"Like I said, they weren't Covington steers," Garner said. "That's an altogether different situation if they were."

"Well, Nate Cooper's got history with the Blackfoot," Clayton said. "And with rustling too, if I recall."

"That's what I've heard."

"I didn't know the man was out of Deer Lodge," Clayton said. "All those years in prison, you'd think he would have wised up. This suggests he has not. Better tell the boys to keep a good count on the stock."

"I did it already."

"Why would he waste his time on those people?" Clayton asked. "They serve no purpose. None. General Sheridan had the right idea—extermination. We should have listened to him back then. Would have been the best thing for everybody, including the damn Indians."

Garner nodded emphatically. "I don't want them getting the notion that there's free beef out there for the taking. I find a single Covington cow on that reservation and I'll settle it the old way. Won't be no Little Big Horn neither, I promise you that."

Twenty

WILLIS SAMUELS SAT AT THE BAR in the Bighorn Saloon, drinking ale from a glass mug and watching the pool game in progress a few feet away. He and his employer, Angus Gibson, had finished running the week's edition of the *Cut Bank Chronicle* an hour earlier. The papers were stacked in the back of the office down the street, ready for delivery the next morning. After they put the edition to bed, Angus had walked with Samuels as far as the saloon.

"Come for a beer," Samuels said.

"The old girl's waiting supper on me," Angus replied in his light Scottish accent. "And by gosh, it's hard to have just one."

The old man clapped Samuels on the shoulder, as if to say that one day you'll understand, and then was off to his house on Cedar Street where his wife of nearly fifty years would indeed be waiting with a warm plate. Samuels watched the portly figure disappear into the dark night before heading inside.

Nate Cooper had been in control of the pool table for over an hour. His first victim was a cowboy just in from Wyoming, or so he claimed. He'd worked the roundup for a sheep man near Buffalo, and was in the Cut Bank area looking for permanent work on a cattle concern. He said he'd had enough of sheep. He'd had enough of Nate too, after getting beat five games straight at four bits a game. After fleecing the sheepherder Nate was now playing a bank teller from town, a chubby baby-face wearing a snug wool suit and bow tie. He wasn't faring much better against Nate, although he could shoot better than the cowboy.

For his part, Samuels was having an enjoyable time just watching, and listening. Since arriving in Cut Bank two years earlier, he'd been starved for entertainment during the hours he wasn't at the newspaper. There were few eligible ladies his age in the town proper and—aside from the odd strawberry social or square dance—even fewer opportunities to socialize. Samuels also suspected that his position as cub reporter at the *Chronicle* was not one to excite any parents who might be considering potential suitors for their daughters. Not that he was overly concerned about that aspect of things. Just twenty-three, he had plenty of time to consider marriage and family. There was one young woman in town who he fancied but she had a swain back in Illinois.

Samuels had taken a circuitous route before arriving in northern Montana. He'd been apprenticing as a tanner in his hometown of Albany when he'd had occasion one night to attend a lecture given at the opera house by Mark Twain. The old boy had been in fine form, adorned all in white—suit, mustache, and shaggy mane. He had spent the better part of the evening telling tales of his career as a young and only occasionally successful newspaperman. Samuels left the hall that night thoroughly inspired and by the time he arose the next morning, he decided he'd had enough of the foul smells and nasty chemicals of the tannery and promptly quit the place. As fortune would have it, the Republican National Convention was about to get underway in Chicago. Samuels bought a train ticket west, convinced that the political hograssle (a phrase he borrowed from Twain) would be just the place for an aspiring reporter to find a job. He had been correct in that; he was hired by the first publisher he approached, Mr. Angus Gibson. It wasn't until after he'd accepted the position that Samuels learned that he wouldn't be breaking stories in Chicago or New York or even Kansas City, but in a tiny town in Montana he'd never heard of. He presently shook off his disappointment in this, telling himself that another writer got his start in such a place, a hamlet on the Mississippi called Hannibal. And west he went.

Although he was a regular in the Bighorn, he had never before laid eyes on Nate Cooper, who seemed to be a character from a different time. The way he looked, and the way he talked, even the bowlegged manner of his stride. He appeared to be in his mid-fifties, with gray hair and mustache and he had more stories than Aesop, stories that he was more than willing to share with the young would-be pool sharks while he took their money.

"I can still see Bill's cards on the table," he was saying now, leaning forward at the waist, studying the felt. "Two ball in the side. Yes, I can still see the hand. Aces over eights." He sank the two. "I myself was not heeled at the time, as I had that very afternoon dropped my Colt off at the gunsmith to have a broken hand spring replaced. Otherwise, I would have done for McCall as he did for Bill. Six ball in the side pocket." He made the shot and then reached for the chalk. "Not that it mattered. In the end, he got the necktie party he deserved."

At a corner table a few feet away, a lively poker game was in progress, some local merchants and a couple of cowboys. The punk Ballinger was in the game, losing heavily and growing irritated with his luck. The more he lost, the more he groused. He was wearing his revolver, the only man in the place so armed.

Samuels ordered another glass of ale as Nate dropped the eight ball to beat the chubby banker. Nate was drinking beer; his glass was on the corner of the bar, not far from where Samuels sat, and he came over to have a drink. He'd had a fair amount already, but it didn't show in his game.

"I win again," he said to the bank teller. "That's four bits."

The teller put the fifty-cent piece on the table. "Again?" he said.

"Loser racks," Nate told him.

After breaking the new rack, Nate continued the story. "But a killing like that leaves a sour taste in your mouth. I had me enough of towns for a while. And Deadwood in particular. Took to trailing cattle from Texas to points north for a few years. I survived five stampedes in three years. Not many a cowpoke can match that."

"Goddamn!" Ballinger yelled as he lost again. He threw his cards down in disgust and turned toward Nate. "I think you're full of shit, old man. You never knew Bill Hickok."

"You can think what you want to, son," Nate told him. "Fourteen in the corner."

Ballinger glared at Nate while he waited for a new hand to be dealt.

"Is that how you ended up in Montana?" the chubby teller asked. "Cattle drive?"

Nate took a moment to chalk his cue tip while he considered the question. It seemed for a moment that he might not reply, the first time all evening he'd displayed any reluctance for speech.

"Well now, that's a different story," he said finally. "Truth is, me and my partner pretty much arrived here at a dead run, with a Dakota posse hot on our heels. I ain't gonna tell you what crime we committed, nor my partner's name neither. But it was the winter of '79 and colder than a witch's tit. We didn't dare go near a town, with the law on the prod. We'd have froze to death—or starved, or both—but the Blackfoot took us in. White Bull was the chief. His father was Lame Bull. Keep in mind this was just three years after the Indians cleaned Custer's clock at the Greasy Grass. They could have made soup out of us but they didn't. They were near to starving themselves, but they took us in. Saved our hides." Nate sank the thirteen ball. "We found out later on that the Blackfoot took a vote on us, keep us or kill us, and we squeaked in by a couple of votes."

Ballinger went bust again, and now he was broke. He got to his feet and turned on Nate. "Is there any chance you could just shut your damn mouth, old man? How's anybody supposed to play poker with you going on like an old woman?"

Nate glanced at Ballinger and then at the cards on the table before turning back to drop the nine ball in the side pocket. Reaching for the chalk, he looked once more at Ballinger. "I ain't so sure I should become a mute on account of you being too stupid to fold a pair of threes."

At the bar, Willis Samuels smiled as he drank the ale.

Monday morning Samuels sat at his desk, drinking coffee and watching Angus's rather large posterior, up on a ladder against a shelf high on the back wall of the newspaper office. He was rummaging through some wooden crates that contained the back issues of the *Chronicle*, from 1878 forward.

"He was known as Kid Cooper back then," Angus said over his shoulder. "He came into the territory with Harry Longley. Full of piss and vinegar, the pair of them, and telling all kinds of wild stories. Nobody knew what to believe, if anything. That was not unusual. It was a rare cowboy who wasn't skilled at embellishing his life story."

"Harry Longley was the partner?" Samuels said. "I'll be damned. He never mentioned that. Cooper claims they were two steps ahead of a posse."

Angus pulled a crate close to him and rifled through it. Dust rose and he coughed. "That's about half true. Story was some Dakota rancher cheated them out of wages. Apparently they got drunk and robbed the man's bank in Fargo, looking to square the debt. We found out later they made off with the princely sum of forty-two dollars. The posse chased them until suppertime and then went home. But they didn't know that, they were convinced they were desperate men on the run. Which is why they wintered with the Blackfoot."

"Where did he get the name Kid Cooper?" Samuels asked.

"He likely bestowed it upon himself," Angus said. "It was a common enough practice back then. If you were of tender years, and considered to be any kind of renegade, you might call yourself Kid. There was the Lonesome Kid and Kid Curry and the Sundance Kid. It wasn't as if you had to meet any special requirements. Come to think of it though, none of the Kids I ever heard of survived long enough to outlive the name. I guess Nate Cooper is the exception to that rule."

"It's hard to picture Harry Longley in that scenario," Samuels said. "To me he typifies the fat cat rancher."

"Not back then."

"You knew them?"

"I knew of them," Angus said. "That was my second year here. I was running the paper out of a tent on Front Street. You know you're in the wrong location when your ink freezes overnight, Willis. I first knew of them the following summer. By then, they were riding herd for Parcell Covington. And both of 'em sparking his daughter, Rose."

"A competition Harry obviously won."

"It wasn't much of a competition after Cooper got sentenced to life in prison."

"Well now," Samuels said. "He never mentioned anything about prison the other night."

Angus pushed the crate back against the wall, and moved on to the next. It would have been a good idea to mark each by year, but he never thought that far ahead when he first began the archives thirty years earlier. Back then he was operating week to week, and just barely at that. His main advertiser had been a drunken dentist who sold laudanum and offered embalming service on the side.

"Well, it's a story worth telling," he said. "Those were especially tough times for the Blackfoot. The Indian wars were over. In 1855, they signed what was known as the Judith River Treaty, giving them a substantial reservation. In the years that followed, as the settlers

and the miners kept pushing in, the federal government started taking back the land they'd promised the Indians, piece by piece."

"Under who?" Samuels asked.

"President Grant started it and Hayes followed up," Angus said.
"The Blackfoot had no say in the matter. They attempted to raise
cattle but then we had three or four winters in a row so severe they
wiped out the herds and what was left of the buffalo. The winter
of '83-'84 over five hundred Blackfoot perished. The tribe didn't
take much to farming, still don't, in fact. As the reservation kept
shrinking, they began to depend on government rations for food.
People will tell you the coming of the white man finished off the
Indians but really it was the end of the buffalo that did it. They
didn't need anything from us as long as they had the buffalo. Even
so, things might have worked out better if they actually received
the allotments they were owed."

"Why didn't they?" Samuels asked.

"Parcell Covington," Angus said. "He was one of the first big
ranchers to run cattle in the territory and he had some influence.
He also nurtured an uncommon hatred of the Indians. Thought
they stood in the way of progress. Statehood even. The Indian
agent, Dudley, was Covington's lickspittle, the sort of man who
falls to his knees in the presence of wealth. Most of the beef and
grain earmarked for the reservation never got there."

"Covington wanted to starve them?"

"Possibly," Angus said. "But I think what he really wanted was
an uprising. Remember, this was only five or six years after Little Big
Horn and right around the time that Dull Knife and the Cheyenne
made their last fight. Feelings were still running high and, make no
mistake, people feared the Indians. Parcell had been a soldier and
was of the opinion that the government mollycoddled the tribes.
He wanted to wipe them out and said so publicly."

"You knew Parcell?" Samuels asked.

"I did. He was a hard man. He fought with the rebels during the
Civil War and he was a bigot from his boots on up. You could sit and

have a drink with the man and he would be as sociable as anybody you ever met. But if you happened to have been born a colored, or an Indian, or a Jew—well, you were no better than a cockroach and he would crush you beneath his heel if the opportunity arose."

Angus found what he was looking for. He tucked the box under one arm and came backward down the ladder. He put the crate on the layout table beside the printer and began to go through the papers inside.

"Nate Cooper owed a debt to White Bull," he said as he searched. "With the Blackfoot near starving, he took to borrowing beef from Parcell Covington and driving them over to the agency."

"While he was working for Covington?"

"No," Angus said. "By that time, I believe he was riding for one of the other ranches. Parcell put the run on him when he realized Nate had designs on Rose. No dirty cowboy making thirty a month was going to woo his daughter."

"You're saying that Cooper went to prison for nearly thirty years for rustling?"

At that moment, Angus found the issue he'd been looking for. "No," he said. "He went to prison for thirty years for killing the agent Dudley." He held up a yellowed front page with the headline:

INDIAN AGENT KILLED IN GUNFIGHT

Samuels got to his feet and walked over to read the story as Angus kept telling it.

"White Bull went to Dudley to register a complaint about the rations. Dudley was in his cups and he put a beating on the chief. Threw him out of the agency store and was putting the boots to him on the steps, in front of a couple dozen Indians. Setting an example, you see. Well, who should come riding up but Nate Cooper. Things came quickly to a head. Dudley threw down on Cooper with a shotgun and Cooper shot him dead."

"That's self-defense," Samuels said as he read the piece.

Angus searched through the issues in the crate. "You would think so. But Parcell Covington testified that he was there that day, and that Dudley was unarmed."

"What about the Indians there? They saw it."

"An Indian's word against that of Parcell Covington wouldn't mean spit in 1882," Angus said. "And probably not today either." He held up another paper:

COVINGTON FITS COOPER WITH A NOOSE

Samuels took it from him. "Says here he got the death penalty."

"He did," Angus said. "I remember very clearly being in the courtroom at the time. But then some high-priced lawyer from Helena got the sentence commuted to life. There were rumors as to who paid for the lawyer. One suggested it was Rose Covington. Another said it was Parcell himself."

"Parcell?" Samuels repeated. "Where's the logic in that?"

"I'll tell you where it is," Angus said. "The day Cooper was sentenced, Harry Longley told Parcell on the courthouse steps that if Nate Cooper hanged, he would shoot Parcell dead. I think Parcell believed him. I know everybody else in the county did."

"And then Harry marries the daughter," Samuels said. "I'll bet that was an interesting wedding party."

"Parcell would not have been invited to the wedding. After he testified against Cooper, Rose turned her back to him. Never spoke to her father again, far as I know. He died, I don't know, has to be close to twenty years ago, from a ball he took in the lung at Chancellorsville."

Samuels opened the brittle newspaper, following the story inside. "There's a quote here from Cooper. He said if Parcell had really been at the agency that day, he'd have shot him too."

Angus smiled. "I recall that very well. The jury didn't know whether to gasp or laugh."

"He wasn't exactly currying favor with the court, was he?" Samuels said.

"Currying favor was not one of Kid Cooper's strong points. Cards and liquor. Fast horses. He was a typical cowboy, to tell you the truth. It's hard to imagine him approaching old age."

Samuels put the paper carefully back in the crate. "From what I saw the other night in the Bighorn, I'm not sure the man would acknowledge any such thing."

Twenty-One

ROSE WAS IN THE VEGETABLE GARDEN when Nate came out onto the porch. It was early, the sun just up, and Harry was still sleeping upstairs. The pole beans Rose had been waiting for had arrived with the weekly mail and now she was on her knees in the dirt, running string for the rows. A wheelbarrow with her gardening tools inside stood alongside.

Nate had found the coffee she'd brewed earlier in the kitchen and poured a cup before walking outside. He stood on the porch for a time, watching the morning, before heading over to where Rose was at work, idly scratching his chest with one hand while carrying the coffee in the other. He was hatless, his hair uncombed, shirttails hanging.

"Sowing the seeds of salvation?" he asked.

"That might be too much to ask for," she replied, not looking up. She had heard his approach. "I would settle for a bushel of pole beans come fall instead." Tying off the string, she glanced up; the sun was behind him and she shielded her eyes with her hand. "Where have you been lately?"

"Taking advantage of the mediocre pool players in Cut Bank for the most part," Nate said.

"That's an admirable vocation. Would fetching me a couple of buckets of water be beneath your station?"

"I expect not." Nate placed the cup of coffee in the wheelbarrow and went to get the water.

"Harry not up yet?" she asked when he returned.

"Still snoring when I came down." He set the buckets on the ground and took up the coffee again.

Rose ran the edge of a hoe along the string she'd stretched, cutting a v-shaped furrow in the soil. "He's going to ask you to run supplies up to the line shacks today. Staples we've been waiting on from the mercantile." She looked up again. "If your busy social agenda will allow it."

Nate nodded, drinking the coffee.

"You can see how young Donnelly's making out," Rose said. "He's awfully green to be up there by himself."

"He'll be all right," Nate said. "If he doesn't poison himself with his own coffee. I advised him to get his girl to come and visit him. Bring him something nice to eat. I told him I used to have a girl visit me when I rode line. You remember that?"

Rose stood up. "Sometimes you talk too much, you know that?"

"I didn't mention any names."

"Your discretion is admirable, Mr. Cooper." Rose got the beans from the wheelbarrow and began to plant them in the rows she'd marked.

"I was out to the reservation again," Nate said.

She hesitated a moment before carrying on with her work. "You're a going concern."

"You know there ain't hardly a child on the place?" Nate asked. "They get sent to the white school over to St. Mary." He had a drink of coffee. "I suppose so they can become refined. That seems to be a popular word these days. Everything is refined. The liquor, and the women. Even the damn kerosene."

"It's important that they go to school," Rose said. She smoothed the soil over the row and then watered it down.

"I never had much schooling and I don't know that the lack of it hurt me none," Nate said. "I always managed to get by . . . on my charm and my good looks." He smiled. "And my expert pool playing."

"You forgot to mention your humble nature."

"Modesty prevented it."

Rose moved on to the next row. "Whatever your charms, Nate, I would hardly hold you up as a shining example to the youth of today. A child needs an education."

He sipped the coffee again, watching her at her planting, her fingers in the dark soil. She was never one to shy away from hard work, or from getting dirty, either. She'd been raised up privileged but never seemed to take to the easy life. It was a good thing, Nate suspected, given her fractured relationship with her father, and her brother later on.

"Why is it you and Harry never had kids of your own?" Nate asked.

She shook her head. "Wasn't meant to be." Glancing over, she displayed the beans in her hand. "Some of these will grow and some won't. That's just the way it is."

"Well, you still got some good years left, Rose," Nate said. "Might happen yet."

"I'm about to turn fifty-three years old," she laughed. "My child-bearing years are gone. We're all of us getting older, although I suspect that some of us are reluctant to admit it."

"Now, now, don't you be too hard on Harry and his toys," Nate said.

"I wasn't talking about Harry."

"I know you weren't," Nate smiled. He finished the coffee, tossing the dregs into the garden. "I figure I'm still about thirty. I don't count those years in Deer Lodge. I got a lot of catching up to do."

"So I hear."

Nate knew that she was heading in the direction of Abigail Jones again and he decided to cut her off. "Did you ever hear anything fishy about a survey they done back in '85, out at the Blackfoot reservation?"

"Not that I recall. What about it?"

"I heard there was some—what's that word—dis-something or other?"

"Discrepancies?"

"That's it."

"What kind of discrepancies?"

"They did one survey and then they did another," Nate said. "The second one cost the Indians a few thousand acres of grassland."

Rose stood now, wiping her brow with the back of her dirty hand. "Where's this coming from?"

"That surly Indian I mentioned before."

"It's the first I've heard it," she said. She regarded Nate a long moment before turning west to look out over the flat range, the range that ran all the way to the reservation in question. "Nothing would surprise me though."

It was mid-morning by the time Harry was up and breakfasted. He and Nate loaded two pack mules with the food going to the camps. After her planting was finished Rose had changed her clothes then hitched a rig before heading into Cut Bank for a meeting of the ladies auxiliary.

Each of the three line riders were to get the same supplies—flour, sugar, bacon, and beans. When the packs were finished, Harry went into the house and came back carrying three bottles of rye as well.

"We don't need to tell Rose about this," he said as he tucked the bottles into the packs. "She thinks those boys are still babies."

"Why don't you fetch another bottle and come along with me?" Nate said. "We'll take a couple lines and try for trout in Willow Creek."

"I'm off to town," Harry said. He pulled his watch from his vest. "I'm late, in fact."

"What's so important in town?"

"I have to meet another buyer, looking for a beef contract. These men are coming out of the woodwork. Chicago can't get enough beef."

"You're all business these days, Harry."

"Ranch doesn't run itself."

Nate tightened a strap on one of the mules. "What happened to all that fanciful talk about sitting back and enjoying the good life?"

Harry laughed. "I'm driving into town in my brand new motorcar and having a free lunch with a cattle buyer. I wouldn't call that breaking my back, Nate."

"I suppose not."

"All right," Harry said, pulling his watch again. "You know where you're going?"

"I still know north from south, Harry." Nate walked around the mules, checking the straps. "Maybe I'll ride out to the reservation and have a visit with old Standing Elk. Him and I can share a drink."

Harry was walking toward the shed and he stopped. "You don't need to be riding out to the reservation," he said. "And you sure as hell don't need to be giving the Indians whiskey."

Nate watched as Harry backed his motorcar out of the shed and started off, the machine barking and backfiring as he adjusted the levers. When he was through the gate and on the road toward Cut Bank, Nate went back into the smokehouse for another side of bacon. Thinking a moment, he went in again, brought out more flour and beans, and strapped everything onto the mules.

Ulysses Elkhorn took the supplies from Nate without a word, carried them into the agency store, and came out a few moments later to stand on the porch, looking down to where Nate was seeing to the mules, unburdened now of their cargo.

"Now you feel better?" Ulysses asked.

Nate looked up at him. "About what?"

"The poor Indians."

"You're the one with the chip on your shoulder, son," Nate said. "Although it don't seem to be getting you anywhere." He held the younger man's insolent gaze a moment. "That story about the survey—you sure about that? It's not just some Indian making up stories about how the white man lied to him?"

"We don't need to make up stories about that, Cooper."

"Show me," Nate said. "You got a horse?"

It seemed for a time that Ulysses would refuse the request, but then he came down off the porch. "We can walk."

The two men started out along the dirt road, heading east. It was mid-afternoon and warm and they kept to the shade of the tall pines. As they walked, Nate glanced over from time to time at Ulysses, who stared straight ahead, uninterested in small talk. Nate took his makings from his pocket.

"Where'd you get that scar?" he asked.

The Indian was quiet for so long Nate didn't think he would reply. "Fighting for my woman," he finally said.

"Where is your woman? I haven't seen her."

"She is gone," Ulysses said. "I won the fight but lost the woman."

Nate lit the cigarette. "Would you have preferred it the other way around?"

Considering this, the Indian almost smiled. "No," he said.

They walked on. "Where's Standing Elk today?"

"In his lodge," Ulysses said. "He's been sick."

"What's he got?"

"Sometimes he spits blood," Ulysses said. "But mostly he is sick in his heart. Do you think he likes to live like this? Taking charity? Scratching in the dirt for vegetables?"

"I expect he doesn't," Nate said.

When they reached the edge of the tree line, near the bullet-riddled reservation sign, Ulysses stopped and pointed to a ridge, running north and south, a couple of miles away.

"I was fifteen years the summer of the survey," he said. "My father and I hunted every day. We would ride north, sometimes into Canada, looking for buffalo. The surveyors worked along that ridge all summer, and we were told that was the border for the reservation."

"When did it change?" Nate asked.

Ulysses began to walk along the tree line, looking for something in the grass. "One day," he said as he searched, "we came back from a hunt. We had been gone nine or ten days. When we returned the surveyors were putting their stakes here. See?"

He pointed at the ground. Nate walked over to see a brass plate there, imbedded in concrete. There were numbers on the plate.

"This was the new boundary," Ulysses went on. "When we asked why, we were told there had been a mistake. That's all."

Nate straightened to look at the range to the east. "How did Covington come to own it?"

Ulysses shrugged. "The next year he started grazing cattle there. We were told to keep away. His men would run us off. Sometimes they would shoot at us for sport. Old man Covington hated the Blackfoot. He would accuse us of stealing his cows."

"Why would he think that?"

"Because sometimes we would steal his cows," Ulysses said. "He hired men with guns. Many Indians disappeared and we never saw them again." He turned to Nate. "That still happens."

"Today?"

"Yes," Ulysses said. "Today."

Twenty-Two

"I THINK SHE'S THE PRETTIEST FILLY that ever there was," Libby Thompson said.

She was standing in the corral with the little roan, stroking the animal's nose with her fingers. Donnelly was on the top rail a few yards away, watching her. She wore a yellow frock with white lace trim and when Donnelly had helped her down from the side saddle she rode, she had smelled of rosewater and lavender, exactly as he imagined an angel would smell. When he told her the filly was hers, she squealed like a little piglet with its tail caught in a door.

As he watched, she pressed her face against the horse's cheek, closing her eyelids and smiling dreamily. Donnelly could look at her all day long—her button nose and blue eyes, her cascading blonde hair, now tied up at the back of her head, the luscious curve of her bosom. She always looked so cool and fresh.

He himself was a little uncomfortable. He had passed the morning making everything perfect for her visit. Swept out the cabin and washed the single kitchen window. Wiped the crumbs from the table to the floor then realized he had to sweep again. He'd bathed in the cold stream, using a bar of lye soap rough as sandpaper. He greased his boots with bacon render and then, while waiting for her to arrive, he noticed a coffee stain on his one clean shirt, the fancy red paisley shirt he kept aside just for her visits. He pulled the garment off and took it to the creek to wash the stain out with the lye soap and, in the process, created a wet spot so large that he eventually dunked the entire shirt in the water. He wrung it out as best he could and hung it on the corral but it was still damp when he spotted Libby approaching along the south bench and he'd been forced to put it on wet.

But that was spilt milk. Nothing could ruin this day for him. Libby arrived with a basket behind her saddle, carrying a Mason jar of buttermilk and half a cherry pie. She had taken the basket inside the shack and when she came out, Donnelly had presented her with the filly that she was now fawning over.

"She's the prettiest filly that ever there was," she said again. "And you, Tommy Donnelly, are the sweetest cowboy in the entire state of Montana. If you climb down from that rail, I will give you the biggest kiss."

Donnelly climbed down.

They kissed for a little while and then went inside, where Libby poured the buttermilk before cutting the pie into three large pieces, one for herself and two for the sweetest cowboy in Montana. Donnelly removed his hat when they came in and was concerned at once about his hair, which he had spent considerable time combing that morning. It was now flat to his head. Aside from running his fingers quickly through it, there wasn't much to be done though, so he let it be. And soon the pie—and the girl— made him forget it altogether.

"I had no notion you could make something this tasty," he said, finishing the second wedge.

"Oh, I didn't make it," Libby said. "Mabel made it. She's our maid."

"It's still tasty," Donnelly said.

"She can cook most anything. Daddy said there's nothing like a colored woman in the kitchen, if you can keep them from filching."

"It's right tart," Donnelly said. He noticed that Libby ate just a few mouthfuls. "Not hungry?"

"I had enough," she replied. "I have to watch my waistline. Mother has engaged a seamstress from Conrad to sew me some new outfits for summer." She hesitated. "Did you know there's a dance next weekend at the community center in Conrad?"

"I was not aware of that," Donnelly said.

"Well, there is. And I shall be attending. If a certain gentleman was interested in dancing with me, I just might oblige him."

Donnelly started to scratch his head but realized he had a fork in his hand. "I ain't much for dancing," he said. "I guess I never had time to learn."

"I can teach you!"

Donnelly nodded uncertainly, reaching for the tin cup containing the buttermilk. "Well, maybe."

"No maybes about it," she told him. "I love to dance. I just love it."

Donnelly nodded once more, to show that he wasn't opposed to the notion, even though he was highly nervous about it. For the here and now, he had other matters to discuss.

"I was thinking," he began. "I've *been* thinking, I should say, about this little spread east of here, runs up hard against the Longley ranch. It's only a section, but I was thinking that maybe, in a couple years, I could offer on it. Be a good place for a man to get his start. Run a few beeves of his own. There's a house there, with a good tin roof."

"What are you suggesting, Tommy Donnelly?"

"I was just thinking."

"Thinking what?"

Donnelly had more buttermilk, taking time to wipe his upper lip with the sleeve of his shirt after he drank. He was suddenly perspiring. "Might be a good place for a young couple to start out, that's all."

"Well, well," she smiled. "Do you have any particular young couple in mind?"

He looked at her and nodded. He'd already spoken all the words he had rehearsed earlier. He had been hoping she would take over the conversation at this point and maybe even tell him what she thought of his plan. Instead, she came around and sat in his lap and kissed him, then leaned back to look at him before kissing him again.

"You are so sweet," she said. "That place sounds like a little piece of heaven."

"It would require hard work," he said.

"We would have the hired hands for that."

"Well, not at first," he allowed.

"We would have to have hired help, silly," she said. "Maybe I could steal Mabel away from Daddy."

"Well, eventually," he said. "If things got rolling good—"

She interrupted him by kissing him again, this time giving him a long and lingering smooch. When she pulled away, her breathing had increased.

"Is that your bunk?" she asked.

Thinking on it later on, Donnelly realized it had been a foolish question. It was the only bunk in the shack. For now he merely nodded, not able to speak, what with his pulse pounding and his heart in his mouth.

"Do you think we might move over there where it's more comfortable?" she asked.

Donnelly thought it was a good idea. Maybe the best idea he'd heard so far in his young life.

Samuels had been waiting for a chance to talk to Nate Cooper and late Tuesday afternoon he got the opportunity. He was sitting at his desk in the *Chronicle* office, his feet up, reading the weekly minutes from the Cut Bank town council meeting when he looked up to see Cooper strolling along the plank sidewalk from the direction of the livery. He went into the Belmont Hotel.

Since there was nothing Samuels could name that was more boring than the weekly minutes from the Cut Bank town council meeting, he got up from his desk, put on his hat, and headed across the street.

Cooper was standing at the bar, nursing a glass of rye, as Samuels entered the hotel. A handful of others were also at the bar, drinking and slurping oysters, and the restaurant to the rear was filling up with the hour. The bartender was Abner Dent, the son of the hotel's owner, a callow young man who parted his hair in the middle and doused himself several times a day with scented witch hazel. He had been sent home the previous year from a college in Wisconsin after failing seven out of eight subjects and was now forced to work at the hotel, at a job he thought was well beneath him.

"I'll have a glass of ale," Samuels told him, approaching the mahogany bar a few feet from where Nate stood. "And another rye for Mr. Cooper, if he's agreeable."

Nate turned a critical eye on Samuels, looking him up and down. "I have never been one to refuse a hospitable gesture."

Abner Dent stood there looking blankly at the two men, as if he was having trouble understanding the request.

"Ale for me, Abner," Samuels repeated. "And a rye over here."

At that point, Abner turned his hand to the task. Nate was still watching Samuels, as if trying to place the skinny young man, dressed in a blue serge suit, his hair at the mercy of a determined cowlick.

"You were at the bar in the Bighorn the other night," he recalled. "Watching the pool game."

Samuels took a step toward Nate and extended his hand. "Willis Samuels. I'm a reporter for the *Cut Bank Chronicle*."

Upon hearing of Samuels' vocation, Nate took his hand warily. "The newspaper," he said.

"I'd like to talk to you," Samuels said.

"Then it ain't a free drink after all."

Abner, having drawn the ale, set it in front of Samuels. Reaching for a bottle behind him, he topped off Nate's drink as Samuels placed a dollar on the bar. Abner took the coin and moved off, wearing his ever-present petulant expression.

"That boy appears dimwitted," Nate said absently. He took a drink of whiskey, regarding Samuels over the rim of the glass. "What do you want?"

"You like to get right to it," Samuels said.

"You saying you don't?" Nate asked. "Man in your business?"

Samuels nodded. "Fair enough. I heard that you spent nearly thirty years in prison because you were railroaded by a man named Parcell Covington. Is that true?"

Nate snorted. "You're goddamn right I was railroaded by Parcell Covington. I watched that bastard put his hand on the Bible and lie through his teeth to a judge and a jury. Claimed he watched me shoot a man down in cold blood. Well, he wasn't there and that never happened. I'd call that railroaded, wouldn't you?

"I would," Samuels said.

Nate took more rye. "But that's old news, son. I don't know what interest it might hold for you. Parcell is dead now, and I only hope that his deceitful act has landed him in hell, where he belongs."

"You're understandably bitter."

"Hold on now," Nate said. "I wouldn't say that. You asked a question and I answered it. That don't mean I'm bitter. I'm still alive and able to take a sip of good whiskey. The past is dead and gone. It would give me no pleasure to dwell on it."

"That's an admirable attitude," Samuels said. "I'm not sure many men would feel that way after thirty years in prison."

"Twenty-eight."

Samuels smiled. "Twenty-eight. You can file this under better late than never, but the *Chronicle* would like to run your side of the story. What we call human interest. And we would like to take your picture too, to run with it."

"I'm not much for getting my picture made," Nate said. "Last time I did, it was at the request of the territory of Montana. But go ahead and print your story if you want. I got nothing to hide."

Samuels had a drink of ale before pulling a notebook and pencil from his coat pocket. "I want to make sure I have the facts straight." He watched as Nate took more rye. The glass was nearly empty. "Would you like another drink?"

Nate wiped his mouth. "What do they pay you over there, son?"

"Twelve dollars a week."

"How about I buy you a drink?" Nate suggested. "I am a successful billiard tycoon these days."

"Obliged," Samuels said.

Nate signaled young Abner, who was admiring himself in the mirror behind the bar.

"Now," Samuels said. "The story, as I have it, is that you came into the territory with Harry Longley in 1879. And that the two of you were outrunning a posse."

"Whoa now," Nate said. "I never said that Harry was the one on the dodge with me. He's a respectable rancher in these parts. We got no call to be tying this to his tail."

"Don't worry, I'm not looking to incriminate anyone. Besides, I have a feeling the town of Fargo has forgiven any and all sins. I just meant that you were cowboys together."

"You can put that much in your paper," Nate conceded. "Harry was a hell of a cowboy. He could throw a rope, bust broncs, turn an ornery bull inside out. And he was the best damn pistol shot I ever saw. You can put all that in your paper, but not a word about that other business. He's worked too hard to put that in the past."

Samuels held up his hands. "Duly noted."

Abner delivered the drinks. After Nate paid, he watched for a moment as Samuels scribbled away in the notebook. "Used to be a man named Gibson ran that newspaper. Skinny Scotsman with big sidewhiskers. He still alive?"

Samuels nodded. "He was about an hour ago. He's my boss. He's not so skinny these days, but he's still got the whiskers and still runs the paper, been thirty-some years now. He's the one who would take your picture, if you change your mind."

Nate stood quietly, tapping his index finger on the bar top, thinking. "He's been there all this time?"

"Yes, sir."

"How's his memory?"

"Sharp as a saber."

Nate nodded. "Maybe I'll get my picture made after all."

They arranged for Nate to come by the newspaper office the following afternoon. He arrived in town an hour early and went to the barbershop at the train station, where he received a shave and a haircut. He allowed the barber to trim his mustache, albeit just slightly. His cheeks still stinging from witch hazel, he walked across town to the *Chronicle* office, where young Samuels and Angus Gibson were waiting on him. Samuels was sitting at his desk in his shirtsleeves, eating an apple. Nate would not have recognized the older man; he'd grown fatter and balder with the years. He had Nate sit in front of a wall painted white while he set up the camera. Nate, his hat in his lap, was impatient by nature and more impatient with the notion of having his image collected.

"You're like molasses in January with that thing," he told Angus.

"One moment," Angus said absently. After nudging the camera a couple of inches forward, he finally clicked the shutter. "Hold for another please." The shutter sounded once more. "There we go."

Nate put his hat on. "Any chance I could get one of them for myself? I got a sister back in Missouri been worrying over me all these years. Maybe she'd like to know what the man looks like she's been praying for."

"Of course," Angus said.

"I'll pay you."

Angus waved the suggestion away. "Stop by later in the week. Thanks for coming in, Mr. Cooper."

Nate started for the door but lingered there, clearly something on his mind. "This young fella says you've been here since back in '78?"

"Yes, sir."

"Would you remember anything about a treaty with the Blackfoot? In 1885, I believe."

"I remember it well," Angus said. "It was part of the government's ongoing efforts to reduce the size of the reservation."

"They are good at that, if not much else," Nate said. "Well, there's an open range just east of there, a few thousand acres I'd say, was supposed to be part of the reservation. And it got changed somehow and ended up part of the Covington ranch. You recall anything about that?"

Angus gave it some thought before shaking his head. "Can't say that I do. It wasn't anything that made the paper, not that I recall."

Samuels was still sitting at his desk. "What's your interest in this, Mr. Cooper?"

"Oh, I just got a curious nature," Nate said. "Lucky for me I ain't a cat." He started for the door again but stopped once more. "You wouldn't happen to know who would have done the survey for the reservation?"

"Far as I recall, Joe Simpson's crew did all the surveying in northern Montana at that time," Angus said.

"You wouldn't know anybody that worked on that crew?" Nate asked. "Maybe somebody still around these parts?"

Angus shook his head once more. "Sorry."

Nate nodded. "Thank you, gents. I'll stop back for that picture."

When he was gone, Samuels glanced over to his boss, his eyebrows raised. "What was that about?"

Angus shrugged but his interest was clearly piqued. "I haven't the faintest idea."

Dusk arrived, and Rose sat by the bay window looking west, a book in her lap. It was a novel she had just started, and she was having trouble becoming engaged in it. The dust cover claimed it was a romantic story of a princess who is kidnapped by a dashing pirate. So far Rose had read the first page three times. She couldn't say whether the book, or the reader, was the problem. She glanced across the room to where Harry was sleeping in the overstuffed leather chair he'd had shipped from California. There was a half glass of bourbon on the table beside him, and the nearly empty bottle on the floor by his feet. His mouth was open and his breathing came in starts, his large belly rising and falling with each breath.

As Rose turned back to the book, her eye caught movement in the yard. Nate Cooper trotted through the gates aboard the chestnut mare, making for the barn, where he dismounted and pulled the saddle and bridle from the horse. He spent the next fifteen minutes brushing the animal down and cleaning its feet with a hoof pick. When he turned her loose in the corral he stood there watching her for a time, his arms draped over the top rail.

After a while he made a cigarette and lit it. As he smoked he began to pace the length of the corral and back, slowly, his eyes on the ground. He appeared restless in thought but slow in motion, as if attempting to calculate some problem in his mind. In the scant light, Rose thought he could have passed for the thirty-year-old he claimed to be. He was still bowlegged and lean, relaxed but deliberate, restless but somehow content in that restlessness, as if he accepted that it was part of who he was. The way he had always been.

She looked over at Harry again, slumbering noisily in the chair. He and Nate had once been two peas in a pod, each one always trying to outdo the other, especially if Rose was around. Harry had been the more handsome of the two, but Nate was more quick-witted and sly. Women had loved him and no doubt still did, even ridiculous women like Abigail Jones.

The two men were not so alike anymore. Fate had seen to that. Rose watched Nate as he paced then shifted her eyes over to Harry in his slumber. She should send him up to bed, she knew, as she had done so many times in recent years. She watched him and tried to remember the way he used to be. He had changed so much, not only in appearance but in attitude. He rarely touched her anymore. She couldn't recall the last time they had kissed with passion. It wasn't something she dwelled upon. In fact, she never really thought about it at all, not until of late.

She went back to the book, to the first sentence, and started again.

Twenty-Three

THE RIDGE ROSE UP OUT OF the badlands to the south and ran north all the way into Canada. It wasn't high, and from a distance of a few miles didn't appear as a ridge at all, especially now, with the spring grass growing in abundance.

Nate passed most of the morning crisscrossing the hog's back, looking in the tangled buffalo grass for any sign of a survey that might have been made, and then abandoned, twenty-five years earlier. He had no notion of what he was searching for, just as he had no notion if he was even looking in the right place. He couldn't know how much surveying had been completed before the boundary had shifted, just as he couldn't know for a fact that the shifting had ever occurred. So he was searching for old stakes, or brass and concrete markers, like the one he'd seen at the reservation a few days earlier. He would have been encouraged by anything—even the remains of a camp that might have belonged to the surveying crew. But the range was giving up nothing; twenty-five years was a long time. Twenty-five years of blizzards and fires and floods; it was little wonder nothing remained but grass.

Moving south for an hour or more, he came upon a narrow valley running down from the ridge to the east. A spring-fed creek came out of some rocks to flow along the bottom of the ravine. The stream was just a trickle, but it ran clear. Not far from the source of the water was a gray shack, with a rusted tin roof and a swayback porch. Behind the shack stood a juniper brush corral, with a small black mule and six or seven goats inside. A flock of chickens roamed the yard. Nate nudged the mare and rode down the slope for a closer look.

Drawing near, he saw a burlap curtain move in one of the windows of the shack and seconds later the front door opened and an old man stepped out onto the porch. He was skinny and gray-whiskered and filthy, wearing overalls with no shirt, and a slouch hat so battered by age it could hardly be identified as such. He held a double barrel ten gauge shotgun in the crook of his arm.

"Something I can do for you?" His voice was hoarse and cracked, as worn as his clothes.

"Howdy," Nate said.

"You can save your howdy. I asked you a question."

"Nothing you can do for me," Nate said. "Just riding by."

A large red rooster appeared from somewhere and began to chase the hens in the yard. The birds scattered in all directions, loudly squawking their distress.

"You ain't riding by, you're sitting still," the old man said. "And you ain't hunting cuz you don't got a gun. So I figure you're on the snoop for something. And this here is private property."

"I thought maybe it was a cotton plantation," Nate said. "You got a name?"

"Briscoe Tuttle, if it's any of your beeswax."

Nate smiled. "You're an unsociable old cob, I'll give you that."

"I'm an old cob with a scattergun, so you might want to button that lip and keep on riding."

The rooster had now focused in on a young male bird, a threat to his domain. The young bird was half its size and terrorized, running one way and then the other, slipping beneath the porch and coming out the other side. The old rooster stalked it relentlessly.

Nate gestured at the little spread. "How'd you come to live on Covington land anyway? Old Parcell would never stand for any squatters. Clayton neither, I'm guessing."

"I own this here fifty acres," Tuttle said. "Bought and paid for. I can show you a deed, but since it's none of your damn business, I'm not inclined to. Just as you're not inclined to tell me what you're doing here." He shifted the heavy shotgun from one arm to the other. "I seen you up on that ridge. You're looking for something. I figured a lost calf at first, but then you got down from your horse and started nosing around. You don't need to climb off a horse to find no calf."

The big rooster caught the smaller one, just for a moment but long enough to tear a chunk out of it. The young one scurried away in a panic, feathers flying. Nate watched its flight before turning back to Tuttle, but the old man was no longer looking at him. He was staring past Nate, his eyes squinting into the afternoon sun.

Nate turned to see a rider at the top of the ridge, sitting his horse and watching them through a spyglass. When the man lowered the glass, Nate recognized him as the Covington foreman who'd intercepted Nate a few days earlier on the range. He was leading a large pack mule and across the mule's back was folded what appeared to be a grizzly bear hide.

"Friend of yours?" Nate asked.

"Ed Garner ain't no friend of mine," the old man replied. "Just another nosy bastard, like you. I wouldn't piss on him if he was on fire."

Nate watched as Garner put the glass away and started off, leading the mule while still holding his gaze on the two men down in the canyon. He headed north, toward the Covington ranch buildings. Nate watched until he disappeared behind the rise before turning back to Tuttle.

"Well, I won't trouble you any further," he said. "I'll leave you to enjoy this little slice of heaven you got here."

"You can kiss my rosy asshole," Tuttle told him.

Nate laughed as he reined the mare around to leave. But Tuttle was peeved over Nate's remark about his holdings and wouldn't let it pass.

"You ain't gonna find nothing," he called out.

Nate stopped, turning in the saddle. "What?"

"You're wasting your time." Tuttle was smiling now, displaying brown and broken teeth. "Just so you know."

"What am I looking for?" Nate asked.

At that moment the young rooster came out from under the porch once more. The big bird was waiting and was on it at once, grabbing it by the neck. The smaller bird screamed like it was being killed, which was precisely the old bird's intent. It managed to break free and then Tuttle shot the old rooster, blowing its head off. He watched a moment as the body flopped bloodily around the yard, then he looked at Nate.

"Don't you know?" he asked.

Twenty-Four

CLAYTON CAME IN ON THE AFTERNOON train. At the Cut Bank station he gave his bag and two bits to a boy and told him to take it over to the livery and have a rig ready for him in an hour. Then he walked down the street to Fran's Diner for supper. The special of the day was Yankee pot roast.

It was early for the supper crowd and, save for a couple of farmers drinking coffee and eating pie at the counter, Clayton had the place to himself. As he was finishing the meal, he heard the door open and looked up to see Sheriff Henry Pearce coming toward him, wearing his semi-automatic Colt and his put-upon expression.

"What is it, Henry?"

Henry, for a change, didn't say a word. Instead, he took the latest edition of the *Cut Bank Chronicle* from his coat and laid it on the table in front of Clayton. The story was featured on the front page and the headline read:

THE RETURN OF KID COOPER

Clayton looked at the paper then at Henry Pearce. He picked up his coffee cup and sipped at the brew as he started to read.

Their week's work finished, Samuels and Angus were playing a game of cribbage and drinking beer when Clayton walked into the office a short while later, carrying the newspaper Henry Pearce had given him. Angus had just counted twenty-four points to take a commanding lead. A skunk was not out of the question.

Clayton walked over and tossed the paper onto the table on top of the cards and the cribbage board. Angus leaned back in his chair to look up at the man.

"Senator Clayton Covington," he said. "Looking like a man who has lunched poorly and is not looking forward to dinner."

Clayton managed a smile. "And you look like a man who will soon be explaining himself in a court of law."

"How so?" Angus asked, reaching for his bottle of beer.

"You've slandered my father in this thing you call a newspaper," Clayton said. He looked from Angus to Samuels, who was calmly retrieving the cards from where they had scattered.

Angus picked up the *Chronicle* and made a show of reading the front page, as if he was just now seeing it for the first time. He took his time with the pretense, while Clayton idled beside him, his color growing red.

"I see," Angus said. "And how is it that we've slandered your father?"

"You're saying that he lied under oath. That's a very serious charge to make against one of the founding fathers of this state, and you will answer to it. Is business that bad, Gibson, that you need to resort to this type of yellow journalism?"

Angus spread the paper out, turning it slightly so Clayton could have a look. "Actually, it is Mr. Nate Cooper who alleges that your father lied under oath. And it would appear that Mr. Cooper was in a unique position to make that observation. As for this newspaper, we were merely quoting Mr. Cooper."

"That's cute," Clayton said. "I'll be showing this to my lawyer in Helena on Monday morning. We'll see how cute he deems it to be." He turned to leave.

"Senator," Samuels called out as he reached the door.

Clayton turned.

"While you are here," Samuels went on, "I was wondering if you might know anything about some inconsistencies in a land survey that was conducted back in 1885?"

"What?" Clayton asked.

Samuels continued. "Regarding a large parcel of range that was allegedly earmarked for the Blackfoot reservation but somehow became part of the Covington ranch."

Clayton shook his head impatiently, as if he was annoyed by a flying insect, before turning to Angus. "Who is this pup?"

"Mr. Samuels is a reporter for the *Chronicle*," Angus replied. "A reporter asking a question of our local senator."

Clayton continued to regard Angus with contempt. "I know nothing about any surveys. I can tell you that the work would have been contracted by the state of Montana – "

"Montana wasn't a state then," Samuels pointed out.

"Then by the *territory* of Montana," Clayton snapped. "I suggest you take it up with whoever was involved at the time. I was not. I also suggest that you be very careful what you print in the future." He made a point of looking around the office. "I have a feeling that this establishment has a limited litigation budget."

When he was gone, Samuels looked at Angus.

"My deal," Angus said.

They'd barely had time to look at their cards when Clayton returned. His anger seemed to have disappeared in the scant moments he'd been gone and his tone was now downright conciliatory.

"Gentleman, let's take a moment here," he said. "I'm well aware of how important a newspaper is to a small town. Especially my hometown. This man Cooper has spent half his life in prison for killing a government employee. He's at an age where I'm sure he would like to justify that—not only to himself but to his maker. I have no desire to press this matter. I'll leave him whatever peace he might find in his . . . rose tinted . . . version of events."

Angus looked at Clayton without speaking. He wasn't about to commend the man for retracting a threat.

"Surely you can understand my initial reaction," Clayton went on. "When I see my family name in that context."

"We will print any rebuttal you'd like to offer," Angus told him.

"No, no," Clayton said calmly. "I will not enter into any kind of back-and-forth with this character. He's been kicked around enough by life. Let us just let the matter lie."

And with that, he showed them his best smile and left again. Samuels looked at his cards and then his boss.

"Well now," Angus said. "Was that a man who's had second thoughts because he has his eye on the governor's chair and would rather not have his family name dragged into a libel suit—or was that a man who's had second thoughts because you asked a question about a twenty-five-year-old land survey?"

Samuels flipped over a one-eyed jack. "Maybe it was both."

Clayton's mood was sour as he drove the rig out to the ranch. He knew he needed to let the matter drop. There was nothing to be gained by suing the only newspaper in his district, and even less to gain by giving life to a story that was nearly three decades old, one that featured Clayton's father and would undoubtedly highlight the old man's raging racism. On the grand scale of things, the *Cut Bank Chronicle* was the smallest of potatoes. A few hundred people might buy it, read it, and then use it to kindle the fire in their potbelly stoves. Better to leave the story there with the ashes, let them both grow cold together. As for the pup reporter asking questions about the 1885 survey, Clayton had no notion where that was coming from, or where it might be going. But he sensed it was something else that needed to remain dormant.

Driving the rig into the yard, his spirits rose when he saw the enormous hide of a bear hanging from a cottonwood limb by the smokehouse. The legs were tied off and staked and old Murphy was busy scraping the hide out. The bear's carcass was in the back of a freighter nearby; a couple of the hands were busy hitching a come-along to it in order to hoist it out. Others had a game of horseshoes in progress by the bunkhouse.

Ed Garner came out of the barn to meet Clayton as he drove up; he took the pacer by the harness while Clayton stepped out of the rig.

"Well, well," he said, indicating the bear.

"Yes, sir," Garner said as he began to unhitch the buggy.

Clayton strode across the yard for a closer look at the grizzly hide.

"Ain't that a bear?" Murphy said as Clayton approached.

"It surely is," Clayton said. "What do you think for weight?"

"All of seven hundred pounds, my guess," Murphy said. "The boys will eat offa him for a spell, if they don't mind a gamey stew. And you'll have a fine rug to show, once I comb the fleas and ticks out of her, and get her tanned."

Clayton's mood was elevated to the point that he felt obligated to invite Garner inside for a drink, breaking his own rule. They sat in the den in the fading light of the day while Garner told of the hunt.

"He killed a big bull calf Wednesday sometime," he said. "Ate about half and left the rest in some rocks below Dutchman's Creek. Line rider came across it and sent word down. I was there at dawn, waiting on him, and here he come, looking for his breakfast. Plugged him below the ear with my Sharps, a good two hundred yard shot. Had to skin him out on the spot, mule couldn't of carried the carcass. Sent the freighter up for it and it still required a block and tackle to load him."

"Good job." Clayton leaned forward to pour more whiskey for Garner. "Now I need to figure how I'm going to get that hide down to the capitol. It won't fit in a steamer trunk."

"Strap it on a pallet and send it on the train," Garner said.

Clayton nodded.

"Something else you should know," Garner said after he'd drank. "The ride back took me past old Tuttle's."

"Yeah?"

"Well, he had company."

Now Clayton took a long drink. It seemed as if his day had been full of unexpected developments. "What sort of company?"

"Nate Cooper."

Clayton didn't say anything for a time. He poured again for himself, shifting in his chair. "Seems like the man is everywhere I turn," he said at length. "Running beef to the Indians, telling stories to the newspaper, and now he's paying that crazy old hermit a social call."

"What's this about the newspaper?" Garner asked.

"Nothing. You say they were talking?"

Garner nodded. "Don't know what about, I wasn't near enough. But they were talking."

"Could have been nothing," Clayton decided. "Looks as if Cooper's on the drift. And old Tuttle doesn't make a lot of sense on his best day."

"That's true."

Clayton got to his feet and walked to the window. Some hands were still throwing horseshoes, in spite of the dying light. Clayton spotted Munson and Ballinger among them; he hadn't seen them before. Munson was sitting and smoking while Ballinger was leaned back against the bunkhouse wall, his thumbs hooked in the belt of the fancy holster he wore. Why would a man need arm himself with a six-shooter to watch a game of horseshoes?

"He's got a lot of energy for an old man," he said over his shoulder to Garner.

"Who?"

"Cooper."

"Seems like it."

"A man that age, you'd think he'd be slowing down." Clayton watched a horseshoe flying through the air, heard the ringing of the iron against the stake. "Maybe he could use some help in that regard."

Twenty-Five

THE BUYER FROM CHICAGO WAS NAMED Hightower and he had set up shop of late in the Belmont Hotel. He was a large man, soft-spoken, with dark curly hair and a small reddish mustache that looked like a caterpillar. He wasn't of the west and, unlike some buyers in their new Stetsons and shiny boots, didn't pretend he was. He'd been buying a lot of beef all across the northern half of the state, and his checks had always cleared, Harry had been told.

They met for lunch on Saturday in the dining room of the hotel. By the end of the hour Harry agreed to send five hundred yearling steers east over the following three months. Hightower wrote a check as a down payment, the rest to be paid upon delivery.

While they were eating, Harry saw Clayton enter the lobby, glancing Harry's way before continuing on to the bar, where he ordered a beer, choosing a place to stand where he could keep tabs on Harry and the buyer. When Hightower got up to leave, moving on to his next appointment, Clayton picked up his beer and came over to sit down. Harry was finishing dessert, pumpkin pie beneath a mound of vanilla ice cream.

"Hello, Clay," Harry said. "How's that bull working out for you?"

"He's doing what bulls do, from what I hear. What brings you to town?"

Harry gestured in the direction Hightower had gone. "Sewed up a beef contract. You ought to talk to that fellow, if you haven't already."

"Who is he?"

"Name's Hightower, out of Chicago," Harry said. "Buying a lot of beef."

"Chicago," Clayton repeated. "I thought maybe he was with Indian Affairs."

"Why would you think that?"

Clayton had a drink of beer. "My foreman saw one of your hands driving some steers onto the reservation last week."

"Not my steers."

Clayton shrugged. "They were wearing your brand."

Harry finished the last mouthful of pie and pushed his plate away. He was not fond of Clayton's coy attitude. "What hand?"

"Some old cowboy. Gray hair, mustache."

Harry shook his head darkly. He looked across the room and got the waiter's attention. "Bring me a rye," he called over.

"What's the matter, Harry?" Clayton asked.

Harry kept his eyes on the bartender as he poured the drink. "Nate Cooper," he said.

"Cooper?" Clayton said. "Why, I heard he was out of prison. Matter of fact, our local newspaper considered him worthy of a story. Mostly fiction, but what can you expect from the *Chronicle?*"

"I haven't seen the paper."

"When did he get out?"

"A few weeks ago," Harry said. The rye arrived and he took a drink. "Been staying at the ranch."

Clayton smiled. "Looks like he's back in the cattle business. Although I wouldn't think a steer would fetch much of a price out at the reservation, Harry."

"I wouldn't think so either," Harry said unhappily.

Clayton drank his beer off. "If memory serves, wasn't it a combination of stolen beef and Indians that got Nate Cooper into trouble the last time?"

Harry, his gaze fixed across the room, just nodded. He'd rather not have this conversation, but if forced to, he'd rather not have it with his brother-in-law.

Clayton stood up. "Well, I'm glad he's your problem and not mine. I'll see you, Harry."

The horse-buying Scot from Wyoming had finally resurfaced, having sent Rose a telegram a few days earlier, saying he would be arriving with some hands to pick up the fifty head of two-year-olds sometime Saturday. Harry had business in town, so Rose asked Nate to help out with the stock in question when the man arrived. The horses had grown a little tamer since being penned, but not much.

McCrae showed up again in a rented rig, but this time he was accompanied by six hands, all mounted on scrawny cow ponies, older nags that had seen better days. The hands themselves were equally as questionable, a dirty sullen bunch, with saddles worn by hard use, and hats and boots of the same description. They dismounted inside the front gate and squatted or sat there in the dirt, smoking and talking in low voices.

McCrae drove the rig up to the porch, where Rose, having seen his approach, was waiting for him. Nate was inside, drinking coffee and reading about himself in the newspaper, wondering if he'd really said all that young Samuels had quoted him as saying. He couldn't be sure; he suspected the reporter might have changed the words around somewhat. He definitely left out the cuss words. When Nate heard the voices, he put his hat on and walked outside. Rose, her hip against the newel post, was talking to the pudgy Scotsman, still sitting in the rig. Rose introduced the two men.

"You've arranged transportation?" she asked then. "I hope those hands are good. These horses aren't going to take much to being loaded into a boxcar."

"We'll not be taking them by train," McCrae said in his lilting voice. "Not at the railroad's prices. Dreadfully dear."

"What do you intend to do?" Rose asked.

"The men there will drive them."

"Drive them?" Rose repeated. "Where you taking them again?"

"Fremont County," McCrae said. "That's in Wyoming."

"I know where it is. That's four hundred miles from here."

"A little over that, by my calculations."

Nate stood quietly on the porch, watching the pink-faced man in the rig. He glanced across the yard to the hands the Scot had hired. Not a one of them had yet to walk over to the pasture for a look at the horses their boss was buying, a strange way for a cowboy to behave.

"I guess you know this isn't open range anymore," Rose was telling McCrae. "There's a lot of fencing between here and Fremont County."

"I believe we will utilize the public thoroughfares," he replied.

Rose glanced over at Nate before trying once more. "These young horses are not exactly gentled. You might tell them they're bound for Fremont County but they could have other ideas."

"I'm sure the men I've hired can handle that," McCrae said. "Shall we have a look at the stock?"

Rose came down the steps as McCrae finally climbed out of the rig. She was beginning to think he intended on completing the transaction without ever getting out of the buggy. She turned to glance pointedly at Nate and he followed along, a bemused look on his face.

"I had about given up on you," Rose said as the three of them approached the pasture. McCrae replied without looking at her. "I am a busy man. I deal in a lot of horse flesh."

"So do I," Rose told him. "And I've been obliged to feed this bunch a fair amount of hay after they grazed the grass down to a nub. Money out of my pocket." She turned to McCrae. "Waiting on you."

The young Scot ignored the jab, or was too obtuse to notice. When they arrived at the pasture, he looked over the top rail to cast his inexpert eye on the herd milling inside.

"There's about sixty head there," Rose told him. "You can pick the fifty you fancy best."

McCrae nodded as he turned to her, apparently finished in his appraisal. "Remind me—what kind of price were we discussing?"

"Remind you? We agreed on a hundred a horse. That makes the price five thousand dollars. I'm assuming you have a bank draft to cover that amount in your coat pocket. Or cash."

"Of course," McCrae said. "As I said, I deal in a lot of horse flesh. I can'nae always remember each individual deal."

Rose turned to give Nate a look, but he was walking away now, wandering toward the cowboys loitering by the front gate.

"Do you have the bank draft?" she asked.

"Let's say I have *a* bank draft," McCrae replied. "In the amount of four thousand dollars. Upon looking at these horses up close, I think that's a fair price."

Rose smiled at the young man and said not a word in reply.

The hands, still sitting or lying on the ground, a couple with their backs to the gate posts, didn't get up as Nate approached. They were a sad-looking bunch, in their forties or fifties, with holes in their boots and an odor about them that suggested a lack of soap or of recent bathing in general. The ones that weren't hungover might have been drunk yet.

"Howdy, boys," Nate said. "Having yourselves a little siesta?"

A couple of them grunted in reply. Nate turned from them to their mounts, standing untethered off to the side, pulling at the grass outside the gate. They appeared too tired or worn-out to wander off. They were a scarred-up lot, their flanks raked with spur marks, mouths damaged by rough use. Not one of the six appeared to have spirit enough left in it to break into a trot. Nate turned back to the hands.

"I hear you boys are planning an old-fashioned drive."

They were quiet for a time until one of them, a sandy-haired man with a goatee, replied. "Looks like we are."

"Green bunch like that, you might make thirty miles a day in good weather," Nate said. "That's two weeks. How do you figure to feed and water them on the way?"

"There's plenty grass alongside the road," the same man said. "The rivers and creeks are running, if you ain't noticed."

Nate indicated the saddle horses at their graze. "You men supply your own mounts, or do these belong to Mr. McCrae?"

"You got a lot of questions."

"I have been burdened of late by a curious nature," Nate said. "So why don't you answer the question? I can see you're too lazy to get up off your ass when somebody's talking to you but it don't take a whole lot of effort to make a simple reply."

"You go to hell," the man said.

"Christ, George," another man said in protest of the attitude. He looked up at Nate. "They belong to the boss man. We brung 'em on the train."

Nate turned toward the pasture, where Rose appeared to be arguing with the young Scotsman. He caught her eye and shook his head. She left off her conversation and started over, with McCrae on her heels.

"All right then," McCrae was saying as they approached. "You can'nae blame me for a wee attempt at negotiating. It's the businessman in me. So it will be the bank draft for four thousand and a personal check for the balance."

As Rose approached, Nate nodded toward the cow ponies outside the gate. He waited as she appraised them, her lips tightening. When she glanced over at Nate, he indicated McCrae.

"His," he said.

Rose turned to McCrae. "I'm not interested in your personal check. And I'm not interested in negotiating, either. I've decided to hang onto my stock, Mr. McCrae."

"What in the hell does that mean?" McCrae protested.

"It means we're finished here," she told him.

The cowboys, seeing their wages slip away, suddenly found some energy. They got to their feet as one, and the sandy-haired man took a step toward Nate.

"This sonofabitch queered it," he said.

"It's good to see that your legs work, son," Nate told the man. "Mind that tongue though, or you might land right back on the ground."

McCrae followed Rose as she and Nate headed for the house. At first he pleaded with her, and then he grew indignant, threatening to sue for breach of contract. Failing in those efforts, he took to calling her names, at which point Nate hit him on his cheekbone, knocking him on his rear end. His cowboys were mounted by this time, but none of them came to his rescue, probably realizing that they'd made the long trip from Wyoming for nothing, and that the man lying in the dirt was as much the cause of it as the man who'd put him there. When McCrae, holding his jaw like a fellow with a bad toothache, made his way to his rig and climbed inside, they were already on the road to town.

Twenty-Six

AFTER McCRAE AND HIS CREW LEFT, Nate and Rose sat on the porch, drinking coffee. Nate was winding his dollar watch, having set it to the clock in the kitchen. The watch was losing about two minutes a week. He couldn't expect too much for the price.

"What do you figure a man like that would want with good horses?" he asked, slipping the watch into his pocket.

"I've been thinking on that," Rose said. "I met a rancher last year in Cheyenne. We were down there for a cattleman's meeting. He said there was a man going around his part of the state, looking for half-wild horses to sell to rodeos. You might not know it, but travelling rodeos are a big business these days. They take them into the cities and people pay two dollars a head to get in. I wonder if Mr. McCrae might just be supplying broncs to somebody for that purpose. The wilder the better."

"That might fit. Why else would a fat man can barely drive a buggy want to buy unbroke horses? He sure as hell is no horse man."

"And now he's got a sore jaw to boot." Rose sipped her coffee. "That was uncalled for, you know. The day I can't handle a man

191

like McCrae is the day I'll move into town. Like Abigail Jones.
Get myself a cute little house and a phonograph machine."

"Jesus H. Christ," Nate said.

"Did you like coming to my rescue?" she asked.

Nate drank from his cup and made no reply.

"Like old times, Galahad," she said.

When they finished their coffee, Rose decided that they might
as well drive the bunch of young horses back to their graze on the
southern slope. There would be no need for leads this time; the
herd had been yearning to get back there since the day Rose and
Donnelly had brought them to the pasture. She and Nate saddled
up and when Rose opened the gate, the horses lit out at a gallop,
heading due south. Nate and Rose followed on point but little was
required of them. The herd was of one mind.

When they reached the slope, the other horses sounded off as
the sixty splashed through the creek to join them. Rose and Nate
sat their horses on the high side of the hill and watched.

"Well, that was an exercise in futility," Rose said. "All it did was
cost me hay."

"What will you do with them?"

"We'll break them, a few at a time. There's always a market
for broke horses. Sell what I can and use the rest on the ranch."
She watched the herd a while longer before turning to him. "You
remember that sorrel colt you gave me?"

Nate shook his head, surprised she would ask that of him. "Did
you think I wouldn't?"

"I couldn't say," she smiled. "Knowing you, you might have
given lots of colts to lots of girls."

"Not on thirty a month, I didn't," Nate said.

Rose laughed. "And here I thought I was special. Now you're
saying the only reason I got a horse and the other girls didn't was
due to your impoverished state at the time?"

"I can't win with you," Nate said. "I ought to give up trying." He
held the pose for a moment. "What did you do with him, anyway?"

"I kept him, of course," Rose replied. "I wouldn't have parted with that horse for anything under heaven. Oh, he was a real knot-head, we ended up gelding him to make him behave, which he did somewhat. He died just two years ago."

"What made you think of him today?"

"A couple of things. Young Donnelly is sweet on a girl from down south a bit, blue ribbon daughter of a rich rancher. In way over his head, I suspect. You recall that filly he took up to pasture with him? Well, he bought her out of this bunch, and he intends to make a present of her for the girl. He's working it off. Sound familiar?"

"Young cowboys and their fancies," Nate said. "Some things never change. You said there was a couple things."

"Yeah," Rose replied. "I thought about that colt when you knocked the dumb Scotsman on his behind. You never knew what I named that horse, did you?"

"I guess I didn't," Nate said, thinking back. "I went off to Deer Lodge around that time."

"I called him Galahad."

Nate laughed. "Did he live up to the name?"

"Some days he did," Rose said. "And some days he didn't." She gave Nate that familiar look. "How about some lunch?"

Riding into the yard, they could hear the clatter of Harry's motorcar approaching. It came over the rise and through the gate at a high speed, the brakes locking in the dirt as it slid to a halt not twenty feet from the two horses, which shied and side-stepped away from the racket and the dust. Harry shut the noise off and climbed out, his face a combustible shade of purple. Nate got the mare under control and reined her sideways to where Harry stood.

"You look like you sat on a porcupine, Harry."

"You been running my beef out to the reservation?" Harry snapped.

"Yes, sir," Nate replied, getting down from the horse.

"Goddamn it, Nate," Harry said. "What in hell do you think you're doing?"

"Feeding hungry people is what I'm doing," Nate said. "People that fed us when we were hungry. I also took 'em flour and beans and sugar. You want no part of it, figure out what I owe you and I'll pay you. If I don't have it, I'll work it off."

Rose had dismounted now. "That's nonsense. You're not paying anything off."

"You stay out of this," Harry told her sharply.

"What did you say to me?" she demanded.

"This has got nothing to do with you."

"Everything on this ranch has to do with me," she said.

Harry glared at her but didn't reply for a moment. He hadn't come back to the ranch to argue with *her*. He turned and took a step toward Nate. "I told you to stay away from the goddamn Indians. You don't have enough brains to realize that place is nothing but trouble for you? What do you figure to accomplish out there?"

Nate gestured to the motorcar. "Seems to me that you're the one that's stuck on accomplishing things, Harry."

"Yeah, and I've done pretty goddamn good at it," Harry told him. "Took a lot of work. You ought to try it sometime, instead of getting yourself wrote up in the newspaper, like you're some martyr. You think you're a hero, after all these years gonna ride in and save the poor Indians? Is that what you think?"

"Harry," Rose warned.

He wouldn't look at her. He stood staring at Nate, knowing that he'd stung him and satisfied, for the moment at least, that he had. Nate stepped over to the mare and swung up into the saddle.

"I don't believe I'm any kind of savior, Harry," he said. "That is beyond my way of thinking. I do believe this though—a man has got to pay his debts."

"You don't pay your debts with my cattle!" Harry shot back.

Rose watched as Nate pulled his hat down low on his forehead, hiding his eyes from them both. He reached forward for the reins.

"All right, Harry," he said softly. He turned the mare in a half circle and, kicking her into a lope, rode out of the yard.

Harry stood watching him defiantly, his face still as red as a ripe tomato. When Nate had disappeared over the rise, he turned toward Rose, standing tight-lipped behind him. She wasn't looking at him; she was watching the road where Nate had gone.

"What in the hell has got into him?" Harry asked.

"He wasn't talking about his debts," Rose said, still looking westward. "He was talking about yours."

She and Harry never said much over dinner. He told her he wasn't hungry, but she ended up warming a pot of venison stew she'd made the day before. Harry sat by the stone fireplace in the great room, drinking, but when she carried the food to the dining room, he followed the aroma and came in to sit down. When he offered to pour wine for her, she declined. She didn't eat but a few mouthfuls of the stew. After clearing the table and washing the dishes, she said she was going up to bed. By that time Harry was back in his large steer hide chair, drinking brandy.

"I expect he never told you about Dutchman's Creek," he said.

At the bottom of the stairs she stopped. "Who?"

"Nate. I know you two were close back then, but I expect that's one story he never told you."

"I don't know what you're talking about, Harry."

"I didn't think so." He took some brandy. "We came out here in '79 and we wintered with the Blackfoot. You know that part, Lord knows you've heard it more times than you can count. Well, there's more to it. You recall that was the winter that Dull Knife and the Cheyenne made that last fight with the army. He led the whole tribe up from the Indian Territory and gave the army fits for months before they finally ran him to ground over to Wyoming."

"I know the story of Dull Knife," Rose said.

"You might recall that the whole damn countryside was scared to death of the Cheyenne," Harry said. "Stories were everywhere, how they was burning ranches and stealing horses, killing every white man they came across. They raped women and killed young 'uns. That's just the truth, Rose. Everybody was terrified of them and that included me and Nate." Harry hesitated, this time taking a large measure of the brandy. "Well, we were hunkered down in a dugout along Dutchman's Creek, the day the blizzard hit. We were flat broke and out of food. Sometime during the day the snow eased up a mite, for just a half hour or so. We looked out and there's a damn Indian standing not thirty feet away. The snow swirling around, it looked like he was holding a rifle. Nate pulled his Colt and shot the Indian dead." Harry was required to take another drink. "Problem was—when we got to the body, there weren't no rifle. That Indian was no more than a boy, sixteen years or so, and he was holding a coup stick."

"Jesus wept," Rose said.

Harry nodded. "We didn't know what to do, so we put him in a hollow along the creek bank and covered him with snow. Left him for the coyotes or the wolves or whatever. A few days later White Bull found us in the dugout and took us to the village. We never told them about the boy with the coup stick. No doubt he was kin to some of them that was good to us. Them that fed us."

Rose stood with her hand on the newel post. "So all these years . . ."

"Yeah," Harry said. "And I figured he never mentioned it to you because, to this day, he has never once mentioned it to me. It tore him up and I guess it's still tearing him up. And now I'm the one paying for it."

Rose stood there quietly for a time. "Looks to me like he's the one paying for it," she said and went upstairs to bed.

Twenty-Seven

Angus Gibson took a rig north on Saturday morning to talk to a woman who had given birth to triplets the week before. The woman and her husband lived on a sheep farm ten miles south of the Canadian border. They already had seven children, with the oldest just twelve years, and neither seemed especially thrilled to see the number jump to ten. Angus arrived at the farm shortly before noon. The babies were as tiny as ground squirrels, all lined up in a wooden box by the woodstove, their eyes just slits, pink faces wrinkled and pinched. But they were healthy, it seemed, and it made for a good human interest story. Angus did a short interview with the woman, who was as tired as a person in her predicament should be and then got a quote from the husband, who asked afterward if the newspaper would be paying anything for the story. He grew somewhat brusque upon learning it would not. Lunch wasn't offered. Before leaving, Angus took some photographs of the recalcitrant couple and the sleeping babies and the seven siblings, a silent lot dressed in patched hand-me-downs.

Thunderheads rolled down from Alberta and rain began to fall as Angus drove the rig back to Cut Bank and by the time he walked from the livery to the office, there was a steady downpour.

There he found Samuels surrounded by the archival copies of the *Chronicle* from 1885. The yellow newsprint was spread everywhere across the room, suggesting that Samuels had devoted most of his day to examining the old editions.

"And what have you found?" Angus removed his wet hat and coat.

Samuels shook his head. "If there was any impropriety surrounding that survey, it never made the newspaper at the time. Not that I can find anyway."

Angus took a moment to glance at some of the twenty-five-year-old headlines. "As I said earlier, it's a story I would have remembered," he said. "Especially if it involved Parcell Covington. There was never any love lost between the two of us."

"Why not?"

"He was an unrepentant bully," Angus said. "And a cruel man who thought that rules were for everybody else. I sometimes implied that in the editorial page. Is there tea?"

Samuels indicated the cup by his elbow. "Coffee."

Angus set about brewing a pot of tea. "Keep in mind you're looking for a cover-up. And if the cover-up was successful you won't find anything. You wish to turn it into a failed cover-up, and to do that you need evidence."

"And I can't find any," Samuels said.

"Maybe there is none to be found. Whoever said there is no such thing as a perfect crime had no imagination. The perfect crimes are the ones you never hear about."

Samuels gestured to the old papers. "The Simpson Survey Company is mentioned now and again in the 1880s. They surveyed the railway lines and the county roads and the streets of Cut Bank too. You don't remember what became of them?"

Angus shook his head. "No. They were here and then they weren't. Nobody would make note of a business like that leaving the area. Presumably there came a time when there was nothing left here to survey."

"Speaking of Simpson," Samuels said, walking to the layout table, "do you remember this?" He lifted a front page to show Angus. The headline read:

Barn Saved from Fiery Fate

Angus came closer for a look. "I do indeed. I had a flare for headline hyperbole back then. The barn belonged to the widow Molly Frick, and that is Joe Simpson's survey crew all right. They just happened along when the fire broke out."

A picture below the headline showed half a dozen men, wearing coveralls and armed with shovels and buckets, standing in front of a blackened yet still erect barn. An elderly woman posed alongside the men, whose names were printed below the picture. In the accompanying story they were identified as being in the employ of Joe Simpson.

"Molly treated the men to Sunday dinner by way of gratitude," Angus said. "One of them ended up marrying Molly's spinster daughter, if memory serves. Of course, in those days you were considered a spinster if you were twenty-one and still unencumbered."

"The names of the men are here," Samuels said. "Any chance one of them might still live around here?"

Angus went over the list before shaking his head once more. "I don't think so."

Samuels put the paper aside. "What about the territorial land records at the capitol? Everything would have been registered there at the time."

"They would have recorded the survey," Angus said. "But we have to assume they would have recorded whatever was given them. Fudged or unfudged."

Samuels had a sip of cold coffee. He was determined to find a way into the story. Clayton Covington's reaction to the question about the survey had occupied his mind all weekend.

"There might be nothing to it, Willis," Angus said then. "We have Nate Cooper, holding a grudge against the Covingtons, and we have the Blackfoot, holding a grudge against the white man in general and, more specifically, against the chain of events that pushed them onto the reservation." He gestured to the scattered newspapers. "And we have absolutely nothing to back up any allegations."

"Nate Cooper didn't invent the story," Samuels said.

"I don't believe he did."

"And I doubt the Indians did."

"I doubt it too," Angus said. "I'd say there's a good chance that it happened. However, suggesting the Indians were cheated out of their land is hardly a breaking story. It's been happening since Columbus arrived on these shores."

"But this involves a ranch belonging to a local politician with grand ambitions," Samuels said. "You told me on my first day here that I needed to follow my gut. I believe this story."

"Believing it and proving it are two different things," Angus said. "We can believe a story all day long and well into the night." He gave Samuels a look. "But we can't put it in our newspaper."

Nate had been in the Bighorn Saloon since he'd ridden in from the ranch, after his confrontation with Harry. He'd ridden straight into a rain squall, coming down from the north, arriving in town in the middle of a torrent, the streets already slick, puddles filling. He'd dismounted in front of the livery and led the mare in out of the deluge, pulling the saddle and bridle from her and rubbing her down with a gunny sack while the man with the crooked back stood by and watched, the rain hammering down loudly on the tin roof of the building.

"This ain't nothing," the man claimed. "Back in the old days we wouldn't have called this a shower."

"Everything was bigger and better back in the old days," Nate said.

He paid the man and headed for the saloon, where he spent an hour sitting alone in the corner, drinking beer and talking to nobody. His sour mood eventually began to lift and he found a vacated chair in a poker game. He lost twelve dollars to a bunch of hands from the Covington ranch before giving up on the cards and moving on to the pool table. By nine o'clock he was playing against the same bank teller he'd skinned a week or so earlier. The young man had been working on his game, he'd said, his tone suggesting that this time he was ready for Nate. The man wore the same brown checked suit as he had earlier; Nate wondered if that was his banking outfit, and his only set of clothes.

It was Saturday night and the place was full of cowboys from the local ranches. Munson and Ballinger were there, having come in after the rest of the Covington crew. They didn't sit with the others though, instead taking a table in the corner, close to the pool table. They drank rye and chased it with beer and they kept a close eye on Nate. Their scrutiny was not lost on him.

The bank teller's game had improved, but not so much that he was in a position to win any money from Nate. They played six times, with Nate taking all but the final game, when he scratched on the eight ball.

"You didn't lose on purpose?" the bank teller suggested as Nate gave him his dollar.

"I only ever once threw a game on purpose," Nate told him, "and no offense, but she was a lot prettier than you, son."

"This old geezer's bullshit never stops," Ballinger said loudly.

He was sitting ten feet from the table, slumped carelessly in a chair, his boots extended onto the plank flooring. He'd been rolling and smoking one Bull Durham after another, grinding the butts out on the tabletop. Nate didn't favor him with a look.

"Another game?" he said to the teller.

"Why not give somebody else a chance?" Munson asked.

He'd been sitting but was on his feet now, leaning back against the wall, a glass of beer in his hand. Nate had looked him over earlier, when he'd come in with the hothead Ballinger. He was a big man, with pig's eyes, and a few days stubble on his chin. He hadn't spoken until now, and had only occasionally grunted in acknowledgment of the stream of nonsense coming from his part-ner.

"Have at it," Nate said. He indicated the teller. "This young fella holds the table."

"I want you," Munson said.

The bank teller was a fragile youth, and smart enough to sense that there was something in the air he wanted no part of. He quickly invented an excuse about being late for an evening meal and within a minute had his coat on and was out the door, leaving a nearly full glass of beer on the rail of the billiard table. Ballinger was on his feet in a flash to claim it.

Nate was not of a mind to take up Munson's challenge, but nei-ther was he willing to turn heel and walk away. He glanced about the big saloon and noticed Samuels from the newspaper, on a bar stool near the front door, watching. Nate hadn't seen him come in.

"Dollar a game," he said.

Munson barely knew which end of the cue to hold. Nate beat him as quickly as possible, thinking that one game might settle things, although in his heart he knew it wouldn't be so. Ballinger kept up a running commentary as the two men played.

"You're hell on wheels with the billiards," he said as Nate moved around the table. "Teach you that down at Deer Lodge, did they?"

"There's no table in Deer Lodge," Nate said. "You'll see . . . when you get there."

"What makes you think I'm going to Deer Lodge?"

"Just a hunch." Nate sank the eight ball and turned to Munson. "That's a dollar."

"Double or nothing," Munson said.

"Pay as you go," Nate advised him.

"Now ain't he a particular one?" Ballinger said to Munson.

Munson put the silver dollar on the felt and began to rack the balls. Nate chalked his cue, feeling the sweat gathering in his armpits. A few of the other cowboys were watching with interest. But none of them had a dog in this fight and when the ball got to rolling, they would allow it to roll. It was Saturday night and they were in the mood for some entertainment.

"What've you been up to, old-timer?" Ballinger asked then.

Nate blew chalk from the tip. "How would that concern you?"

"It might," Ballinger said. "I do believe I saw you riding on the Covington range the other day. You been warned about that."

"Did you now?" Nate asked as he broke the balls. He made the three off the break and then dropped the five in the side pocket.

"I saw you," Ballinger said again. "I saw you talking to that old goat farmer."

Nate gave it some thought. So that's the way it was. "You didn't see me," he told Ballinger. "But I got a feeling that the man who did is the one sent you here tonight."

He made the seven and the four, then attempted a bank on the ace but missed. There was a back door out of the place, but Nate couldn't persuade himself to use it. Even if he did, they would follow, and being caught in the dark alley would be worse than in the saloon. He watched as Munson managed to sink the twelve in the corner.

"Why you bothering that old man, anyway?" Ballinger asked.

"Who said I was bothering him?"

"I did," Ballinger persisted. "You been bothering a lot of people. Locked away down to Deer Lodge all them years and now you don't know how to act. That's how I see it." He paused a minute, enjoying himself immensely. "That what happens when you get old? You just become a damn nuisance? Why don't you tell us, old man—what is it you're good for these days?"

Nate kept his eyes on the felt. "Good for nothing, I guess. Maybe you and me should start a club."

Ballinger stiffened in the chair. He pulled his legs under him and leaned forward. "That's pretty funny. Now why don't you tell me what you were asking that old man?"

Munson missed an easy side shot. Nate drank off his beer and set the empty glass on the rail. He decided it was going to be whatever it was going to be. He called the two in the side and made the shot.

"What was I asking the old man?" he said as he circled the table. "I was told the old boy had a talking jackass. Ace in the corner." The ball dropped. "And in all my years I have never seen such a thing as a talking jackass. Bank on the six."

Ballinger watched, his face tight as Nate made the shot before crouching down to eye level for a close look at the eight. He called the shot and hammered the ball into the corner pocket. Straightening, he smiled at Ballinger.

"Turns out, if I wanted to see a talking jackass—all I had to do was come here and wait for you to show."

Ballinger came out of the chair like a shot. Nate was ready and smashed him flush in the face with the fat end of the pool cue. He turned to see Munson coming for him and swung the cue around in an arc, breaking it across the big man's forearm. Munson kept coming, reaching out and clamping his huge right hand on Nate's shoulders. Nate grabbed a pool ball from the table and slugged Munson on the temple with it. Munson grunted but held on.

Now Ballinger came back, swinging wildly at Nate, knocking his hat off and raining blows on his head and shoulders. Munson muscled Nate around and pinned his arms from behind, giving Ballinger easy access to attack. Nate leaned his weight back into Munson then drove the heel of his boot into Ballinger's balls. The little man screeched in pain, his face contorted, but in seconds he was back, enraged now, throwing punch after punch into Nate's face. Nate felt Munson suddenly let loose of him and he went down.

Now he was aware of somebody else in the fray. Young Samuels had come across the room and climbed on Munson's back. Letting go of Nate, Munson had turned and slugged Samuels flush in the face, knocking him across a table and onto the floor. From his landing spot, Samuels looked up at the bartender.

"Get Sheriff Pearce!"

Nate, rising on one knee, heard Munson laugh at the suggestion and then he and Ballinger went to work on Nate again, knocking him back to the floor and giving him a few kicks before finally leaving off. Apparently it wouldn't do to kill him, not with a saloon full of witnesses. Nate went into a fetal position until the kicking stopped. When he got to his feet, the two men were gone.

Twenty-Eight

S<small>AMUELS TOOK</small> N<small>ATE DOWN THE STREET</small> to the *Chronicle* office, the two of them making their way along the wet sidewalk in the drizzling rain. Inside, he heated water and filled a basin in the back room. Nate stripped his shirt off and cleaned his face. There was a cut above his left eye and, other than that, a few bruises and lumps. His ribs were painful where he'd been kicked. Whether they were broken or not was hard to say. It wouldn't be the first time if it was so; Nate had been underneath a few horses in his day.

Samuels stood by and watched. He himself had a mouse under his left eye; he would have a doozy of a shiner come morning.

"I can fetch the doctor," he said as Nate tried to stop the bleeding from the cut.

"Hell," Nate said. "I been beat up worse by temperance ladies in Kansas City."

Smiling at that, Samuels went back into the office to his desk, where he kept a mickey of rye. He poured into two glasses and had a drink. When Nate came out of the back a few moments later, buttoning his shirt, Samuels nodded toward the second glass. As Nate drank, he took notice of the yellowed newsprint spread about the room.

"Yes," Samuels said to the question not asked. "I've been looking into your survey story and to tell you the truth I was just about to give up on it." He regarded the damage to Nate's face. "But somebody certainly turned loose the hounds tonight, didn't they?"

Nate drained the glass and sat down gingerly in a chair, mindful of his ribs. "Some men don't appreciate getting bested at billiards, I guess."

"You don't believe that," Samuels said.

Nate chuckled. "Well, my heart wants to, but these knots on my head tell me otherwise." He indicated the bottle. "Could I have another dose of that painkiller?"

Samuels handed the bottle over. Nate poured and drank, coughing as he did.

"I'd say tonight had something to do with that old goat farmer I come across on the Covington range. The old boy made a peculiar remark as I was leaving. Told me I wouldn't find nothing."

"That was all he said?"

"Pretty much," Nate replied. "He wasn't the most sociable man I ever run across."

"Those cowboys tonight," Samuels said. "You figure they work for Clay Covington?"

"First of all, don't call them cowboys. I don't know what they are, but they're not cowboys. And they're working for Covington. I already had a run-in with the little one, the one who fancies himself John Wesley Hardin. He was with Covington's foreman at the time. He's the one saw me talking to the old hermit."

"So he sent you a message tonight," Samuels suggested. "Or was it Clayton?"

Nate thought about it as he drank again. "That business with the survey would have been with Parcell, not Clayton. Though I suspect Clayton would've known about it."

Samuels poured more rye for himself. The mickey was nearly gone now and he reached over to splash the remainder in Nate's glass. "The worst kept secret in Helena these days is that Clayton's going to run for governor come fall. The last thing he needs is a scandal, even if it is tied to his father and not him. Clayton still owns the land in question."

Nate indicated the newsprint all around. "But you said you were about to throw in the towel."

Samuels nodded. "I haven't found a shred of evidence."

"Then where's your scandal?"

"In the wind, I suppose." Samuels took a drink. "But then there was tonight in the Bighorn. And the old hermit with the peculiar comment."

He waited for a reaction from Nate, but the older man seemed to be fading. He sat slumped in the chair, the glass balanced precariously on his knee. It was the first since Samuels had met him that Nate seemed tired, or even close to his years. The cut above his eye was beginning to clot, the thin trickle of blood drying now, turning dark. Samuels wondered that he could still be upright; a beating like that would put most men, younger men included, in the hospital.

Nate suddenly realized he was being watched. He straightened in the chair and nodded toward the back room. "I see you got a cot back there. I don't fancy riding off into a rain storm at this hour."

"You're welcome to it."

Nate drank the whiskey off in a gulp and got carefully to his feet, his left elbow held tight against his damaged ribs. As he made his way toward the back, Samuels gathered his coat to leave. Walking toward the front door, he turned.

"You didn't get that old hermit's name?"

Nate had to think a moment. It had been a long day, what with the scallywag Scotsman and his miserable crew, the argument with Harry, and finally the dust-up in the saloon. It seemed as if his conversation with the goat farmer had happened a month ago.

"Tuttle," he said remembering. "Briscoe, I believe."

Samuels nodded and turned off the electric light switch inside the front door as he left. Nate went into the back room and sat on the cot, feeling the pain in his side and a weariness in his bones. He was too old for barroom brawls. And maybe he was too old for all of it. Could be that Ballinger had been right about that, even if he was wrong about everything else. After a moment he pulled his boots off and placed them on the floor beside the cot. As he made to lie down he heard the front door open and then the lights flickered on.

"I'll be goddamned," he heard Samuels say.

Nate walked out in his stocking feet to see the younger man charging about the office, searching the yellowed newspapers for something. When he found it, he beckoned Nate over. His forefinger rested on a photograph beneath a headline regarding a barn fire.

"Is that your man?" he asked.

Nate leaned over for a look. The man in question was quite obviously the miserable hermit from the goat farm, albeit twenty-five years younger. He appeared to be wearing the same hat and his expression suggested the same sour disposition.

"That's him," Nate said.

Samuels moved his finger down to the caption below the photo, where the men were identified by name.

"Right here," he said. "B. Tuttle."

Nate's eyes went from the name back to the photograph. The men with their tools and their soot-lined faces, staring into the camera lens. A dowdy woman alongside. The scorched barn in the background.

"What was he—a firefighter?"

"No," Samuels said. "He was a surveyor."

Twenty-Nine

T HE PERSISTENT KNOCKING ON THE DOOR downstairs woke Clayton. It was Sunday morning and the clock on the night table read five past ten. He lay there for a moment, thinking the noise might cease, before getting out of bed to walk over and glance out the window overlooking the yard below. Across the way a few hands were sitting outside the bunkhouse, drinking coffee and no doubt nursing hangovers from their adventures in town the night before, those that had even returned at this point. There were puddles in the yard, and the road out front was mud. The sun was shining now, but the rain might have altered Clayton's plans for the day. He saw no rig by the hitching post in front of the house. Whoever was pounding on the door was an employee, and he could guess who.

He turned to look at Nancy, cocooned beneath the blankets on the bed. Her eyes were open and she was smiling at him with an expression he knew very well. There was a time when his wife used to smile at Clayton like that of a Sunday morning. It had been a few years though since that had happened. The casualties of familiarity.

"I'll be back before you know it," he told her. "Don't you move."

"I'll save my moving for your return," she said. "So best you hurry."

He liked the way she talked to him, he decided, while he pulled on his pants and shirt and went downstairs to open the door to Ed Garner, standing on the porch, his hat in his hand. Before he spoke, the foreman took in Clayton's appearance; the mussed hair, the sleep-encrusted eyes.

"I assumed you were awake."

"I am now," Clayton said. "What is it?"

"I'm leaving for the day and needed to talk to you beforehand," Garner said. "Figured you to be heading back to Helena today."

"I'm here for the week," Clayton said. "My secretary's with me. We're working on a special project."

"I didn't know of that."

"What did you need, Ed?" Clayton demanded.

"Just wanted you to know that Munson and Ballinger caught up with Nate Cooper last night in town."

"And?"

"I believe the problem has been resolved."

Clayton watched Garner's eyes for a moment. They were flat though, giving away nothing. But that was the way of the man, the reason he'd managed to get away with so much for so long.

"I take it Cooper is still alive?"

"Yeah," Garner replied. "It was a public meeting, with lots of witnesses." He hesitated, confused for the moment. "Did you want him dead?"

Clayton shrugged. "Makes no never mind to me. As long as he has been educated."

"I've been told he has. Given that Ballinger was involved, I was told it in more ways than I needed to hear. But Munson backed it up. I will say that both men are somewhat marked up from the encounter. Ballinger in particular. His nose looks like a mashed toad."

"Those old cowpunchers can be tough," Clayton said. "Even if they are relics. Was there anything else?"

"No, sir."

Garner left and Clayton went upstairs to the bedroom where he found Nancy sitting up, her back to the headboard. While he'd been gone she'd found the recent copy of the *Chronicle* and was now reading about Nate Cooper. Clayton took the paper from her and tossed it onto the floor.

"Don't read trash, my dear."

She'd been wearing a nightgown when Clayton left and now she wasn't. It was cool in the room; Clayton admired her nipples as he stripped down and joined her beneath the sheets.

"Was there a problem downstairs?" she asked.

"Not at all," he told her, leaning over to kiss her breast. "More of a solution, in fact."

"I thought perhaps you were going to run off and do . . . ranch things."

"I'm staying with you," he said. "We have to work on the campaign."

"Is that what we're doing, Senator?"

"Of course. Besides, the weather might just have spoiled a surprise I had planned."

"Ooh," she said. "What surprise?"

"My new motorcar has arrived in Cut Bank. A brand new Hupmobile. It's on a flatcar at the station right now, ready for unloading in the morning. But I fear that yesterday's rain might have made the roads impassable. These are not the paved streets of Helena, my sweet."

"Which is why, Senator, we need the highway bill to pass," Nancy said smiling. "Which is why we need to have you elected as governor. By gosh—I guess we are working."

"That *is* why you're here," he said.

"Of course it is." She kissed him. "Tell me about growing up here. It was just you and your sister, wasn't it? In this big old house?"

"Yes," Clayton said, not warming to the subject. "And my father."

"When did your mother pass? You were young?"

"I could not have been younger. She died giving birth to me." He laughed. "And my sister has never forgiven me that transgression."

"That's not so."

Clayton shrugged. "It was a strange upbringing. My father was not a warm person. He was wounded in the Civil War, on the losing side, and he never really got over it. He thought I was weak because I wasn't interested in breaking horses and roping steers and all of that. That absurd and archaic notion that a man needs to get beat up and dirty to become a man. My sister was of the opinion that my father treated my mother badly. She was rebellious from an early age, and quite vocal. Always going with this cowboy or that one, the purpose of which, I'm convinced, was to aggravate my father. She ended up marrying one of them."

"Are you close now?"

"Hardly. She disowned my father decades ago over some incident. Never once spoke to him afterward, even when he was dying."

"That's terrible," Nancy said. "What was the incident?"

"I don't recall," Clayton decided to tell her. "Something trivial, I'm sure."

Thirty

SAMUELS WAS AT THE OFFICE OF records in the basement of the Cut Bank courthouse when it opened Monday morning. He had, during his two years in town, become friendly with the clerk there, a young woman named Susannah Braun. She had come out from Illinois on the same train as Samuels, to stay with her recently widowed aunt, and had ended up taking the job at the courthouse when it became available. She'd finished high school and taken two years of college, so she was more than qualified for the position. Samuels had once asked her to a church social and she had turned him down, explaining that she had a beau back home in Kankakee. Still, they had become friends and Samuels found that she was always willing to help out with anything he might need while working on a story. He suspected her job, filing deeds and wills, was boring. Assisting Samuels in whatever he was researching was quite likely a welcome respite.

"Oh my," she exclaimed when he walked in. "Your eye."

"Oh, it's nothing," he insisted.

"Whatever happened?"

Kankakee beau or not, Samuels was not above making his own case as a man to be reckoned with. "Just a little Saturday night

214

brouhaha at the Bighorn," he said. "I'd clean forgotten about it until you mentioned it."

He feigned modesty in refusing to provide her with any more details of the event. He would not lie to her, but neither was he anxious to tell her he'd been eliminated from the fracas by a single punch. As a potential suitor, his best ally at this point might very well be her imagination.

He found what he was looking for after an hour's search in the county land records. He thanked the sympathetic and increasingly curious Susannah and went up to the street. Walking to the office to report to Angus, and wondering how he might get in touch with Nate Cooper, he glanced in the window of Fran's Fine Diner to see the man himself sitting at a table. Samuels turned back and went inside.

Nate was having a breakfast of hen's eggs and sowbelly and fried potatoes. Samuels had eaten something earlier at the boarding-house, but he ordered coffee.

"You look like a real hard case with that shiner," Nate told him.

"I'm not certain but I think it makes me more interesting to the women," Samuels told him. He thought about it further. "One woman anyway."

"Watch your step there," Nate warned him. "A woman is a con-founding creature. She'll tell you she likes you one way and then turn around and try to reform you."

Samuels nodded at the sage advice. He'd had little experi-ence with the fairer sex and welcomed any advice that might be offered. He indicated Nate's own bruised face. "How are you feeling?"

"Like a puppy with two peckers," Nate told him.

Samuels took that to mean that the old cowboy was suffering no after effects from the fight, although he couldn't imagine how that might be true, after the barrage of punches and kicks the man had received. Allowing the matter to slide, he pulled his notebook from his coat pocket.

"I've been to the courthouse," he said as he opened it. "I did some title searches. Briscoe Tuttle bought fifty acres of the Covington range in 1892."

Nate drank his coffee. "Well, the old bird claimed he had a deed."

"Apparently land was going pretty cheap back then," Samuels said. "He paid a dollar for it."

Nate smiled as he set his cup down. "Parcell Covington could squeeze a nickel so hard it would turn into a dime. And yet he lets fifty acres go for a dollar?"

"I would refer to that as suspicious behavior," Samuels said. "Especially considering the comment that Tuttle made to you. But you're wrong about one thing. Tuttle bought the land in '92. Parcell died two years earlier."

Nate glanced out the window. It was a typical Monday morning; the town was stirring, freight wagons rolling along the muddy street, cowboys on horseback, men in suits headed to their offices or retail concerns. Nate looked at Samuels.

"Then I guess that silver dollar landed in Clayton's pocket."

"I would assume so," Samuels said.

Nate forked the last of the fried potatoes into his mouth before leaning back in the chair to drink his coffee. "They put on a pretty good breakfast for thirty-five cents," he said absently.

"I eat at the boardinghouse where I lodge," Samuels said. "It's porridge most mornings. I might see an egg or two on the weekend."

Nate indicated the notebook on the table. "So is that what you consider evidence?"

"I need to talk to Angus about it," Samuels replied. "Although I know what he's going to tell me."

"What's that?"

"That it was not a crime for Clayton Covington to sell this man Tuttle fifty acres of land, regardless of the price. And when I mention that two of Covington's men assaulted you after you were seen talking to Tuttle, he's going to tell me that a barroom brawl of a Saturday night is as common as bedbugs in a town like Cut Bank."

Nate laughed. "Sounds as if you know your boss pretty well."

"I do." Samuels picked up the notebook. "However, I also know he's going to tell me to keep looking." He did a fair impersonation of Angus Gibson's burr. "Connect the dots, lad. Connect the dots."

They walked out of the diner together. The sun was full up now, and the day was warming quickly. The livery, where Nate was headed, was a few hundred yards beyond the newspaper office. They walked along the plank sidewalk.

"What's this about a woman taking to that shiner?" Nate asked.

"Susannah, who works at the courthouse," Samuels said. "I've admired her for quite some time, but she has a sweetheart back in Illinois."

"He's in Illinois but you're right here in Montana. That ought to give you a leg up."

"I'm not so sure," Samuels said.

"Well, you need to be. Women like that." Nate stopped walking. "Lookit here."

Samuels followed his eyes. Clayton Covington was standing on the freight platform at the railway station down the block from where they stood. Four men, using ropes and come-alongs, were carefully rolling a fancy new motorcar from a flat car onto the platform. Clayton, dressed in a black suit and wearing an open road Stetson, was supervising the effort. Nancy, her face half hidden by a parasol, was off to one side, watching.

As was usually the case, there were several Indians hanging around the station and now one of them, an older man with a blanket around his shoulders, shuffled over to Clayton with his hand out. Overseeing the operation, Clayton turned and bumped into the Indian. Angry at the inconvenience, he shoved the man forcefully, knocking him from the platform onto the rail bed below. The Indian landed in the gravel and laid there, either hurt or feigning it. After a time he looked around, as if seeking sympathy from some quarter or another.

Samuels glanced at Nate. "There's our senator's empathy for the Indians."

"They shouldn't be begging," Nate said flatly. "Who's the girl?"

Samuels turned back to see Nancy climbing down from the platform. She stepped over to kneel beside the Indian on the ground.

"I don't know. Not the senator's wife."

From where they stood it appeared that Clayton had sharp words for the girl but she ignored him, setting aside her parasol and helping the Indian to his feet. Just then the motorcar landed on the loading dock and rolled to a stop. The men unhooked the ropes as Clayton began an inspection of the machine. It wasn't until he walked around the car that he spotted Nate and Samuels across the street. He reacted, looking away at once. After a moment's consideration, he stepped down from the platform, to where the girl was still attending to the stricken Indian. Clayton spoke to the man before handing him a coin.

"Looks like the *Chronicle* carries some weight in this town," Nate said.

"Maybe it's you he's worried about."

Nate shook his head. "These days Clayton Covington wouldn't know me from a load of hay."

He walked with Samuels as far as the newspaper office. They stood outside in the sun there while Nate made a cigarette and lit it. Samuels glanced through the window, where Angus Gibson could be seen inside, setting type.

"I'll see what the boss has to say about Clayton and Tuttle and the rest of it," Samuels said.

Inhaling the tobacco, Nate blew a couple of smoke rings into the clean morning air. He hadn't said anything since they'd left the scene at the railway station.

"What will you do now?" Samuels asked.

Nate thought on it as he continued to blow the rings. "These past couple of days have got me thinking that maybe I've had my fill of this place. Might be time to drift. According to Harry Longley, they're making some good rye whiskey up in Canada. There are worse reasons to set out for a place." He drew on the cigarette again. "I don't know. Everywhere I look since I got out of prison, I've been running up against what they call progress. I was always of the opinion that progress made things easier. But it don't look that way to me. If anything, things seem more complicated. Is that the whole idea of progress—to complicate matters?"

Samuels had no answer to that and didn't attempt to invent one.

Nate hadn't really been expecting a reply. He extended his hand and Samuels took it. "I'll let you get to work, young fella. You got dots to connect."

Nate walked over to the livery and saddled the mare. He mounted up, the pain in his damaged ribs taking his breath as he did, and rode down Main Street through the center of town, heading south. When he drew near the train station, he reined the horse to a stop. Clayton and another man were leaning over the engine of the motorcar and as Nate watched, the machine fired up. Nate was far enough away that the mare beneath him didn't react, or maybe she was getting used to the noise by now. Nate couldn't say the same for himself.

Nancy was standing by, watching, an expression of admiration on her face; whether it was for Clayton or the new automobile was impossible to say. Maybe it was both. Clayton turned to beckon her over and the two of them got into the motorcar and seconds later the machine lurched forward. Clayton aimed the vehicle toward the main road, heading south toward the Covington ranch.

Nate watched them disappear, then tied the mare to the rail in front of Gill's store and went inside to buy tobacco and cigarette papers. He bought a nickel's worth of hard candy as well before mounting up and heading out of town.

The sun that had shone all day Sunday had dried things considerably after the storm, but not completely. The old county road was deeply rutted and marked by low spots. A quarter mile out of town, the new Hupmobile foundered in the mire, spun its tires and then bogged down. Nate rode up to find Clayton standing outside of the vehicle, assessing the situation. Clayton regarded him unhappily.

"Hello, Clay," Nate said. "Your machine's stuck in the mud."

"I'm aware of that."

Nate tipped his hat to the young woman in the motorcar. "Good morning, ma'am. I'm sorry to see you're having troubles. I've been hearing that these machines were the greatest thing since Moses parted the waters. And yet here you are, bogged down in the Montana muck."

Nancy regarded Nate openly but made no reply.

"This your daughter, Clay?" Nate went on. "If she's heading to the ranch, she could always climb up behind me. I don't mind."

"We don't need your help, Cooper," Clayton told him.

"So you know who I am," Nate said.

"I saw your picture in the local paper. Along with your fictions."

Nate ignored the comment. "Well, the offer's there. Funny, Rose never mentioned having a niece."

"She's not my daughter," Clayton snapped. "She's none of your business." He turned away for a moment, regarding the wheel half buried in the mud. Stymied as to what to do about the motorcar, he looked back at Nate. "Are you even familiar with the concept of minding your own business, old man? I see under that hat that your face is a mess. Did you fall off your horse?"

"No," Nate said. "Matter of fact, I had a run-in with a couple of your hands. When did you start hiring nincompoops, Clay?"

"Looks as if they were more than a match for you," Clayton said. "I hope you're not too old to learn a lesson when it would behoove you to do so."

"Clay," Nancy said. "There's no need to be rude."

"That's okay," Nate told her. "I don't know what behoove is."

"It means you'd better wise up, old man," Clayton said. "Your days are finished. If you were smart, you'd find a rocking chair someplace out of the way."

"I'm in the way?" Nate asked. "Seems to me that you're the one clogging up the road, Clay."

Clayton walked around the motorcar now to confront Nate. Save the mud on his boots and the cuffs of his trousers, he had grown into a distinguished-looking man, a figure well-suited for his position in life. To Nate he was still the same snot-nosed kid he'd always been, a whiner and a backslider, always looking out for himself, and the easy way out of things. Nate recalled a time when Clayton, no more than eighteen or nineteen, had called Rose a strumpet, standing on the front porch of the Covington ranch house. Rose had punched him flush on the jaw, knocking him over the railing and into a flower bed below. Nate had particularly enjoyed the exchange, since Clayton had called Rose the name because she'd been out riding with him. Now it seemed Clayton was determined to put on a show for the young woman watching.

"That machine is the future," he said. "And you are the past. Look at you. Gray old man on a worn out saddle. They ought to put you in a wild west show or a museum. Your days are gone and everybody knows it but you."

As he spoke, though, his eye caught movement in the distance. He turned to see a farmer coming over a rise in a buckboard being pulled by two tall mules. The team could be the solution to Clayton's problem but it was more than a quarter mile away, angling for town. Clayton looked reluctantly at Nate, wishing he had curbed his tongue somewhat.

"Do us a favor, old-timer," he smiled. "Be a good man and ride over and fetch that team."

"You got something wrong with your legs, Clay?" Nate asked.

"You're the one riding a horse," Clayton pointed out.

"But you're the one stuck in the mud. I don't need a team."

Clayton nodded benignly, not wishing to show his displeasure. He glanced at the woman. "I'll be back shortly. This man won't bother you."

He set off at a good pace, determined to intersect the buckboard's path before it moved too far off. Nate watched him striding away before turning to the young woman.

"Those mules will do the trick." He touched his thumb and forefinger to the brim of his hat. "Good day to you, ma'am."

"I read about you in the paper too," she said quickly.

Nate was nudging the mare around to leave and now he stopped. "I guess I was near famous for a day or two."

"Is it true what you told the reporter?" Nancy asked. "Was that man Dudley cheating the Indians out of their due?"

"He was."

"Then why weren't the authorities involved?" Nancy asked. "Why did you take it upon yourself to settle matters? Or is that what they call frontier justice, Mr. Cooper?"

"Dudley was the authority at the agency," Nate said. "He was also pointing a double barreled shotgun at my belly button and about to pull the triggers. I thought it would *behoove* me to shoot him before he made a hole in me."

Nancy smiled at the word. "You're a quick learner."

"Some would say otherwise."

She let the smile fade. "Do you still visit the Indians, sir?"

"From time to time."

"And what are their circumstances today?"

"I would say none too promising," Nate replied. "What is your interest in the tribe anyway?"

"I work for the senator," Nancy said. "Perhaps there is something that can be done to help them."

Nate smiled.

"Did I say something amusing, Mr. Cooper?"

"Not on purpose, you didn't," Nate said.

There was a shout and both turned to see Clayton a few hundred yards away, waving his arms and calling out to the farmer in the buckboard. After a moment the man swung the rig toward them.

"Looks as if you are about to be saved, young lady," Nate said.

"You didn't answer my question."

"You mentioned you worked for the senator," Nate said. "You wouldn't like my answer."

He touched the horse with his heel and loped away. Atop the rise he stopped and looked back. The farmer had unhitched the mules from the buckboard and was positioning them in front of Clayton's motorcar. They would have the machine out of the mud in no time. Clayton would, of course, pay the farmer for the effort. Nate could imagine him tossing a dollar to the man.

It seemed to be the going price of things.

Thirty-One

Angus Gibson sat back in the oak swivel chair, a cup of tea balanced on his ample belly and his eyes on young Samuels, who stood leaning against the printer, having just finished telling his story.

"First of all," Angus told him, after a moment's digestion of the facts. "There's no law on the books against Clayton Covington selling a parcel of land to some hermit, no matter what the price. And secondly, a Saturday night donnybrook down at the local gin mill is as common as fleas in this neck of the woods. To suggest that it is connected to this tainted survey story is a stretch."

Samuels made a futile attempt not to smile. Angus eyed him suspiciously before continuing.

"On the other hand, there are questions that beg answers here. Based on what you've learned, I would say that a conversation with Clay Covington is in order. What is his relationship with this man Tuttle? And then a version of the same questions should be posed to Tuttle himself. If one or both choose to misrepresent themselves, then we need to know why. So let us get this on record. I am always in favor of allowing a man to explain himself."

"Or incriminate himself."

"That as well," Angus said quietly. He sat looking at the ceiling, his mind working. "But before you do all that, Willis, I suspect that a trip to Helena is in order. The *Chronicle* can't be asking questions about a survey we've never seen. We need to examine the original document. And who knows who you might encounter down there, plugging away in the hall of records? Maybe somebody who was there at the time in question, somebody who noticed some irregularities in the filings but has kept his suspicions to himself these twenty-five years." Angus smiled. "Waiting for the intrepid Willis Samuels to appear."

This time Samuels was allowed to smile as well. "When were you thinking?"

"No better time than the present," Angus said, pulling his watch from his vest pocket. "If you hie to the station, you can just catch the morning train. Visit the courthouse this afternoon and be back here by midnight. Tally your expenses, of course."

"I'd best get moving," Samuels said. He walked over and got his coat from the hall tree by the front door. He hesitated there, his mind going back to Saturday night. He glanced back at Angus. "Funny how things turn out. If I hadn't been in the Bighorn Saturday night, I never would have been involved in the fight. And Nate Cooper and I wouldn't have come back here. He never would have identified Tuttle's picture in the paper. And I wouldn't have been looking over the records in the courthouse this morning. We would still be ignorant of all of this."

"Serendipity, lad," Gibson told him.

"It was vicious," Samuels said. "What they did to Nate Cooper. They could have killed him. I think if it wasn't for a room full of people, they would have."

Angus nodded slowly, watching the young man. "Are you nervous about the assignment?"

"A little bit," Samuels admitted. "But I'll hold up my end."

He got into Helena shortly after two o'clock and went directly to the capitol building off Lockey Avenue. Samuels had been in the hall of records before but had never had reason to examine any of the old land surveys. They were in the basement, it turned out, and under the eye of a Mr. Henderson, a tall stooped man with wire spectacles and gray hair combed over a bald head. He looked to be in his sixties, which gave Samuels hope until he learned that Henderson had been in Helena for only twelve years, having worked most of his life at a copper mine in the Missoula area. He had moved to Helena to be near his daughter after her husband was killed in the war against Cuba. He shared all of these details with Samuels within five minutes of meeting him.

Henderson found the original Blackfoot survey after a quarter hour or so of searching through the files, stacked ceiling to floor in the large basement warehouse. He spread it out on a wide-topped table, and took the time to explain the various symbols and markings on the document. Samuels studied the pages, not knowing what he was looking for, and not knowing if he would recognize it if he found it. Everything appeared in order but then he had no frame of reference that might allow him to notice if things were not. The only thing familiar to him was the name of Joe Simpson, Surveyor, typed at the bottom of each page. The documents were in excellent condition. Presumably they wouldn't have been handled much over the years.

"Tell me," Samuels said when he'd gone over the pages a second time. "Would there be a listing anywhere of the men who worked the survey?"

"I doubt that very much," Henderson replied. "I assume this man Simpson would have such a thing. If you could track him down."

"Is he still in the business?"

"I haven't heard of him since I've been here." Henderson indicated the shelves all around them. "His name is on most of the surveys done in the northern part of the state, back in the early days. But nothing that I can recall in recent years."

Samuels turned again to the pages of the survey. "Would you have a date when this was filed?"

"That would be upstairs, in the registry. I can check for you." He made his way from the room.

While he was gone, Samuels shuffled through the survey for a third time. The western boundary of the Covington ranch was clearly marked, running hard up against the reservation, where the tree line began and the range ended. The coordinates of longitude and latitude meant nothing to Samuels. It occurred to him that he might have made the trip for nothing, but then that had always been a possibility. At least he knew the survey existed. He would have preferred to discover that it did not, that it had somehow disappeared from the records over the years. Now that would have been a suspicious occurrence.

"July 17, 1885," Henderson announced when he returned.

"And that would be the day these documents arrived here," Samuels said. "Everything on this table?"

"That's right."

"And they've been here ever since?"

"Yes. They don't go traveling."

Samuels found himself at the end of his futile questions. "I guess you can put this away. I appreciate your time."

"Part of my job," the clerk said. "Not sure what your newspaper's after, but it's good to see the official papers. We get people here from time to time. Most of them are lawyers, investigating mine claims. Every time some goober hits upon a vein somewhere, seems as if a dozen old panners decide it once belonged to them."

Samuels watched the man gather the survey and put it in order. "You said official just now."

"Did I?" Henderson asked.

"You did. What makes this survey official?"

"The state stamp. See here, on the back of every page."

In fact, Samuels had seen the stamps and not paid any attention to them. Henderson held a page forward to show him. The stamp was in red, an official type of seal, typical of government documents.

"Given the year, this is actually a territorial stamp," the clerk said. "But it's the same thing."

Something caught Samuels' eye. "There's a date there, beneath the stamp."

"Yes, they're always dated." Henderson shook his head as he realized. "There was no need for me to go upstairs to check the filing date. It's right here."

Samuels was no longer listening. He reached over to take the document from the man. "The date here is August 23, 1885."

"That can't be right." Henderson picked up another page from the survey and saw the same August date. "Why in Sam Hill would the dates be different?"

"I can think of a reason," Samuels said.

"And what is that?"

"There are two different dates because there were two different surveys."

Henderson took a moment. "That's damned suspicious."

"Isn't it now?"

Thirty-Two

IT WAS LATE AFTERNOON, THE SUN dipping behind the foothills, when Tuttle made his way to the brush corral to milk the two nannies. He'd built the enclosure against a high rock ledge, and from there he had extended a short overhang, with cottonwood limbs for rafters and rusted corrugated steel for a roof. The mule and the goats—three kids and a billy and the two milking nannies—were able to find shelter there, from the sun or rain or snow. The corral was twenty-five feet square and built of juniper saplings bound with rawhide rope.

The old man butchered a couple of goats every year, one in the spring and one in the fall, and he used the milk from the nannies for drinking and making cheese. If he got the chance he would kill a Covington calf if a stray wandered too close, butchering it quickly and cutting the meat into strips which he dried for jerky before any of the hands happened along, looking for the animal. Goat jerky and beef jerky looked the same hanging in the sun. The bones of the calf he would burn in a fire pit in the yard and the rawhides were cut up and braided for rope.

Today Tuttle tied the nannies in the shade of the tin roof while he milked them. The billy didn't like the old man, or anybody else,

229

getting close to the nannies, and Tuttle was forced to tie him off across the corral or risk being butted while he worked. The mule stood hipshot, watching the old man at his chore. The milk from the goats nearly filled the wooden bucket.

Nate had left the mare tied off to a willow sapling below the bench to the south of the old man's spread and approached the place on foot, keeping to the boulders strewn above the narrow stream. He found a spot a couple hundred yards away where he could hunker down out of sight to watch the cabin, waiting his chance. He wanted to approach on his own terms; he'd seen what the old boy had done to the rooster. When Tuttle made for the corral, leaving the shotgun behind, Nate began to move.

He was sitting in a rickety willow chair on the porch, smoking a cigarette, when the old man came shuffling around from the corral, carrying the near to overflowing bucket. He was muttering something to himself, his eyes down, and he practically walked right up on Nate before seeing him. The shotgun he had left leaning against the cabin wall was now resting across Nate's lap.

"What in the hell?" he sputtered.

Nate smiled. "You're such fine company, I couldn't keep away."

The old man's eyes narrowed as he set the bucket on the ground. "Do you intend to rob me with my own scattergun?"

"I'm not after your riches," Nate said. He opened the double barrel and shucked the shells before leaning the gun against the porch railing. "I'll settle for some information."

"I got none for you so git along."

"I think you do," Nate said. "Or you wouldn't have said what you did, last time I was here."

Tuttle squatted in the dirt then, beside the bucket, which had already begun to draw flies in the fading afternoon sun. "What did I say?"

"You told me I wouldn't find anything," Nate said.

A yellow mother cat, her teats hanging almost to the ground, came out from under the cabin and made a move for the milk. Tuttle swatted her away with the back of his hand, sending her sprawling.

"I said that?" He smiled as he dipped his dirty fingers in the milk and then licked them off.

"You said that," Nate told him. "I've figured it out since then, most of it at least. You worked for the survey crew that laid out the reservation, back in the summer of '85. Somebody got paid off that summer, and the stakes got moved a few miles west. I'm not saying it was you. But it was you showed up here a few years later, and it was you bought this place for a dollar."

Now the old man made a point of glancing about, his eyes going from the rocks above the creek to the high ridge to the north. "You alone this time?"

"I was alone last time."

Tuttle dipped his fingers again in the milk. "Who you working for?"

"Pardon?"

Looking up at Nate, the old man took more milk and in the process deposited a fly in his mouth. He spit it out. "Ain't nothin' free in this world," he said. "Hundred dollars a year was middlin' in '92, but it don't fetch much now."

Nate took a moment, thinking on it. "That's what Clayton pays you to stay shut up? Hundred a year?"

Tuttle stared steadily up at the porch, milk trickling down the stubble on his chin. The determined yellow cat was approaching again, this time coming up on the old man from behind.

"But what's he paying you for?" Nate pressed. "You gotta have more than just a story, or he'd of sent you packing from the start. His word against yours ain't exactly a dogfall. What do you have that Clayton's afraid of?"

"I asked you before who you're working for," Tuttle repeated.

"I'm not working for anybody."

"You're a damn liar. What's it to you, what stakes got put where? And why you nosing around, sneaking up on a body? I expect somebody's paying you. And if they're paying you, they're gonna be paying me. That's the size of it."

"Paying you for what?"

The yellow cat made her move again and this time the old man grabbed her by the scruff of her neck and flung her twenty feet from him. She hit the ground and rolled in the dust before scooting under the cabin to safety. Glancing up at Nate, the old man jerked his thumb over his shoulder, in the direction of the open range to the west.

"The original markers is still out there," he said. "Brass plates set in concrete. And I'm the one knows where they are."

Nate looked past the old man, toward the range he'd indicated. Tuttle cackled like a hen.

"Go ahead and look for 'em. They're set ground level, in a few thousand acres of sweet grass. Find yourself a needle in the haystack while you're at it, you dumb bastard."

Nate glanced back at the old man, squatting in the dirt, his filthy clothes hanging from him as he sucked the goat's milk from his fingers. There were more flies in the bucket now. Nate indicated the property around them.

"How'd you manage this?"

Tuttle laughed and milk spittle flew from his mouth. "So now you want my life story to boot. You take a long damn time to get to the matter at hand, and the matter at hand is money." He slurped more milk. "All right then, if that's the way you want it. I left here with Joe Simpson's crew for Idaho, the spring of '87. Few years later, I took me a fall off a bridge trestle, stove my back. Simpson paid me off, and poorly at that. I pissed it all away, what there was of it, and then I was flat. Only card I had left to play was this 'un."

"So you and young Clayton made a deal," Nate said.

The old man nodded vaguely at the memory. "He was a big noise, on some council or such with them that brung statehood. And he didn't want no trouble from me. Wasn't the land so much that worried him as it was his name. You're fixing to be somebody important, you gotta keep that name clean, you see?"

Now the old man stood. He stretched his back out a moment, his hands resting on his hips. He appeared pleased with himself, pleased with the circumstances of his day.

"But I always knowed you would show up," he went on. "Somebody like you. And I always knowed it would figure to my advantage when you did. Like I say, a hundred dollars covers mighty little now'days. I been giving this matter considerable thought since you was here last. This is my determination on that—you tell who you're working for and I'll show 'em the goddamn markers. The price is five thousand American dollars."

"Well," Nate said and that was all for the moment. Hearing about the markers, if the old man could be believed, had excited him. But the price tag had tempered that considerably. He couldn't lay his hands on a tenth of that money.

"You wouldn't want to show me just for the showing?" he asked.

"Do I look like a fool?"

"No, sir," Nate said. "But I thought maybe you'd like to do the right thing. You know, the Christian thing."

Tuttle scoffed. "What are you offering me—heaven? No thank you. I prefer the hard coin, if you don't mind. I got no interest in heaven." He smiled at Nate, showing the rotten brown stubs of his teeth. "I intend to live forever."

The rifle shot roared like a cannon and Nate watched as Tuttle's chest seemed to explode into pieces as the slug ripped through him from behind and thudded into the cabin wall. The old man was dead before his expression could change, before his legs left him and he pitched forward, landing on the bucket of milk, knocking it over in the dirt. He rolled onto his side and was still.

Nate jumped at the sound of the shot and ran off the porch to his left. He ducked down alongside the cabin wall and then a second shot sounded, ripping into the wood a few inches above his head. He turned and ran up the slope of the canyon, trying to keep the building between him and whoever was doing the shooting. He heard one more shot as he scrambled through the rocks and made his way to the mare. Mounting up, he galloped off to the south, his injured ribs jabbing him with each step the horse took. He put three miles between him and the old man's spread before he finally slowed the mare, blowing hard, and reined her to a halt.

Dismounting below the crest of a hill, he loosened the cinch under the mare and left her there, still heaving, while he walked back to the ridge for a look. It was open range before him, but there were swales and gulches deep enough to hide a rider. Nate watched for half an hour before he convinced himself he was not being pursued. When he walked back to the mare he gave her some water from his canteen, tightened the cinch, and set out again. As he rode south he kept turning in the saddle to watch behind him. Somewhere back there was a devil on the loose.

Thirty-Three

Young Donnelly was on the flat below the line shack, and he was afoot, working the roan filly on a long lead, turning as the horse circled around him at a trot. She was a pretty horse and she moved like she knew it—her head up, her pace quick and sassy. When Donnelly gave the rope a flick she broke into a canter smooth as silk.

Nate sat his horse on the bench a quarter mile away, watching for a time. He wouldn't interrupt the youngster at his work. It was late in the day, the shadows of the foothills stretching over the broad meadow where the cattle grazed, the animals spread out along the flat until they were out of sight. Nate rolled a cigarette and smoked as he watched Donnelly and the filly. He was suddenly and unexpectedly jealous of the young cowboy—of his simple life, and his youth, and his innocence. Nate must have been that way himself at one time, but he couldn't remember it being so. It seemed there was always trouble around him, sometimes of his own design and sometimes not, from the time he'd left the family farm in Missouri to this very day, when he had just a few hours earlier watched a dirty hermit being assassinated in his own yard. Not only had Nate watched it, he in all likelihood had caused it.

As Nate smoked the cigarette down, Donnelly led the filly back to the corral behind the cabin and loosed her inside where his saddle horse stood, its head over the top rail. The boy went into the shack. By the time Nate eased the mare down the slope and through the shallow creek, there was smoke rising from the rusty pipe above the roof. Nate stopped a hundred feet from the door and helloed the house.

The young cowboy was about to fry up some trout he'd caught earlier and he invited Nate to supper. They ate the fish along with some brown beans and hardtack the boy had made a few days earlier. It wasn't until they had their fill and were sitting outside, drinking coffee, that Nate told the young cowboy about the incident at Tuttle's spread.

"Good golly. Are you certain the old man was dead?"

"I've never been more certain of anything," Nate said.

"You never saw the man who shot him?"

"I didn't stick around for an introduction," Nate said. "He was looking to do for me as he did for old Tuttle. So I lit out."

Donnelly sipped from the tin cup. "And you figure it was because you were asking about that survey you mentioned?"

Nate nodded. "The old man told me about the markers and five minutes later he was dead in the dirt. If those two things aren't connected, it's the biggest damn coincidence since Noah built himself that boat right before the rain started."

"You think the man heard you then?" Donnelly asked. "I mean the man with the rifle."

"I doubt that," Nate said. "The shot came from up on the ridge. I suspect he made his own conclusions before he started shooting."

A coyote called from the foothills and Donnelly turned in his chair. He removed his hat and held it up against the setting sun while he searched for the animal, concerned for the stock.

"Coyote," Nate said. "He's no threat."

Donnelly kept looking a while longer before dropping his hat. "What will you do now?"

"I wish I knew the answer to that. I do know one thing—I'm gonna keep my head down for a time until I figure some things out. So far I have been set upon in a saloon by thugs and shot at by somebody who has no qualms about killing. I'm beginning to take it personal."

Donnelly nodded at that but had no comment. Nate took a drink of the boy's coffee, which had gotten somewhat better over the weeks. He realized now that there was something off about the youngster; he seemed down in the dumps and had said little while they ate. Usually a cowboy shunted up to a line shack for the season welcomed company like the coming of spring. Nate drank the last of the coffee and set the cup on the arm of the chair. He stood up, indicating the corral.

"I saw you working that filly earlier. A fine-looking animal. You have your saddle on her yet?"

"Not yet," Donnelly said. "I've been delinquent in working her. Today's the first I even had a rope on her since a week Sunday."

Nate walked over to the corral for a closer look and Donnelly followed. The roan moved to meet them; she sniffed at Nate and then pulled her head away. Behind them, Nate's mare sounded her opinion of the meeting.

"You got that chestnut jealous," Nate told the filly. He looked at Donnelly. "I hear you're making a present of this horse to your girl."

"That was my intent. No more."

So that was it, Nate thought. He knew the boy was out of sorts and he should have realized there was a woman involved. With a cowboy that age, there wasn't much—other than the loss of a woman or a good horse—that could take the starch out of him. He could drop a month's wages in a poker game and still wake up the next morning on the sunny side of things. But the heart—that was another matter.

"Well, what happened?"

"I wish I could say," Donnelly replied. "We seemed to be getting on just fine. She would ride up here of a Sunday and pass the day."

"She bring you preserves?"

"A cherry pie one time," Donnelly said. "First time she came, I told her the filly was hers as soon as I got her broke to saddle. She squealed like a little girl. You'd of thought I gave her the moon." He fell quiet for a time. "Then a week ago Sunday we met in a little spot we have, in a stand of pine trees on her father's ranch. Well, she didn't stay but twenty minutes. Said she had to get home for some do."

"Maybe she did," Nate said. "Women are awful fond of their teas and lunches and such. It's a mystery."

Donnelly shook his head. "That wasn't all. She told me that day she didn't want the filly. Said she couldn't accept it because that would mean we had between us a commitment. That was the word she used."

"I've heard that word myself on occasion," Nate admitted. "Although I don't recall ever using it."

The young cowboy exhaled heavily. The filly came close to him and put her nose out. Donnelly ran his hand across her forehead. "I can't help but wonder if she would have kept this filly if it wasn't given to her by somebody who's part Indian."

"How long you known this gal?" Nate asked.

"Going on a year."

"And you figure she's just noticing now that you got some Indian blood?"

Donnelly glanced over. "I suspect not." His eyes returned to the horse in the corral, as if the animal might explain to him the mysteries of the feminine mind.

"I'm just going to tell you something that you won't want to believe right now but that you'll one day find out is true," Nate said after watching the boy a moment. "And that is there's more than one woman in the world."

And Nate was right. Donnelly did not want to believe it, and he would not believe it, not until life took a hand and showed him it was so. There was nothing but time for that. (Nate wasn't sure he believed it himself, however.) The boy did manage a smile though, as if showing his appreciation for the effort, and he seemed to pull himself out of the depths, if only a little.

"You'll pass the night?" he asked.

In less than an hour it would be full dark. Under ordinary circumstances Nate would be more than happy to spend the night. It meant a roof over his head and besides that, he enjoyed the boy's company. He was of the opinion that he was going to make a good man, once he figured certain things out.

But Nate didn't know the whereabouts of the assassin who had killed Tuttle. Maybe he was trailing Nate and maybe he wasn't. If he was, Nate was not about to put Donnelly in his path, although he realized he may have done that already by stopping for supper. Either way, he knew he had to make tracks. He doubted the young cowboy's life would mean any more to the man than had Tuttle's.

"I believe I'll move on," he told the boy. "I was wondering if you could spare some beans and a little bacon? I might not see a town for a spell."

"You're welcome to stay."

"I know it and it's appreciated. Another time."

Nate saddled the mare while Donnelly went into the cabin for the food. He also brought a spare blanket, having seen Nate was without. Nate tied the blanket behind his saddle and tucked the provisions in his jacket. When he was in the saddle, he nodded toward the corral.

"You know, the girl that does get that filly is going to be a lucky woman."

Donnelly smiled uncertainly at the notion. A thought came to him then.

"Hold on." He went into the cabin and returned a moment later, carrying a Winchester rifle. "You'd better take this. In case that man is after you."

Nate shook his head. "You need to hang onto that. I don't know that he won't show up here. If he does, you haven't seen me and you've never heard of me. Don't connect yourself to me, you understand?"

"How would I know him?" Donnelly asked.

Nate gestured toward the rifle in the boy's hands. "One thing, he won't be toting no thirty caliber. He shot old Tuttle with a Buffalo gun of some sort. Spencer or Sharps would be my guess. You'll know him by that. And don't you be careless with him if he does show. He so much as touches that rifle, you shoot the sonofabitch first and worry about it later."

Donnelly nodded, uneasy at the suggestion.

"I don't expect you'll see him," Nate said to quiet the boy's mind. "But take extra caution if you do."

He reined the chestnut mare in a half circle and rode off. After splashing through the creek and moving up the slope beyond, he stopped and looked back. Donnelly was still standing where he had left him, watching. When Nate held up his hand, he lifted his hat above his head and waved back.

Nate rode west into the foothills. The dark came on quickly when the sun fell below the foothills and he kept the mare to a walk, fearful of gopher holes. It took him three hours to reach Turtle Creek and another half hour to climb to the ruined Covington line shack on the flat above. The moon was up by then and he could see his way, spotting the derelict building from below the plateau. As he drew near, he noted none of Covington's hands had been there to repair the cabin. He was happy for that; it meant that the place was still empty. He'd seen no stock on the way; he guessed the summer range was not being used.

Near the cabin, he stripped the saddle from the mare and hobbled her on the creek flat, where there was ample graze for the animal. He broke up some dead cottonwood limbs and once he had a fire going inside the shack he heated some beans and cooked two thick slices of bacon. He ate at the table, by the faint light of the moon coming through the broken window pane. Afterward he went outside and smoked, looking eastward, toward the Covington ranch. The night was clear enough that he could see the lights of the buildings and those of Cut Bank too, twenty miles in the distance.

He smoked the cigarette down and thought about what he should do. He was pretty damn certain it had been Covington's foreman who had shot Tuttle. He'd been the one who had seen Nate talking to the old hermit earlier and Nate knew the man to carry a large bore Sharps.

He was just as certain that Garner would shoot him if given the chance. Nate was not obliged to give it to him and that was enough right there to instruct him as to what he should do next. *Vamos*, as the Mexican cowboys down around the Rio Grande used to say. They would yell it at the beginning of a drive, and their women would shout back *vaya con dios*. Some of those vaqueros could cowboy. They grew up on horseback and they had no fear. Nate had buried one of them in Kansas in '77, after he rode his horse off a cliff during a stampede. They found him under the dead horse, his neck snapped, his head turned around backward.

Nate rolled another Bull Durham and lit up. A day's ride and he could be in Canada. He doubted anyone would follow him there. In fact, those in pursuit would probably be content knowing he had left the country. What had them stirred up were the questions about the survey. Well, they'd taken care of at least a part of that problem when they killed old Tuttle. He wouldn't be telling any stories to anybody now, not in this world anyway.

It was true that Nate still had the story but it was secondhand at best. He knew about the markers but he didn't know where they were. If he could somehow find them, then he could turn the information over to young Samuels from the *Chronicle*. Once the

newspapers got hold of the story, there would be nothing Clayton
or his foreman could do about it. Even a man with a buffalo gun
was no match for the press. But how could Nate find the markers?
It was like the old man said; finding a needle in a haystack.

He really didn't think that Garner was presently tracking him.
He doubted the man was capable of it for one thing. It was an art,
tracking a man across open range; there were few who could do
it well in the old days and there would be even fewer today, in a
world where men like Harry and Clayton rode around in stinking
loud motorcars. One of those contraptions would be easy enough
to track; a blind man could do it.

No, it seemed unlikely that the foreman was on his trail. But
that didn't mean that it would be wise for Nate to show up in
town, or within ten miles of the Covington ranch. He'd already
had two run-ins with men working for Clayton, the second one
involving gunplay. If nothing else, Nate could take a hint.

After smoking the second cigarette he stubbed it beneath the
toe of his boot and went inside. He spread the blanket young
Donnelly had given him on the cot and rolled himself in it. He lay
awake for a time, looking at the moonlight where it came through
the roof, and thinking about Canada.

Thirty-Four

WHEN SAMUELS ARRIVED AT THE *Chronicle* office the next
morning, Angus was already there, standing at the back of
the room, brewing the first of what would be a half dozen pots of
tea over the course of the day. Samuels sat at his desk and told his
boss about the discrepancies in the dates on the survey. When he
had heard the story, Angus turned from the steeping pot, his bushy
eyebrows rising.

"Well," he said and he didn't say anything else for a moment.
He poured tea for both men and walked over to hand Samuels a
cup before sitting down at his own desk. He blew gently on the hot
brew before taking a tentative sip.

"And what reason were you given for the discrepancies?" he
asked.

"None."

"Who were you dealing with?" Angus asked.

"A fellow named Henderson," Samuels said. "He's been at the
job for over ten years and claims he's never seen this before."

"He's never seen it before," Angus repeated, sipping the tea. "I
don't suppose there's anyone there with firsthand knowledge of
the filing?"

Samuels shook his head. "I did ask. I was told that a survey could be revised but the revision would be noted in the file. For this, we have the mismatch on the dates and that's it."

"That is something though, isn't it?" Angus said. "All right, it's time for you to talk to Clayton Covington about this. And this old fellow Tuttle as well. The senator seems to be up from Helena for the week, he's been seen tooling about in his new motorcar." He hesitated, thinking on it. "But talk to Tuttle first. We would be loath to tip Clayton off and then have him get to Tuttle before you do. He might influence the man's thinking."

Samuels nodded. "Of course we know what Clayton will say. That he wasn't involved in the survey and that he knows nothing about it."

"I suspect he will," Angus replied. "That's when you quit addressing him as Mr. Covington and begin addressing him as Senator. This newspaper is investigating a land swindle that just happens to concern his district. It has to be of interest to him, whether it involves his property or that of someone else. He can't ignore it. He can ignore us, but the bigger papers will pick up on it, and there will be questions, especially in a gubernatorial race."

"And the fact remains that he did sell Tuttle that property for a song," Samuels said. "Why?"

"Why indeed?" Angus repeated. He smiled. "You're about to have a busy week, Willis."

Samuels stood. "First off, I need to find Nate Cooper. I need directions to Tuttle's place."

"Cooper's staying at the Longley ranch, isn't he?"

Samuels took his watch from his pocket. "I might catch up to him there. It's too early in the day to find him at a saloon or billiard parlor."

"Finish your tea, lad," Angus told him. "We're not barbarians."

Samuels drank his tea and then walked to the livery and rented a rig. He started for the Longley ranch as the morning sun cleared the buildings in town. The roads were mostly dry now, although occasionally he was forced to skirt around a mud hole, bouncing the rig over the rough prairie. Samuels had grown up in a small town; he was a green hand with horses and had yet to get accustomed to driving a buggy. He preferred a seasoned horse; the one he'd been assigned today was on the skittish side. It was an hour's drive to the Longley ranch.

Harry Longley was in the yard washing down his motorcar which, by the looks of it, had managed to find one of the mud holes Samuels had avoided. The axles were caked in muck, the fenders splattered. Pulling up in the rig, Samuels didn't see Rose at first and then he did. She was off to the south side of the big barn, hoeing a garden where a few green sprouts were showing. Seeing him, she left the hoe in the dirt and started over, removing her leather gloves as she did.

"Mr. Samuels," she said. "How are you today?"

"Fine, fine," Samuels said. He was aware that Harry was watching him with interest and, quite possibly, disdain. It was the first Samuels had actually been to the ranch and he suddenly felt like an interloper.

"What can we do for you?" Rose asked.

"I was looking for Nate Cooper," Samuels said.

"We haven't seen Mr. Cooper for a couple of days," Rose said. She would make no mention of the row between Harry and Nate. "Mr. Cooper is a bit of a rambler."

Having heard, Harry started over. "What's he done now?"

"He hasn't done anything," Samuels said. "Well—there was an altercation in the Bighorn the other night, but he was not an instigator. I was there and witnessed it."

"What kind of altercation?" Rose asked. "Was he hurt?"

"He is some beat up, although I doubt he'll admit it. He was set upon by a couple of men."

"Is that where you got that eye?" Rose asked.

Samuels put his hand to his face. He kept forgetting he had the black eye, which was strange, considering it was his badge of honor. "It was," he admitted.

"You boys do like to play rough," Rose said. "What was the fight about?"

"Apparently these two were not happy about the fact that Mr. Cooper had been talking to Briscoe Tuttle."

"Tuttle?" Harry snorted. "What's anybody want with that old toad?"

"It seems he might have information about the reservation survey from back in '85."

Harry's face grew red. "That goddamn survey again. I told Nate to leave that alone. And leave the goddamn Blackfoot alone while he was at it."

"Hold on," Rose said sharply. She turned to Samuels. "Who were the men in the Bighorn?"

Samuels hesitated, just now realizing he was obliged to name Rose's brother. "Well ma'am, they work for Senator Covington."

"Cowboys?" she asked.

"Mr. Cooper said that they didn't qualify as that."

Harry began to mumble under his breath. Samuels realized he was getting sidetracked.

"I came to ask Mr. Cooper if he could give me directions to Tuttle's goat farm. I want to get his side of the story."

"You need to leave well enough alone," Harry told him. "Nobody cares about your survey, nor the damn Indians neither. Leave it."

"You don't tell Mr. Samuels his job," Rose said calmly. She turned to the reporter. "I can show you the way."

"The hell you will," Harry said.

Rose ignored him. "I'll just be a minute." She started for the house.

Samuels was forced to stand under Harry's glare while he waited. He made a show of admiring the property—the house and the barns, the horses milling in the corral. When he looked back at Harry, the glare hadn't diminished. Samuels was obliged to cast about for a topic of conversation.

"That was a welcome rain last week—" he began.

"What in Jesus' name is going on around here?" Harry demanded. "I have had enough of this. Everything is upside down." He turned to walk toward his motorcar, then stopped and came back. "What do you know about Nate Cooper anyway?"

"I can't say I know him well," Samuels said.

"I can," Harry said. "He's a troublemaker and he's never been nothing but that. You'll find out soon enough, following him around. You keep poking a hornet's nest, boy, and see where it lands you."

Harry walked away and once more applied himself to the cleaning of his automobile. When Rose came out of the house, ready to travel, he never glanced her way.

Rose knew that Tuttle had a cart and a mule that he drove into town three or four times a year so she reckoned that the old cattle trail that led to his place would be passable in the rig Samuels had rented. Leaving the ranch Samuels suggested that she take the reins so he could make notes along the way. Rose, sensing that the youngster was ill at ease handling the buggy, had agreed.

The rough road passed within a half mile of the Covington ranch house, dipping through a swale to come up just west of the place. Glancing over as they crested the ridge, Rose noticed a gathering of men around the bunkhouse. She pulled the rig to a stop.

"How's your eyesight, Mr. Samuels?" she asked. "What do you see down there?"

Samuels turned in the seat for a look. "Bunch of men standing around a buckboard. I'd say that's the senator in the dark suit."

"Look at the mule, off to the right. Is that a pack across its back?"

Samuels squinted, holding his hand out against the high sun. He took his time deciding. "No, ma'am. That appears to be a body."

Whatever conversation was being made around the bunkhouse came to a sudden halt when Rose drove the rig into the yard. She barely glanced at her brother as she reined the buggy to a stop alongside the pack mule. Ed Garner stood a few feet away, staring at her, his ugly broad face pinched as if he had a pain somewhere. Among the other hands, Samuels had pointed out Munson and Ballinger to Rose as they had driven through the front gates.

"The pair from the Bighorn," he'd said.

Rose got out of the buggy to have a look at the body draped over the mule's back. The man's threadbare coveralls were black with dried blood and bluebottle flies were thick on the wound, buzzing loudly. She didn't have to see the face to know who it was.

"What's going on here?" she asked.

"Murder," she heard Clayton say from behind her. "That's what's going on."

Samuels stepped down from the rig now as well. "Is this Briscoe Tuttle?"

"It is," Clayton said, walking over. "Or it was." He spoke to Garner. "You might as well head into town and fetch Henry Pearce. Looks like we're going to need an old-fashioned posse."

"What happened?" Rose asked.

"He was shot by Nate Cooper," Clayton said.

"That's a lie," she told him.

At that, Ballinger sauntered over. His stare fixed on Rose, he stood on Clayton's flank, his upper lip pulled back over his teeth like a dog protecting its master. Rose took note of both the sneer and the Colt revolver on his hip.

Clayton, having been called a liar in front of his employees, gave Rose a long look and then waved his hand as if dismissing her before turning back to the hands.

"Let's get this man off the mule."

"I said that's a lie," Rose repeated.

Clayton turned. "Why are you even here?"

Samuels interjected before Rose could reply. "What happened?"

Clayton looked at him. "I'll just tell you what happened. Briscoe Tuttle has always kind of kept an eye on the stock for me, watching for strays or whatever. It gave the old man something to do. It's common knowledge that Cooper's been stealing cattle and selling them to the Blackfoot. Harry Longley can verify that. Looks as if old Tuttle caught Cooper in the act and confronted him. So Cooper shot him dead, plain and simple. My foreman heard the shot. When he showed up, Cooper made a run for it and got away." Clayton paused. "For the time being anyway."

Samuels moved forward for a closer look at the body. "You say he confronted Cooper? This man's been shot in the back."

"Well, that's the kind of man Cooper is," Clayton said. "You know his history. You wrote that fanciful story about him. Briscoe Tuttle never harmed a fly."

"I expect he'll be a saint by sundown," Samuels said. "Is that why you sold him that farm for a dollar?"

Clayton hesitated, glancing quickly at Rose and then away as he formed a reply. The question had clearly taken him by surprise. "That was a favor to the old man. He was squatting out there any- way and I didn't have the heart to run him off. It worked out pretty well for me because, as I say, he would keep an eye on things. Until today, that is."

Samuels stepped nearer to Clayton. "You're saying there was no arrangement between the two of you because of information he might have had regarding the reservation survey."

Clayton frowned. "Tuttle had information about the survey that you're so fascinated with? What kind of information?"

Rose could almost admire her brother's ability to lie so easily, and so convincingly. He wasn't persuading her of anything though, and neither was he impressing young Samuels.

"That's something I intended to ask him," Samuels replied. "Today, in fact."

"Go ahead and ask him," Ballinger said.

The suggestion drew laughter from some of the men. Ballinger preened, basking in it. Rose stared at him for a moment, wondering why her brother would hire a man like that. He was no cowboy.

And it was rare to see anyone, other than a lawman, carrying a handgun these days.

"Looks to me like you missed your chance, young man," Clayton told Samuels. "A day late and a dollar short, as they say. Maybe old Gibson ought to use that as the masthead for his newspaper."

"Let's go," Rose said, having heard enough.

Samuels nodded. He'd gotten all he was going to from Clayton and it didn't amount to beans. He climbed into the rig. As Rose flicked the reins, Clayton stepped in front of the horse and held it by the cheek piece.

"Mr. Samuels," he said. "With regards to these incessant survey questions. It seems that you're bird-dogging a story that doesn't exist. A story you got from Nate Cooper. Thirty years ago, Cooper was a rustler and a murderer. And today he's both those things once again. Shouldn't you be writing *that* story?"

Thirty-Five

HARRY SAT AT THE BIG OAK desk in his study, drinking bourbon and going over the figures from the previous year's beef sales. He had read them before and there was no reason to do so again but the numbers had a calming effect, reassuring him that all was right with his world, even as certain events might suggest otherwise.

He heard the slap of the reins and the creak of the harness as the rig came into the yard and then he heard Rose's voice as she said something to Samuels. The horse and buggy moved off almost immediately, a squeaking wheel indicating its departure. The front door opened and a few seconds later Rose was in the room. She was worked up, her face flush.

"We have to find Nate," she said. "Somebody killed old Tuttle and he's being fitted for it."

Harry looked up from his papers. He took a drink as he considered the news. "Who's doing the fitting?"

"Clayton," Rose said. "Saddle two horses. I'll change my clothes and get some grub together."

She went upstairs and changed into trousers and a shirt, then went down to the kitchen and packed saddlebags with biscuits and cheese and some roast beef from the ice box. As she filled a canteen she looked out the window, expecting to see Harry by the barn with the horses. She heard a noise and turned to see him standing behind her in the doorway, the refilled whiskey glass in hand.

"You going to saddle those horses?" she asked.

He stared at her, saying nothing, his breath rising and falling heavily. The saddlebags over her shoulder, she walked past him and into the front room. When she returned, carrying a Winchester .44-40, he was sitting at the table with his drink. She stopped and looked at him for a long moment before she spoke.

"Fine," she said. "I'll go by myself."

"You're not going anywhere."

"But I am."

Harry slammed his hand on the table with such force his glass jumped, sloshing rye over the rim. "How do you know he's innocent, Rose? How do you know what he's capable of? He's killed men before, what makes you think this is different? You think you know him?"

"Yes. I know him."

"You knew him for a short time thirty years ago," Harry said. "And you know where he's been those years since. He's a goddamn stranger, Rose. We'll let the law handle it."

"For Christ sakes, Harry. The law is Henry Pearce. He'll handle what my brother tells him to handle. I'm going after him."

Harry came out of the chair and grabbed her roughly by the arm, pulling her toward him. Rose slapped him across the face and when he wouldn't let go, she hit him again, harder this time. Harry stepped backward, stunned.

"Neither one of us ever bossed the other," she said. "We won't start now." She turned again for the door.

"Leave it be! What the devil are you thinking?"

She stopped in the doorway, looking out toward the barn. "He'd do it for you, Harry," she said without turning. "He'd do it for you in a heartbeat."

She walked out, saddlebags in one hand and the rifle beneath her arm. She led the buckskin Daisy from the corral and gave her a measure of oats as she saddled the animal. She wanted the horse well nourished; she had no idea how long she would be gone and only a faint hunch as to where she was going. After tightening the cinch, she tied the saddlebags on and shoved the Winchester in the scabbard.

Harry came out of the house as she mounted up. He must have been watching her from inside. Maybe he'd been waiting for her to change her mind but after all these years he should have known better. He walked toward her and stopped maybe twenty feet away. She sat there in silence, reins in hand, waiting for him to say he was coming with her. Waiting for him to be the man he'd always been. Or maybe she was waiting for him to be the man he used to be.

"Don't come back," he told her. "If you go, don't come back."

And he turned and walked to the house.

It was Sheriff Henry Pearce's posse in name only. Clayton was in charge. There were five men in all, setting out from the Covington ranch. When they got to Tuttle's farm, Clayton and Garner sat their horses in the yard while Pearce wandered about the property and Munson and Ballinger went inside the house. The old man's goats and his mule, grown thirsty no doubt, had escaped the flimsy corral and were grazing in the grass along the creek. A few brown hens were scattered in the yard, running this way and that as they tried to keep out of the paths of the visitors. When the men had arrived, a dozen cats were lounging on the porch boards in front of the shack. They slipped beneath the building when Ballinger and Munson approached.

Pearce had taken his sweet time arriving at the ranch from town and it was late afternoon by the time they reached the hermit's spread. They wouldn't accomplish much before nightfall. Both Clayton and Garner knew it to be an exercise in futility coming there, but they were the only ones in possession of those facts. Pearce had insisted that he see the crime scene, as he deemed it.

Clayton had no intention of getting down from his horse. He hadn't been to the farm in ten years or more. The old man had smelled and was a miserable being in general. After their arrangement was made in '92, Clayton had wanted nothing more to do with him. It was strange how things worked out; instead of being a liability the old man now just might help to rid Clayton of the small problem that was Nate Cooper and the bigger problem that was the survey. Looking at the pool of dark congealed blood in the dirt, he turned to Garner, speaking softly.

"Where was Cooper?"

"Sitting in that rocker on the porch," Garner said.

"Cooper's on the porch and the old man was in the yard," Clayton said. He paused. "Seems opposite of what you might expect."

Garner shrugged. Before he could make a reply, Munson walked out of the house, carrying a bureau drawer, which he proceeded to dump onto the ground. A few scraps of paper fluttered about.

"What's all that?" Clayton asked Garner, his voice still low.

"I went through it before," Garner said. "Nothing there. Whatever information the old man had, it was in his head."

Clayton nodded, pulling his watch from his vest pocket. "We'll allow Henry to think he's doing something a bit longer. Let him play detective."

Ballinger came out of the house, gnawing on a stringy length of jerky. "What are we supposed to be looking for anyway?"

"Clues," Henry Pearce told him. Having looked inside the brush corral, he was standing in the middle of the yard now. His pants were hitched high and he wore his holster, with the heavy Colt semi-automatic, on a belt around his thick waist.

"What clues do you need?" Ballinger laughed. "One, you got a dead man and two, you know who done it. Why ain't we after him?"

"We will be," Pearce said. "Soon enough."

Ballinger shook his head to show his impatience. "Can't be soon enough for me. I got a score to settle with that old sonofabitch." He tore a piece of jerky from the strip. "I will tell you one thing," he said absently. "Goat jerky tastes a lot like beef jerky."

"Let's get them out of here," Clayton said to Garner and he nudged his horse forward to address Pearce. "Late in the day to head up country and we're poorly provided for, Henry. We'll go back to the ranch, make a fresh start at first light. And we'll bring this man to justice."

Pearce made a pretense of considering this before nodding his agreement. Clayton turned in the saddle to point behind him.

"Henry, you take the two hands and swing back along the ridge there, look for sign. Ed and I will head down the other side, see what we can turn up. We'll see you back at the ranch by nightfall."

The sheriff mounted up and the two men followed suit, Ballinger still complaining about what he saw as their inaction. Clayton waited until they were out of earshot before turning to Garner.

"We have no idea what that old man might have told him."

"No, sir," Garner said. "But they was sure enough talking. Back and forth for some time, and I kindly doubt it was about the weather, or the price of eggs at market."

"I doubt it, too."

The cats began to make their way from beneath the house again, coming out tentatively, watching the two men in the yard. Soon they scrambled back onto the porch. A large calico, missing one eye, climbed on the rocker and sat there on its haunches, cleaning itself.

"We need to err on the side of caution," Clayton said. "We have to assume that Cooper knows too much. And it appears he's all of a sudden cheek to jowl with our friends at the local newspaper."

"On the other hand, he might be gone," Garner said. "He was running hard last I seen him, heading south. He could be halfway to Colorado by now."

"No, he won't run. If Tuttle told him anything, he'll want to take it to the newspaper. But he's already been beaten up and shot at. He'll be wary about showing up in town. But he might take it to the reservation."

"I wish he would," Garner said. "That way we could settle everybody's hash." He gestured south. "I still think he lit out."

Clayton shook his head. "He's too proud to run. He might not have a pot to piss in but he's got his pride. Maybe not having a pot to piss in is what makes him that way. All he's left with is pride." He glanced at Garner. "Not that it's worth anything. He's a dinosaur. He's extinct and he doesn't know it."

It was nearly a two-hour ride back to the ranch. They kept to the high ground and neither man said much. Approaching the buildings from the south they could see Henry Pearce, riding in from the west with Ballinger and Munson. There were a few hundred yearling steers spread out on the range below where Clayton and Garner were riding. Clayton reined in and sat there for a long moment, thinking.

"Take Ballinger and Munson, and a couple mules," he said. "Kill three or four steers, skin them out and have the boys dump the hides on the reservation. Tell them to swing around to the south and come in from behind. Hide them in a gully or a sinkhole or whatever."

Garner required a few moments to put it together. "But don't hide 'em too good?"

Clayton nodded. "Henry Pearce is going to need a reason to go onto the reservation. Rustling is as good as any. If we happen upon the man that killed poor old Tuttle in the process, then that's just our good luck."

Thirty-Six

R OSE CLIMBED ALL AFTERNOON, POINTING THE buckskin mare southwest. For the first hour or more Harry was on her mind and she found herself turning in the saddle constantly to look at the ground she'd covered, thinking she would see him riding to catch up, even though in her heart she knew it wasn't going to be so. The look he had given her before walking back to the house had assured her of that.

By late afternoon she was riding across the Covington range. She skirted a few miles to the south to keep out of sight of the ranch house, and she watched the countryside in the distance for signs of Clayton and his posse, as he had called it. Growing up, Rose had often heard of posses, romantic and possibly apocryphal tales of honest citizens out chasing down desperados. Rose had always considered a posse to be on the side of the law. She didn't have that opinion of this one, not with it being made up of Henry Pearce and whatever thugs her brother might have recruited.

It was an hour before dark when she arrived at the meandering lower banks of Turtle Creek. As she got closer she began to doubt her instincts. He wouldn't be there and if it turned out he wasn't, she had no notion as to where he might have gone. Considering

257

that, she presently had a frightening thought. What if he was already dead? What if whoever shot Tuttle had killed Nate too, and Clayton's little manhunt was just a charade, part of the set up? They'd ride around for a couple of days and then come back, saying he'd slipped past them, all the time knowing he was buried in the foothills somewhere.

As she rode south along the creek flat, the story grew in Rose's mind until she could hardly stand to think about it. Kicking the buckskin into a lope, she rode the animal hard for a mile or so, following the winding stream up the slope. As the horse began to tire beneath her, she rounded a bend in the creek and came upon the abandoned line shack. There, hobbled outside, was Nate's chestnut mare.

Rose's heart nearly burst.

She reined in, her pulse still racing. A thin plume of smoke drifted from the chimney pipe, disappearing into the dusk. And then Nate walked around the side of the shack, carrying an armful of dead tree limbs. Intent on his task, he didn't see her at first, and then he did. He continued on to the front of the cabin, watching her all the while. There he stopped and smiled.

"I hope you remembered the strawberry preserves."

"You're going to have to settle for a fifth of rye."

Nate dropped the firewood outside the door. "Well, I'm told a beggar can't be choosy. Why don't you climb down?"

They sat outside the line shack, on rickety backless chairs from inside, and drank rye from the bottle while they ate the biscuits and cheese Rose had brought with her. The buckskin grazed alongside the mare on the flat below them. Rose's saddle and saddlebags were on the top rail of the corral, or what was left of it. She had finished telling Nate what she had ridden all day to tell him and he had been sitting quietly since.

"How'd you know I'd be here?" he finally asked.

"You're getting predictable in your old age."

"I am?"

Rose smiled. "No. That's the one thing you're not."

Nate reached for the bottle and had a drink. "So I shot old Tuttle, did I? How'd I manage that without a gun?"

"They're not concerned with minor details," Rose said. "They'll tailor the story to fit. Garner claims he saw you, right after you did the deed."

"Well, somebody saw me," Nate said. "Because whoever shot that old man was shooting at me too, with a damn buffalo gun. Just lucky for me I'm so spry or I'd be in the dirt with old Tuttle."

"Garner carries a Sharps," Rose said.

"I know it."

"He likes to brag on his marksmanship. Competes in the fall fair in town."

Nate shook his head. "Well, there was nothing fair about how they shot that old man. He might have been a sour apple and a bottom dealer but I can't say he deserved back-shooting."

"That reminds me," Rose said. She got up and walked to the saddlebags to retrieve the Smith & Wesson .44 she'd brought along, then pulled the Winchester from the scabbard and brought both rifle and pistol over and handed them to Nate.

"I figured you'd best be armed at this point," she said. "It was them started the shooting."

Nate slid the revolver from the holster and spun the cylinder to check the load before setting it and the rifle aside. He sat thinking it had been a long time since he'd fired a gun and then recalled that it wasn't so. He had visited that sonofabitch Willard a few weeks back and he had fired a shot that day. Strange that he'd practically forgotten it already. But he had killed varmints before in his life and never dwelled upon it afterward.

He looked over at Rose. She was taking a drink from the bottle, watching him. Goddamn, but didn't she ride all that way just to warn him? There wasn't another woman like her.

"Where's Harry in all this?" he asked.

"Nowhere," she said, capping the bottle. "He wouldn't come. And he's mad as hell that I did."

"Well, he's right to keep out of it," Nate said. "And he's right to advise you to do the same. It's my affair, Rose."

"I'll decide what's right for me. Harry can do what he wants." She paused, looking at him a long moment, eyes narrowed as she figured what to say. "Remember the first day you came back—when you didn't recognize him riding into the yard? Well, I have that problem myself these days. Recognizing him. And it's got nothing to do with his beard or the size of his belly. Was a time the two of you were like two sides of a coin. No wonder I couldn't choose between you." She paused again, now looking away from him. "Things change over the years, that's to be expected. The funny part—I never knew how different he was until you came back. It's like he's lost the best part of himself. He gets excited about things like motorcars these days. And brandy from France or wherever. And he always hated the rich ranchers—right up until he became one."

Nate looked at the capped rye bottle on the ground but he didn't reach for it. "Don't be too hard on him. You've made a good life together, the two of you. And like I said, he's a smart man to keep away from this mess here."

"Maybe he is," Rose admitted. "It just seems to me that . . . he was a better man when he was hungry."

"Hell, maybe we all are," Nate said, getting to his feet. "But it could be those good old days are only good when you're looking backward at them. I can recall plenty of times being cold and hungry and not liking it one damn bit." He gestured toward the shack. "Hell, I can recall freezing in there. Wet wood, chimney wouldn't draw."

"I can recall being real cozy in there," Rose told him.

"Well," Nate said hesitantly. "There was that too."

"You just blushed, Mr. Cooper."

"I don't believe I did."

"Maybe you just took a sudden sunburn." She smiled at him a moment before letting him off the hook. "Would you have the slightest notion what you're going to do next?"

Nate nodded. "I've been studying on it some, even more so since you told me what Clayton's got cooked up. I figure one trumped up murder conviction is about all I can handle in this lifetime."

"I can get you the best lawyer," Rose said. "The money's there."

"I appreciate that," Nate said. "I do. But I think the smart move might be to drift. Not that I have any reputation to speak of for making the smart move. Whatever the case, I need to put a few things straight first. I'll head to the reservation tomorrow. The Blackfoot need to hear what Tuttle told me. I'll trust young Samuels at the newspaper to keep the story alive. You might not know it to look at him, but the boy's got some sand." He paused, looking off to the west, to where the sun was just now dipping behind the mountains. "You want to spend money on a lawyer, hire one for the Indians. Maybe they'll get that range back. And then might be Clayton will have to forget about being governor."

Rose's mind was on the earlier statement. "Where will you go?"

"Canada."

"What's there?"

Nate shrugged and now reached for the bottle. "Plenty of ranches, I expect. There's cattle country up there in Alberta. I should be able to find a job." He smiled around the bottle neck. "Top hand like myself, right in my prime."

"I'll go with you."

Nate swallowed the whiskey. "Hold on now. You got yourself all wound up over this business with Clayton. You can't go with me, Rose."

"I can do whatever the hell I want."

"But that's just a theory," Nate said, getting to his feet. "Fact is, I was a poor choice thirty years ago and I'm a poorer one now. You've built yourself something, Rose. You can't just leave it behind on account of your brother's dirty dealings. Hell, that'd be like letting him beat you."

"I don't care about Clayton," she said. "You think I'm doing this for you but you're wrong. I'm doing it for me. It's hard for me to explain but I'm feeling like I did when I was twenty-two years old, when you and Harry first came out here. I was excited by you, and I don't mean purely by what goes on between a man and a woman. I was excited because I felt like I was living a life. I would wake up every morning wondering what would happen next. Do you have any idea how long it's been since I felt that way?"

"I expect that's just life though," Nate said. "That's what twenty-two feels like."

"But I feel like it again," she persisted. "I am astonished that I do. And I want to keep feeling that way, for as long as I can. So let's go to Canada, Nate Cooper. Let's live our lives."

Nate shook his head. "We can't do that to Harry."

"Harry's made his choices," Rose said. "He wouldn't come with me today. He was the one that turned away first. I don't want to hurt him, but I need to make choices of my own." She stood now as well, moving closer to him and taking the rye from his hand. She sipped from the bottle, watching him.

"You're the confoundest woman I ever met," Nate said.

"I'm not trying to be."

Nate exhaled, turning from her. He stood looking at the old shack. "You got no idea how many times I've been here over the years. I guess in prison everybody's got a place they go to. In their head anyway. Locked inside those walls, this is where I would come. I could see that cabin, and I could hear the creek running. I could taste those strawberry preserves and that fresh baked bread."

"What else?" Rose asked.

"Everything," Nate said quietly. "Every single thing."

Rose capped the bottle. She put her hand behind his neck and kissed him on the mouth. "Go inside and stoke the fire. I'll be right behind you."

Thirty-Seven

OVER BREAKFAST THE NEXT MORNING CLAYTON informed
Nancy she would be heading back to Helena on the noon
train. He said that a ranch hand named Fields would take her into
town after they had eaten and she had time to pack her things.

"Why am I being dismissed?" she asked.

"You are not being dismissed," Clayton smiled. "But I'm sure
the mail at the office is piled as high as the windowsill. I need you
there. I'll be joining you as soon as I tend to some matters here."

"You're referring to this manhunt," Nancy said.

Clayton, pouring coffee for both of them, nodded.

"How can you be so certain that Cooper is the guilty party?" she
asked.

"I am not certain. That is for a judge and jury to decide. But my
foreman saw him at the scene of a murder and furthermore he saw
him running away from that scene, looking guilty as Judas Iscariot.
Sheriff Henry Pearce has issued a warrant for his arrest based on that."

Nancy reached for the coffee. "Why do you need to be involved?"

"It's a big job, tracking a man in country like this," Clayton told
her. "And just between you and me, Henry Pearce is not exactly
Allan Pinkerton."

"And what if Nate Cooper is not the guilty party?"

"Then he will go free," Clayton said. "And we will endeavor to find the real assassin." He paused. "You are aware that he has killed unarmed men in the past, are you not?"

"He claims otherwise."

"Do you believe everything you read in the newspaper?"

Before Nancy could respond they heard boots on the porch outside and then a knock at the door. Clayton went over and opened it to Ed Garner. The foreman was about to speak when he saw Nancy at the table.

"Ready to ride?" Clayton asked.

"Just waiting on the sheriff," Garner said.

"He'll be moving at a snail's pace, per usual." Clayton hesitated before looking over at Nancy. "You can get your things together, my dear. I need to talk to Ed a moment."

"Dismissed again," Nancy said smiling.

She got to her feet and headed for the back stairs. Clayton watched as she ascended, thinking of the conversation they'd just had. He turned to Garner.

"We'll talk outside."

In the master bedroom, Nancy began to pack her bags. After a moment she went into the bathroom for her toiletries. Looking out the window there, she saw Clayton and the foreman, in conversation by the hitching post, where two saddle horses were tied, rifles in the scabbards. She couldn't hear what was being said. She walked across the hall to a guest bedroom directly above the two men and quietly lifted the window there.

"We both know what he's like," Clayton was saying.

"The most chickenshit sheriff I ever come across," Garner agreed. "Him and his due process."

"We can't expect him to contribute in any way but he'll stay in line once the job is done," Clayton said. "But I need you to be clear on just what we're doing here. We have no way of knowing what Tuttle might have told Cooper."

"How are we gonna find him?" Garner asked. "That old man knows this back country. And he may very well have gone to town. To the newspaper."

"If he had shown up in town, Henry would have sent word by now. He'll head for the reservation."

"How do you know that?"

"Because he always heads there," Clayton said. "That's his history. As far as I'm concerned, he's no better than a damn Indian. We need to find him and we need to silence him."

Garner nodded. "What you're saying is you don't want him dead or alive."

"That's what I'm saying," Clayton said. "Be certain that Munson and Ballinger are clear on that as well."

"They won't require any convincing." Garner paused. "As long as you can handle Henry Pearce."

"Don't you worry about Henry Pearce," Clayton said.

As he turned back toward the house, Nancy closed the window and returned to the master bedroom, where she sat on the bed, staring at the carpet at her feet. She felt hollow inside, as if something dear had been taken from her. When she heard Clayton coming up the stairs, she stood and resumed her packing.

The man named Fields drove the rig in to the train station and then lifted Nancy's bags from the back. He lingered, waiting as she bought her ticket to Helena, and then lingered even longer, suggesting that he wait until she was safely aboard the train before heading back to the ranch. The train was not due for over an hour. It occurred to her he was in no hurry to get back to work. When he began to tell her the rather uneventful story of his life she thanked him once more for his service and sent him on his way. He reluctantly took his leave, driving the rig slowly south out of town.

When he had gone, she sat on a low wooden bench on the platform outside the waiting room, her bags at her feet. From there she could see along the main street of Cut Bank. She could see the millinery and the barbershop and the swinging doors of the Bighorn Saloon.

She could see the office of the *Cut Bank Chronicle* as well.

As she sat there she went over all the things she had been considering these past few weeks. All that she had allowed herself to consider. To dream even. And what she had considered was that she was to be instrumental in getting Clay Covington elected to the highest office in the state later that year. Furthermore, she had dared to dream she would be at his side when he was sworn in, and that she would eventually be his wife. He clearly did not love the woman he was now married to, and he had—on numerous occasions in the past week—declared his love for Nancy. It was only natural for her to believe that she would in due time be the wife of the governor. It seemed like a fairy tale to even imagine it and yet at the same time it seemed so close to being true. So close she could almost taste it. She had even, in her mind, begun to redecorate the governor's house.

But dreams were like everything else. They lived and they died. And most of the time they did not come true. This dream was no different. She could see it flying away, over the mountains and into the mist.

When she opened the door to the newspaper office, she came upon a young man sitting at a desk, eating a sandwich while he made notes on a pad. She remembered the name from the article she'd read.

"Are you Willis Samuels?" she asked.

"Yes," Samuels said. "What can I do for you?"

Thirty-Eight

NATE AND ROSE RODE TO THE Blackfoot reservation under a clear morning sky, the air so cold they could see their breath. They'd had coffee and biscuits at the line shack before setting out. Neither one of them had spoken very much since rising. It didn't seem they needed any more words. The night in the shack hadn't changed anything; Rose was still determined to go to Canada with Nate. When it came to stubborn, she was more than a match for Nate Cooper, or anybody else he'd ever known.

After saddling the horses, Nate stood for a time, looking off to the west in silence, as if thinking on the day to come. He turned and went inside the cabin to douse the fire. When he came back, he was wearing the revolver around his waist and carrying the Winchester. He nodded to Rose and they mounted up.

They rode north onto the open range, where the plush spring buffalo grass, wet with dew, soaked the horses' legs to the hocks. By the time they turned west into the foothills, the sun was full up, although the air remained cool. It was mid-morning when they came upon the fading and bullet-riddled sign marking the reservation. Going forward, they passed two Indian youths, chasing a paint colt that had broken its tether and was now trotting along just out of their reach, toying with them.

They found Ulysses Elkhorn in the store, sweeping the place out. He was no longer surprised to see Nate Cooper riding up the dirt road out front, but he was somewhat intrigued that he had a woman with him this time. A white woman. The only white women that ever came onto the reservation were the ones determined to save the Blackfoot children from living their lives as heathens.

Ulysses' niece was helping him in the store and when the two on horseback arrived, he sent her to fetch Standing Elk from his teepee. There was a pot of coffee, still warm, on the potbelly stove. Ulysses poured for Nate and Rose and then, when he noticed Rose looking critically at the bare shelves, suggested they sit outside in the sun. He didn't want her pity; it was worth nothing to him. They drank the coffee and waited for Standing Elk, who had emerged from his lodge and was making his way slowly along the road, his pace hindered by arthritis and worn hip joints and by wounds from wars fought in another lifetime. His eyes brightened when he saw Rose.

"I know this woman," he said.

Rose got to her feet. "Hello, Standing Elk."

"You are Rose," he said. "You used to bring me sweets."

"I have been delinquent in that," Rose said.

Standing Elk dismissed the apology with a shake of his head. He sat on the steps with Rose and listened while Nate repeated the story Briscoe Tuttle had told, or at least as much as he'd told before somebody with a buffalo gun had decided to shut him up.

"I know that goat farmer," Ulysses said. "He is crazy in his head."

"Well, a crazy man can speak the truth as good as anybody," Nate said, "if he's got hold of the facts."

Ulysses looked away, toward the corral beside the store. He was still distrustful of Nate Cooper. The horses the two had been riding were tied off to the railing, still saddled. Ulysses watched them a moment, sipping the bitter coffee.

"You believe these markers are there?" he asked.

"He offered to show me where," Nate said. "For money. You can't sell something you don't have."

"But now he is dead," Ulysses said. "How can we find the markers? Do you think you can find them, Cooper, because you talked to a crazy man who is now dead?"

"You're a pessimistic sonofabitch for certain," Nate said. "No, I don't think I can find them. There's six thousand acres out there. But a few hundred Indians might be able to. You know the general vicinity and you know what you're looking for."

"Covington would never allow it," Ulysses said.

"He might not have a choice," Rose said. "This is going to be in the newspaper. And not just the local newspaper; the big papers down at the capitol. Clayton is awful worried about his image, these days more than ever. What he wants to allow and what he can allow might be two different things."

"I thought he was your brother," Ulysses said.

"He is."

The Indian smirked. "We were taught that the Bible tells us to love our brother."

"Well, that's the thing with the Bible. You need to separate the wheat from the chaff. Otherwise, you'll just end up chasing your tail."

"What does that mean?" Ulysses asked.

"Some brothers just aren't that lovable."

Standing Elk smiled. Rose stood now, looking across the reservation, toward the teepee the old man had emerged from.

"Is that your garden?" she asked.

The old man nodded. "Do you have a garden?"

"I try," Rose said. "Will you show me?"

The two of them set out together, walking along the dusty road. Nate set his empty cup on the railing and watched as they went into the sparse vegetable patch a hundred yards away. Rose's presence drew stares from the other Indians, some sitting in front of their cabins or teepees, others at work at their morning tasks. After a time, Nate got to his feet.

"They get to talking about string beans and we'll be here a while," he said. "I'll just loosen the cinches on those horses."

Ulysses trailed him as he walked over to the corral and stepped inside.

"I suppose it will look bad for us," he said. "Asking for that land."

Nate shrugged. "I have to believe it'll look worse for them, stealing it from you in the first place." He flipped the stirrup up on the chestnut and unfastened the cinch before moving on to Rose's mare. "Keep in mind there's a politician involved," he added. "People generally have a low opinion of them to begin with."

"All these years, the goat farmer knew this."

"He wasn't a man to ride the river with," Nate said. "Besides, Clay Covington was paying him to keep his trap shut, although I kindly doubt that can be proved now. But you can never tell—maybe if the story gets out, somebody else who worked the survey will tell his side of it. Twenty-five years ain't that long a time. There's got to be men still around who were involved. Who knows but there's not a copy of the real survey stored away in somebody's steamer trunk."

Finished with the cinches, Nate came through the gate and closed it, looping the rawhide rope over the post. As he and Ulysses walked out onto the road, he looked over to where Rose and Standing Elk were kneeling in the old man's garden. When Standing Elk made to rise, Rose reached out to steady him. Ulysses turned to Nate.

"And what about you, Cooper?" he asked. "I still don't know why you have your nose in this. Are you going into the cattle business with us?"

"No, sir," Nate said. "I'm heading to Canada."

"When?"

"Right shortly here."

Rose and Standing Elk were now returning along the dirt road. Ulysses looked at Rose as he spoke. "You're going there alone?"

Nate hesitated, considering the question as he had been considering it since waking up that morning. Waking up with Rose beside him in the bunk, her body warm, a slight smile on her lips even as she slept. It was a morning he hadn't anticipated, a morning he had stopped even imagining many years ago. It was a morning that thrilled him and yet filled him with guilt.

The first shot kicked up the dust at their feet and the second whizzed over their heads. Nate turned toward the sounds of the gunfire to see Munson and Ballinger, riding hard toward them, pistols in their hands. Nate ran at once toward Rose and as he did he heard a soft grunt and saw Standing Elk collapse on the road, his legs folding under him like they were twigs. Grabbing Rose by the arm, Nate pulled her through the corral gate. Looking back, he saw Ulysses running toward the store.

Nate pushed Rose. "Get behind the horses!"

Turning now, he watched as Munson and Ballinger rode past at a gallop, holding their fire now, trying to get a bead on Nate in the corral. Fifty yards along they whirled their mounts and came back. Nate glanced at Standing Elk, lying motionless in the road. He pulled the .44 and stepped through the gate to meet the two riders.

Munson was in the lead, at full gallop, rifle in one hand and the reins in the other. He snapped a shot at Nate and Nate shot him twice in the throat, flinging him backward from the horse. Ballinger had swung his horse wide and now charged toward Nate from the side, leaning low over the saddle. As Nate moved to his right for a better angle, Ulysses came out of the store carrying an ancient shotgun. He loosed both barrels at Ballinger and the blast caused the horse to rear. Ballinger fell from the animal, landing heavily on his back. He got slowly to his feet, fighting for breath. His revolver lay ten feet away. He glanced at the gun then turned to look at Nate, who stepped into the road and put three bullets in the little man's chest. Ballinger dropped to his knees, a look of surprise on his face, before falling to the dirt.

And then dead silence, as if time was suspended. The cordite hung in the air like wood smoke. Ulysses hurried down from the steps and ran toward his father's body. There he knelt, his hand on the old man's chest. Other Indians came out from cover now; some approached Ulysses.

Nate looked at the two dead men on the road, then turned to find Rose. She was standing inside the corral gate, her expression one of shock, of disbelief of what had just occurred. She stared at Nate, walking toward her. Seeing he was unhurt, her face relaxed and she exhaled. Then she looked past him and screamed.

The roar of the Sharps rifle was deafening, like a sudden crack of thunder on a quiet evening. The slug hit Nate in the upper rib cage, flinging him against the corral, snapping the cottonwood railing in half. He collapsed there as Rose rushed to his side. As she dropped to her knees beside him, he grabbed the broken railing with his strong right hand and held fiercely to it as he held onto his life for a few seconds more. He smiled at Rose to reassure her, and then his hand let loose of the rail. He rolled over into the dirt and was still. Frantic, Rose knelt over him and tried to stop the bleeding from his chest but there was nothing to stop, nobody there to save. Finally, she put her arms around him and gathered him to her breast.

Moments later, she heard the horses and looked up to see Ed Garner on a big gelding, drawing near, the Sharps carbine across the pommel. Behind him, sitting their mounts a cautious distance away, were Clayton and Sheriff Henry Pearce.

Garner climbed down from his horse and approached, leveling the barrel of the rifle at the body on the ground, wary of Nate Cooper even now. Six feet away he stopped, his eyes moving, seeking something. Rose looked up at him.

"You goddamn sonofabitch."

Quick as a cat, Garner grabbed her by the hair and flung her aside like she was no more than a rag doll. Turning back, he warily prodded Nate with the barrel of the buffalo gun, then flicked open Nate's coat, first one side and then the other. Still not finding what he was after, he knelt in the dirt and rolled the body over. There was nothing underneath.

He felt Rose's presence before he saw her. She leaned into him from the side, and a split second before she spoke he felt the barrel of the missing .44 jammed beneath his chin.

"Looking for this?"

She pulled the trigger and blew the top of his head off.

She got to her feet, stepping away from all that was left of Ed Garner, before turning on her brother and Henry Pearce, now just a few yards away and noticeably anxious about what they had just witnessed. Before Clayton could move, Rose pointed the .44 at his head and pulled the trigger. He yelped like a frightened dog and the hammer came down on an empty chamber. Knowing it was to no avail, she pulled the trigger again. And again.

Then Henry Pearce was beside her, his big belly preceding him and his Colt automatic in his hand. He wrested the empty .44 from her and when she resisted him, he slapped her twice across the head, knocking her into the red dirt of the road.

"Kill her," Clayton hissed. "Do it, Henry."

"I don't think you will," Ulysses said. He was walking toward Henry Pearce, carrying the shotgun.

The scattergun was empty but Henry, kneeling over Rose, didn't know that. He was afraid of Indians in general and now he stood there, the fear rising in him, not knowing what to do, a familiar feeling for him. He heard noises and looked up to see Indians coming out of the teepees and shacks. A half dozen, and then a dozen more. All walking along the dirt road toward the sheriff. Soon there were scores of Indians there, all watching him, waiting to see what he would do with the woman at his feet. The fear in Henry

Pearce was so great that he couldn't swallow. The gun in his hand felt like a blacksmith's anvil.

He was saved by the creak of a buggy spring.

Willis Samuels was sitting in a rig fifty yards away, near the agency store. It was anybody's guess how long he had been there, or how much he had seen. Clayton regarded him unhappily for several moments before turning back to Henry Pearce.

"Let her go, Henry," he said. "Her little adventure is over."

Pearce turned Rose loose. She got to her feet.

"It's not over," she told her brother. "It will be over when I kill you."

Thirty-Nine

ROSE SAT IN THE DIRT BY the body of Nate Cooper, watching his face. His eyes were closed, mouth open slightly. From time to time she brushed his hair back from his forehead, for no other reason than she wanted to touch him. There was blood on Rose's hands and clothes and in the dirt of the corral.

Clayton and Henry Pearce had ridden off, leaving their dead associates behind, with Pearce saying he would send a wagon for them. Rose hadn't looked at them as they left. Neither spoke to her.

Around her the Indians, already in mourning, were gathering, seeing to the body of Standing Elk, rolling the dead chief into a blanket and carrying him off. Some had already begun to cut pine saplings for the burial scaffold. Ulysses Elkhorn came and stood by Rose for a time. He didn't say anything and after a while he went off, following those who had taken his father. Flies began to hover above Nate's wound and Rose busied herself brushing them away.

It was the youngster Samuels who finally convinced her that they should transport Nate's body back to Cut Bank. He spoke to her quietly for several minutes until finally she got to her feet. Her eyes were blank but she nodded her agreement. It was impractical to put him in the little buggy so they tied him over the back of the chestnut mare he'd been riding these past weeks. They left without speaking to anyone, Samuels in the rig and Rose leading the chestnut.

A few miles out from the reservation Rose's thinking began to clear. The Cut Bank cemetery was no place for Nate Cooper. She didn't want him there, nor did she want some Methodist preacher talking over him, telling stories about the man he'd never met and knew nothing of. She didn't want Abigail Jones wailing at the gravesite, bemoaning the loss of her great true love. He didn't belong to any of them. He didn't belong to anybody.

They buried him by the line shack on Turtle Creek. Young Samuels followed her up to the summer pasture in the buggy, or at least until the going got too rough and he was obliged to leave the rig behind. He walked the last few miles alongside the horses. It was hard going and his shoes were ill-suited for such a trek but he never complained. Nate had been right about the young man.

The two of them took turns digging in the soft ground of the creek flat, using a broken-handled spade Rose had found beneath the shack. It was late in the afternoon when they finished and without ceremony they rolled the body into the grave. It took but a few minutes to cover it over. And that was that.

"Are you going to say some words?" Samuels asked.

"No," Rose said after consideration.

The reporter shifted his weight from one foot to another. "I guess we should be going then."

"You go on."

"I can't leave you here all alone. Night coming on."

"I'll be fine," Rose told him. "You can ride his mare back down to your rig. Leave her off at the ranch if you don't mind. It's on your way."

Samuels nodded.

Rose looked at the sky. "Best get moving. You'll want to make it to the county road before dark." She saw that something was troubling the boy. She kept her eye on him until he spoke his piece.

"I've been worrying," he finally began and then stopped. "I've been worrying how I can write about this. The guilty parties, which are Garner and Munson and Ballinger, are all dead. I expect your brother will distance himself from the whole situation, and Henry Pearce will back him up on it. And that's not right, Mrs. Longley."

"None of it is right," Rose told him. Looking at his earnest face, she was envious of him—that he still lived in a world where he thought things would just naturally turn out the way they should. As if right had some sort of advantage over wrong.

"But what can I do?" Samuels persisted. "I can't put in the paper that these men were doing Clayton's bidding, even though we know it to be true. I can't write it when I have no proof."

"Write about the survey," Rose said. "Get that story out there, get the newspapers down at the capitol interested." She paused, suddenly realizing something. "What made you go to the reservation today?"

"I had a woman come see me at the office. She said the posse was heading for the reservation. And she suggested that they had no intention of taking Mr. Cooper alive."

"What woman?"

"She is the senator's . . . friend. Or was."

"I'll be damned," Rose said. She regarded the fresh grave a moment before turning back to Samuels. "Write about the survey. Let me worry about my brother."

When Samuels was gone, she went inside and lit the old stove to make coffee. There were pine limbs left from the previous night, her last night with Nate Cooper. Pouring a cup, she went and sat on the mound beside the grave to drink it.

It was quiet, with just the sound of the creek and the soft whirring wings of swallows, diving for prey, to cut the silence. Listening to the water gurgling across the rocky stream bed, she thought of how it sounded tonight just as it had when she'd first come to this shack to see Nate Cooper, thirty years ago. The creek was the same and everything else had changed. Thirty years from now, the creek would still be the same. And thirty years after that. It wasn't forever but it was as close to forever as anything could be.

She drank the coffee as the dusk arrived, the air growing cool. She hoped young Samuels made it to the road before darkness fell. She feared he would get lost in the foothills. If nothing else, the horses knew the way home.

After a time she had a thought and got up to walk to the old corral, now broken up and largely gone. She found two lengths of lodge pole pine and made a cross, tying it with a length of rawhide rope from her saddle. Using a flat rock from the creek bed, she hammered the cross into the ground at the head of the grave. The cross wouldn't last either, but it was there for now.

Standing by the grave, drinking the gone-cold coffee, she thought of Samuels, of how he asked if she would say anything over the burial. What would she say? That the man buried there was a great man? He wasn't and Rose wondered if anybody ever truly was. Nate Cooper had done some bad things. He had robbed a bank in his reckless youth, and he had killed men. He had trifled with the affections of more women than Rose wanted to know. He had squandered too much time at poker and billiards. He had known prison, and the inside of a few brothels. There was no evidence to suggest that he was a great man.

But Nate Cooper had a true heart in many respects, and Rose was vain enough to believe that she knew that heart better than anybody else. Not only did he have a heart but he followed it, sometimes against his better judgment and sometimes downright foolishly. That heart, flawed and fickle, did not make him a great man but it made him a good one, and maybe that was as high as anyone could reach.

Forty

SAMUELS SAT ACROSS FROM HARRY LONGLEY, the glass of bourbon in his hand. He hadn't wanted a drink. It was nearly midnight and they were in the living room of the big ranch house.
Harry was drunk, although somewhat coherently so. His appearance and his actions were that of a man who had been drunk for a
couple days and while he would not be getting sober anytime soon,
he was past getting any drunker.

Samuels had shown up an hour earlier, trailing the chestnut
mare behind his buggy. Harry had heard him talking to the foreman in the yard and had come out on the porch and asked him
inside, asked him in a manner not really a request. Samuels had
been hoping to travel on; he had ten miles to go to Cut Bank. He
had spent an anxious few hours crossing the range after leaving the
line shack, worried that Clayton Covington might decide silencing
Samuels would work to his advantage. Samuels attempted to find
solace in the hope that all of Covington's bad men were lying dead
at the Blackfoot agency. He could hope it but he couldn't know
it. He had been overjoyed to see the lights of the Longley ranch.

Inside the house, he was obliged to drink with Harry, which was
a comfortable enough situation, and to tell Harry the events of

the day, which was not, considering Rose Longley's involvement. Harry, however, had not so much as raised an eyebrow when he heard that his wife had shot Ed Garner's brains out, nor had he shown any emotion upon hearing Nate Cooper was dead. He continued to drink, looking not at Samuels but at a huge buffalo head mounted above the stone fireplace across the room, as if the creature held his interest and nothing else. Samuels now backtracked to tell of Briscoe Tuttle's story.

"Apparently Clayton was paying Tuttle a hundred dollars a year to keep quiet," he said in finishing. "It's all going to be in this week's paper."

"Clay's not going to like that." It was the first Harry had spoken in some time. His voice was cracked and thin. The voice of a man who was defeated and knew it. Accepted it even.

"I expect he'll deny it," Samuels said. "But he can't deny that he sold the old man fifty acres for a dollar. That smacks of conspiracy."

Harry nodded vaguely as he drank. He seemed to be through with the conversation now, even though he was the one who had insisted upon having it. Samuels took the opportunity to drink off his own glass and get carefully to his feet, which were painful from the blisters he'd developed following Nate Cooper's body up to the line shack. He was looking forward to soaking them in the copper tub at the boardinghouse.

"I should be getting back." When there was no response, he added pointlessly, "I just wanted to leave off that horse."

Harry sat looking at the buffalo head. He seemed near to falling to pieces, sitting in the chair, the life drained out of him, his world a shambles. Samuels got as far as the door before he turned back, thinking he should leave the man with something of a positive nature.

"I have to say I was real happy to get to know Nate Cooper these weeks," he said. "He was a character. The last of his breed, I would think."

Harry's breathing was shallow.

Samuels made one last effort. "Did the two of you really rob a bank in Fargo?"

"We did."

"I didn't know for certain," Samuels said. "I knew Mr. Cooper liked to spin a yarn. I could never tell if my leg was being pulled. Like the one about him being there when Wild Bill Hickok was shot."

Harry took a drink. "Nate was there when Bill Hickok was shot."

"He was?"

"Hickok wasn't playing poker by himself," Harry said. "There was nothing false about Nate Cooper. Oh, he might of lied to a couple dance hall girls when he told them he loved them, but other than that, he was straight down the line. He was a helluva cowboy too. And he was the best damn pistol shot I ever saw."

"According to him, you were."

Harry scoffed at the suggestion and reached for the bottle.

Sensing that Harry was suddenly not adverse to conversation, Samuels stepped back into the room. "Is it true you told Parcell Covington that you would kill him if they hung Nate?"

"I did," Harry said. "And I would have."

Samuels nodded, seeing Harry Longley as he had not in the past. "Well, I hope you realize that you bought your friend an extra thirty years, Mr. Longley. That is no small accomplishment."

"Is it?"

"I think so," Samuels replied. He hoped for something more from the drunken man in the chair but it wasn't forthcoming. "Well, good night," he said after a time and made for the door.

"Where has Rose gone?"

Samuels found he was obliged to quit his leaving once more. "The last I saw, she was at a line shack in the foothills. Where we buried Mr. Cooper."

At that Harry barely nodded. He took more whiskey and his eyes went back to the buffalo. Samuels hesitated a long moment, deciding.

"She says she's going to kill her brother."

Forty-One

CLAYTON DID NOT SLEEP WELL AND rose early. When he did sleep he had dreams of his sister, and when he was awake he had thoughts of her. Of her threat and of the expression on her face when she made it. In his vocation, Clayton associated daily with men whose word meant nothing. He would not for a moment assume that his sister was anything like those men.

Sometime during his fitful night, he'd decided he would head back for Helena on the morning train. He rose at six and bathed, then drank coffee in the kitchen, keeping an eye on the yard and the road out front. After packing his valise, he strapped on the shoulder holster carrying the Iver Johnson .38 revolver before putting his coat on. He usually transported the gun in his luggage and couldn't recall the last time he had fired it. But it had passed the night, loaded, beneath his pillow and he would carry it today, at least until he arrived in the safe confines of the capitol.

He looked at the clock and saw it was time to go. He walked out onto the porch. The Hupmobile was parked in the yard a few yards away, the morning sun catching the black enamel of the paint and the brass lights. Clayton went down the steps and over to the motorcar, pulling his handkerchief from his pocket to wipe a dead

June bug from the windshield. As he stowed his valise in the back, he heard a horse whinny. He whirled, his hand going inside his coat.

Sheriff Henry Pearce rode his fat mare into the yard at a walk. Pearce was smoking a cigarette and eating a greasy biscuit at the same time. Leaving the revolver holstered, Clayton cursed himself for being careless. If Henry Pearce could surprise him, anybody could.

"What brings you here at this hour, Henry?"

"I wanted to give you a report." Pearce climbed down from the horse and draped the reins over the hitching rail.

"You could have saved yourself a ride," Clayton said. "I'm headed in to the station."

"I'm not a mind reader," Henry pointed out.

"So what is your report? You get things all smoothed out? I imagine you spent long hours in the Bighorn last night, bragging on how you broke up a Blackfoot rustling ring and shot down the murderer Nate Cooper in the process."

"You could be grateful to me, you know," Pearce said. "Just once, you could appreciate the things I do."

"I am much obliged to you, Sheriff Pearce," Clayton said sarcastically. "Now what do you have to say?"

Pearce missed the tone or at least decided to ignore it. "Those Covington hides prove that the Indians were stealing your beef. Munson and Ballinger were working for you as range detectives. They followed the rustlers onto the reservation and gunplay broke out. They were killed by Nate Cooper, doing their jobs."

Clayton kept an eye on the landscape as he listened. In the corral beyond the barn, a dozen or so hands were breaking some young horses, the men riding each other in the process, calling out encouragement and insults in equal amounts.

"What about the reporter Samuels?"

"We don't know what he saw," Pearce said. "But he can't dispute the story that the Indians were rustling. We have just cause,

Clayton." He paused. "You still have the problem with the survey story though. I don't believe the newspaper is gonna let that one go."

"I'm not worried about that."

"Why in the hell not?"

Clayton put one foot on the running board of the motorcar while he hooked his thumbs in his lapels, mocking the classic politician's pose.

"How's this sound?" he asked. "When I heard the rumors concerning this matter, the Covington Ranch initiated its own investigation. And we discovered that an unscrupulous surveyor back in '85 took advantage of the situation and convinced my father, whose mental capacities were failing at the time, to agree that the boundary lines be fudged. I was shocked to learn quite recently of this deception. But I have now decided, in the interest of fair play, to cede the land in question to the Blackfoot Nation. To take effect immediately."

Henry Pearce nearly fell over. "You're gonna give them the range? All that blood, and now you're gonna just hand it over to the goddamn Indians?"

"This kills the story, Henry," Clayton said. "It's six thousand acres. I've got twenty times that. I go from bad guy to benefactor." He laughed. "Hell, I might even get the Indian vote."

"That's the damnedest thing I ever heard," Pearce said.

"It's simple. Whatever malfeasance may have occurred, it was perpetrated by my old man—not me. That the sins of the father not be visited upon the son."

Henry Pearce continued looking at Clayton, shaking his head. The next voice belonged to neither man.

"You got that last part wrong, Clay."

Both Clayton and Pearce turned quickly to see Harry Longley, standing by the corner of the house, holding the reins of a large black gelding in one hand. Harry's eyes were bloodshot and he was hatless and coatless in the cool of the morning. He had a Colt revolver stuck in his belt. He looked leaner and meaner than he had in many years.

Clayton, greatly relieved it was Harry and not Rose in his yard, took in the disheveled man for a few moments. At first glance, Harry appeared too drunk to stand up.

"What are you doing, Harry?" he said pleasantly.

"You got the last part wrong," Harry said again. "About the sins of the father."

He let go the reins and stepped closer. He hesitated when he noticed the Hupmobile, his eyes flicking over the car. Clayton saw and nodded quickly to Pearce, who moved to his right to flank Harry.

"You look like you haven't slept in days, Harry," Clayton said then. "Let's go inside and get a drink."

Harry shifted his gaze back to Clayton. "I made a promise to your father once. I promised him if they executed my friend, I would shoot him dead."

"Cooper brought this on himself, Harry," Clayton said. "The man was a criminal and he died a criminal's death. What did he expect?"

"Who said you could execute my friend?" Harry asked, his voice finally breaking.

"Sheriff Pearce here was in charge." Clayton turned to Henry Pearce as he said it, giving him a sharp look that told him it was time to act. "You'd better talk to him."

Harry offered Pearce but a glance before going back to Clayton. "You were in charge, Clay. And we're not going to talk because you're a lot better at it than me. I'm here to keep my word."

Clayton made a motion with his hand and Henry Pearce went for his gun. He had the semi-automatic out of the holster and was clumsily bringing it to bear when Harry pulled the Colt and shot him precisely between the eyes. In that instant, Clayton reached for the pistol inside his coat and Harry put his next shot in the middle of Clayton's chest. Clayton stumbled backward to fall into the gleaming motorcar. He lay there, gasping for a couple of minutes, blood bubbling from his lips. He died on the plush leather seat.

At the sound of the shots, the hands from the corral came running toward the house. Seeing Harry amid the carnage, gun in hand, they stopped short. He turned to look at them, and they merely stood there, looking back. After a time, he stuck the revolver in his belt and climbed onto the gelding and rode off.

Forty-Two

AFTER THINKING SHE WOULDN'T, ROSE FINALLY slept. She had stoked the fire before rolling into her blanket in the bunk and lain there for a couple of hours, her mind going back over the events of the day, her thoughts suffering over what might have been if this had happened, or if that had not. Finally she dozed off. It was full daylight when she awakened and the stove was cold. She hadn't realized how exhausted she had been. Outside in the sun, she had cold coffee and the last of the biscuits from her saddlebag, spending one last morning with Nate Cooper. After saddling the buckskin, she had a long look around, knowing she would never come there again. Before setting out, she loaded the revolver.

When she got to the Covington ranch, Harry had been there and gone. One of the hands had ridden into town to contact the state police. From the back of the mare, Rose looked at her brother and Henry Pearce and then rode off.

Harry was sitting on the porch, slumped in the wicker settee there. Rose stripped the tack from the buckskin and gave her a thorough brushing and a large measure of grain before turning her loose in the corral.

She walked toward the house under Harry's sad eyes. Climbing the steps to the porch, she saw the Colt revolver resting atop the newel post. Rose looked at it before moving over to sit beside him. Neither of them said anything.

After a time Rose leaned over and rested her head on his shoulder.